CINNAMON ROLL SET UP

A CINNAMON ROLLS AND
PUMPKIN SPICE ROM-COM

by

GENNY CARRICK

Cover design and illustration by House of Orian

Edited by Cindy Ray Hale

ISBN (ebook): 978-1-957745-16-9

ISBN (paperback): 978-1-957745-17-6

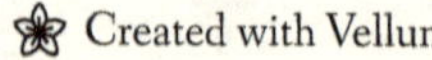 Created with Vellum

Also by Genny Carrick

Love in Sunshine series

Just Act Natural

Mad About Yule

Travel standalone

The Loch Effect

For everyone holding out for a book boyfriend. May you find a non-fictional man who's even better than you imagined.

And for every guy named Maverick, Knox, or Ransom—I believe in you.

Reader Expectations

Heat Level: Kisses only, light innuendo, minimal mild swears

Notable Tropes: Matchmaking gone wrong, cinnamon roll hero, friends to lovers, shy hero, secret pining, coworkers in a bookshop, text messages

Triggers: Indifferent parent (present), death of parent (past), scary moment in a haunted house

Style: First person present, dual POV

Stress Level: Low

Ending: HEA guaranteed

Chapter 1

Georgia

Some people are extra with a capital E. Over the top. Flashy. Do the absolute most.

Hi. It's me.

My best friend, Miles, however, is not extra. He's subtle with a lowercase s.

"What do you think?" I nudge him with my elbow. We've been staring at Dogeared Bookshop's front window for two whole minutes now, taking it in. Soaking it up. Reveling, if you will.

Or possibly hating it. He hasn't given me an indication yet.

Three shallow shelves fill the lower half of the window, and I spent the morning putting all of our most fall-feeling books front and center. I strung ropes of fake leaves along the window border, scattered red and white felt mushrooms around the books, strategically placed real miniature pumpkins, and sprinkled in pinecones I collected throughout town. It's a cornucopia of fall-themed goodness fit for a little woodland family of squirrels to make a home in.

"It's autumn on steroids," he finally says in his trademarked deadpan.

"So you love it?"

He turns to me and his mouth quirks into a smile. "I can smell the apple cider from here."

I breathe a little easier. I've been told that I go overboard on occasion. Well...most occasions. I can't remember him ever complaining, but I still like to have his approval. "You could have said that a minute and a half ago."

"I needed to appreciate it first."

I kind of like that about Miles. He doesn't give knee-jerk praise or empty words. He takes his time to decide what he thinks and isn't easily swayed by everyone else's opinions.

Still. I didn't want to stuff all of those fall decorations back into my car and come up with something less festive and more blah. Magnolia Ridge, Texas is big enough to have some nice variety downtown, but small enough to keep that cozy, everyone-knows-everyone feel. Most shops take holiday decorating seriously and go all-in with their windows, but there's always an outlier that declines to join in the fun.

I refuse to let Dogeared go down the path of boring windows.

Miles leads us back into the bookshop, where the scent of coffee and brown sugar swirls through the air. Dogeared is one-third café and bakery, two-thirds bookstore. And I fully adore all the thirds of this little shop.

He brushes invisible crumbs from one of the café tables before moving behind the front counter. We've got a small glass display case full of pastries to round out our offerings, and although we don't have much of a selection of food, it never goes to waste.

"I always love your windows," he says. "You've got a real talent for them. Everyone walking by will be impressed."

"Don't just sweet talk me. Give me a raise already."

"Done."

Fun fact: Miles *owns* Dogeared, but he's never made it weird. After five years working together, our boss-employee dynamic has shifted into more of a co-parenting BFFs-type thing. The shop is our baby, and we spoil it rotten.

It's stuffed with cozy reading chairs, quiet spots where visitors can play board games, and a bright eating area. Oh, and lots and lots of books. Curated, of course, but there's a little bit of everything.

When I first moved back to my hometown after college, Dogeared was the only place I applied to work. It wasn't much more than a few rows of books back then, but Miles and I transformed it into a place where people feel at home. More often than not, I do my freelance book cover design right here in one of the comfy chairs while Miles dreams up his next novel.

Oh, fun fact number two: he's also a writer.

"You have a better eye for visuals than anyone. You've got... pizzazz." He wiggles his fingers in a goofy attempt at jazz hands.

I snort. "I love everything about that except *pizzazz*."

"You're the most pizzazz-y person I know."

While I like to wear the brightest colors thrift store aisles have to offer—case in point: the orange, red, and yellow-striped sweater I've got on now—Miles leans toward a more muted style. He tends to dress in sepia tones, like he's stuck in an old-timey photograph. He makes it work, though.

Between his messy dark hair, clean-shaven face, and the subdued cardigans and sport coats he likes to wear, he's got a real "Cute Adjunct Professor" vibe going on. Basically, he's everything you could ever want in a bookstore owner.

"Then I guess I'm ready to bring my pizzazz to the Harvest Festival. I've loaded up on the perfect sweaters for the occasion."

If a fall sweater doesn't blind you with faux foliage or have a giant pumpkin on it, I don't want it.

"Thank you for agreeing to that."

"Quit it with the gratitude. It's going to be fun." Miles answered the community's call and signed Dogeared up for some volunteer positions during Magnolia Ridge's Harvest Festival over the next two months. It's really just the Saturday farmers market but with more fall flair and lots of games for kids. Which is probably what we'll wind up manning, but I'm down for anything.

"Tell me about the sweaters." He knows I live for my thrift shop runs.

I smile sweetly. "No spoilers."

"You do have an outstanding eye for style."

My older brother, Sam, gets right to the point and calls it *overkill*, but I'll take the compliment.

"Speaking of my outstanding eye for style…" I put my hands on his laptop where it sits on the counter. "May I?"

He nods and shifts to give me room. "Of course."

I open the laptop and pull up a new browser tab, quickly navigating to the *Found & Freebies* listing that's been on my mind for the last twenty-four hours.

"Look at this beauty." I click through the photos, sighing a little over each one. "A rotating bookshelf. And they're just giving it away."

He sweeps his fingers beneath mine to take control of the laptop's trackpad, moving through the pictures again. "Is this for the shop or for your apartment?"

"I'd take it, but I was thinking I'd bring it here. It would fit perfectly in the back corner. Maybe we could fill it with our middle-grade books."

"Are you going to paint it?"

A sound of disgust escapes me. "You think I'd keep a plain white *anything*?"

He looks like he's fighting amusement. A common expression for him. "Only under extreme duress."

"I feel like that's a yes on the bookshelf."

He lets loose that adorable smile of his that he doesn't reveal nearly often enough. "Yes. Sure. Get it."

"You won't regret it! And if you do, the bookshelf will magically find its way to my apartment."

Commandeering his trackpad again, I close out the *Found & Freebies* tab, and his main browser window pops open. The picture that takes over the screen is a star field with *Andromeda Awards* written out in bold, futuristic text.

"Wait." I grab his biceps and give his arm a little shake. "Did you...?"

Without waiting for an answer or even finishing the question, I click through to the award categories. There, under *Rising Star* is his name: Miles Forrester.

"Miles!" His eyebrows twitch at my shriek, but I plow on. "Why didn't you tell me you were nominated?"

"I was getting around to it."

Another fun fact about Miles: he's humble to a superhuman degree. When people praise the café's baker, he always says he'll pass on the compliment even though *he's* the one in the back every morning turning out pastries. I'm one of the few people in Magnolia Ridge who knows that he wrote the books in the Quantum Station series. Heck, most people don't even know his first name, they just know him as "that bookstore guy."

Which is a real travesty because Miles is probably the best person in this town. Including me, and I'm awesome.

"We shared our Wordle stats this morning! You fed me an apple danish! I spent an hour messing around in the window!" I'm probably going blue in the face, but I don't care. This is huge news, and he just sat on it. I could never.

"I was...waiting for the right time?" His mouth tips into a cringey smile.

I plop myself onto the wooden stool beside him. "The right time is now. I need all the details."

He lifts a shoulder. "There aren't many details. I received an email yesterday. I'm nominated. That's really it."

"How can you be so calm?" I jostle his knees with mine as though I can jumpstart his enthusiasm. "This is monumental. Aren't you excited about it?"

Another smile peeks out. "I might be in shock."

Exactly what I mean about humility. He's written two funny, engaging, plot-twisty science fiction bangers and is surprised at every success he has with them.

I put both my hands on his cheeks and give them a little tap. "You need to celebrate."

His face tugs into a grin beneath my palms. "I did just find a new bookshelf for the store."

I laugh at his dry humor. "Celebrate with something even more exciting than a free bookshelf."

"Does that exist?"

"I'll find you something." Magnolia Ridge doesn't have a wild nightlife scene, but Miles likes to keep things low-key anyway. Maybe dinner at his favorite Indian food place. A slice of pie. Holing up in his apartment and watching one of his odd comfort movies.

I've never known a guy so committed to the Muppets, but he's got me hooked too.

"There's going to be an awards ceremony," he says oh-so casually.

"Awards ceremony?" Good thing nobody's in the shop right now because I can't stop shrieking. I spin back to his laptop and click on a couple of tabs until I land on the ceremony info. The Andromeda Awards are one of the biggest honors in science fiction and fantasy writing, and the pictures of past winners prove it. Men and women decked out in swanky clothes holding their crystal prizes aloft. "Ooh, they call it a *gala*. And it's in Austin. Are you going? You have to go."

Austin's only about thirty minutes south of here. Not much of an excuse to avoid attending.

"Seems like I should."

Those fancy award winners look pretty coupled up in the pics. Like an Oscars red carpet, but with genius writer nerds answering questions like "Where do you get your inspiration?"

"Are you going to take a date?"

He pauses as if his brain needs a second to reboot before he can answer.

"I know you're not huge on dating, but this is a big night for you. You should have someone special by your side."

He blinks his big hazel eyes at me. "I was going to ask you to go with me."

He's the absolute sweetest. But it's a little embarrassing how much we've become each other's default plus one. We spend so much time in the store together, whether working or doing our own thing, it's stretched into our personal lives. I don't really care about mine, but he at least deserves a shot at something more.

"As much as I'd love the excuse to wear a slinky dress, you need a *romantic* date for this."

He makes a weird, strangled sound. "Slinky?"

I suck in a breath as the perfect solution sparks a little light-bulb over my head. "I'll help you find a date."

Miles coughs like something went down the wrong pipe. "You'll...what?"

I can't stop grinning as I pat him on the back.

"I'll help you find a date. I'm the perfect wingwoman because I know you better than anyone, and I'm completely impartial."

Chapter 2

Miles

Impartial.

Not among the feelings I'd prefer Georgia have about me. My list includes words like smitten. Enamored. Flat-out in love.

But I guess I've always been a dreamer.

This isn't going the way I'd thought it might when I got the idea to ask her to go to the gala with me. I was supposed to be daring and blast through years of holding my tongue to tell the woman I'm crazy about that my feelings for her are more than just friendly. That I want her by my side at the awards ceremony because that way, even if I lose, I'll still come out a winner.

Instead, she's ready to bust out a PowerPoint presentation on why she's my ideal matchmaker. My daring just went *whoosh* like it was blown out an airlock.

"I already know your likes and dislikes, so I can narrow down the best options." She beams as if nothing could make her happier than sifting through my dating choices. "And we have two months before the gala, so if one doesn't work out, we have time to try again."

"So much confidence in me."

Not that she should. I haven't dated much in the last couple of years, but there's a very specific reason for that.

Her.

"You know what I mean. True love might not strike right away. It might take two or three dates."

Or five years working side by side.

I hired Georgia because she's confident, outgoing, and has a genuine love of books. I honestly didn't think she'd stick around long, given her degree in graphic design. But she's stayed right here, and after a year or so, proved she has a brain for business as well as visuals. I've gone along with all of her plans to improve Dogeared and never regretted a single decision. She helped me expand the café from just a coffee counter to a pastry bar complete with a deluxe espresso machine. I helped her reupholster the plush chairs she found for the reading spaces. We spent one wild Monday repainting the whole place a rich, inviting hunter green.

And somewhere along the way, we moved from largely indifferent coworkers to mutually invested teammates to close friends who lean on each other through our best and worst moments.

With a side of unrequited love on my part.

I close my laptop and face her. The wide, hopeful grin she flashes twists right to the center of my heart. I've learned to live with the constant butterflies, but the longing ache in my chest is new. How can I miss someone who's standing right in front of me?

I know before she ever finishes her sales pitch that I'm going to agree to her plans. I'd do anything for that smile. Even pretend I'm not in love with her.

"I kind of set up my brother and his wife, you know." She sounds like she's about to hand me a letter of recommendation. *Georgia Donnelly, Matchmaker Extraordinaire.*

"I know. You pretended I was sick."

"And you didn't even have to fake anything! It worked out perfectly."

She's just too adorable, even when she's scheming against all my most secret hopes.

I don't read much romance, but Georgia does. Through years of listening to her rave about her favorite books, I've learned a few things.

The two sexiest words in the English language are "You're mine."

Rolling shirtsleeves is required.

And matchmaking never, ever goes to plan.

"Acting as your boss's matchmaker probably violates some kind of OSHA regulation."

That earns an eye roll.

"Now you want to play the boss card?"

She's right. It's too late to draw that line in the sand. I can't enjoy movie nights at her apartment with her cuddled next to me and then try to claim something goes against our professional relationship. That went out the window the first time we hugged and I realized I never wanted to let her go.

"It was worth a shot."

"Nice try. What's your next move, smart guy?"

"Um, evasive actions?"

She darts her shoulders from side to side. "I'm too speedy for you."

I laugh, but the dread forming a knot in my stomach is hard to ignore. "Why do you want me to have a date to this so badly?"

I'm stalling. Her reason doesn't matter. I'm going to crumple like a spaceship succumbing to a black hole either way.

Theoretically. No one really knows what happens inside a black hole.

Not the point.

She stills, and her smile loses its challenge. It's just bright, sweet Georgia. "Because you're a wonderful guy, and more people should know that."

Under any other circumstances, those words would knock me out.

She takes my hand like she's making a vow. It twists the ache in my chest even deeper, but I hold on tight.

"I shouldn't be the only one lucky enough to keep you company."

She's not, but I appreciate what she's saying.

"And we really need to break the unlucky streak in this store. Getting you a girlfriend would be a big win for Dogeared's morale."

Both of our other employees were recently dumped. Hannah and her boyfriend ended their engagement, so she quit to regroup—I've been picking up her hours in the store ever since. And Arlo's been a sad, mopey mess since his breakup, living in a bubble of the most depressing country music he can stream. His shifts change the whole aesthetic of the store from light and cozy academia to foreboding bookshop of cursed souls.

But I focus on her more troubling point. "I thought you wanted to find me a *date* to the gala, not a girlfriend."

It's semantics, but hey—we work in a bookshop. I can quibble over word choice.

Georgia just grins. "One naturally leads to the other."

"I love your optimism." *Among other things.*

"I can tell you're leaning toward letting me be your match-maker." She squeezes my hands tighter, pleading with me.

I don't bother asking why *she* doesn't try to break Dogeared's employee unlucky-in-love streak herself. It's the same reason I haven't been more upfront with my feelings for her. Georgia is a firm believer in romance—as long as it's fictional. Bring her a book with a couple on the cover, and she's ready to fall in love.

But a real, living, breathing person? She loses all interest. She's gone on fewer dates than I have these last few years, and that's saying something. I can't count how many times I've heard her say, "The only good boyfriend is a book boyfriend."

Last I checked, I'm fully non-fictional.

Letting her set me up goes against my ultimate goals...but maybe I can still salvage this.

"I'll agree to let you set me up."

She squeals, bouncing on the balls of her feet.

"On one condition," I add. She sobers, waiting. "If the dates don't work out, you'll go to the Andromeda Awards ceremony with me."

She laughs, patting me on the shoulder like I'm talking nonsense. "Trust me. You won't need me to be your backup gal."

Georgia Donnelly is the main character in the love story I want to write, and she has no idea. If only I could admit to her she's anything but my second choice.

Chapter 3

Georgia

I get out my phone and start scrolling through contacts, looking for someone who could be a good match for Miles. Now that I've got this idea in my head, I'm super excited about it. He's seriously the best, and although he never mentions it, I'm wondering now if he might be lonely.

He needs more than a couple of guy friends and me in his life. He's the first one to drop everything for someone else—he deserves to get something back in return. He should be appreciated and adored for exactly who he is. He deserves big, open, all-consuming love.

So yeah, I might be looking to find him more than just a date to a party.

"Red flags and pet peeves?" I prompt.

"I thought you already knew all my likes and dislikes."

"In normal life, sure. But in romantic life, I don't know as much." We don't talk a lot about dating, but that's because neither of us really do. I know he had a girlfriend for part of the first year I worked here, but after that, I haven't seen or heard that he's been with anyone seriously. And everything I know about Miles tells me he doesn't see anyone casually.

He drops his chin onto his crossed arms on the front counter, stretching his absurdly long torso. "Are we really doing this?"

"Yes. It will be good for you. And amusing for me."

"Okay, Gandalf."

I love it when he catches my movie references.

"Red flags," I sing.

He sighs. "Inauthenticity. People who rain on everyone else's parades. Gossip."

I nod along, not really needing to write that down. I knew as much already. "Green flags? What are you looking for?"

He stares at me so hard my stomach flutters.

In my first year or so working for him, this little stare down actually intimidated me. If you don't know him, his reserve can come across as aloof or even unfriendly. I was half-convinced he was on the verge of firing me my first couple of months at Dogeared. But I've learned he's just a massive cinnamon roll, and he's staring because he would rather rip the pages from every book in this store than actually have an argument.

So I just stare back. I can wait.

"What cover are you working on now?" he asks.

"It's so cute. It's a couple on a blanket by a lake, but don't bother trying to distract me. It won't work."

"You're very laser focused."

I narrow my eyes on him. "I can out-stare you."

He nods lazily but doesn't look away.

I don't break. It's not like he's hard to look at. He's got thick, dark eyebrows that always make him seem extra happy—or in his current state, extra glum. He looks younger than his age, but thirty-two's not that old to begin with. And he's got nice, full lips.

Right now, they're twitching, but I'm ninety-nine percent sure he's just trying not to smile.

He is, in short, a lovely specimen of a man, and the only reason he doesn't have a bunch of women lined up out the door to date him is that he doesn't let many people get past his quiet outer shell. But I'm going to crack that shell like an M&M and usher some lucky woman to the chocolatey goodness inside.

"Where did your mind just go?" he says. "The expression on your face..."

"You're an M&M. And I'm going to crack you."

His mouth twitches again. "Sounds about right."

"You could just tell me your dating preferences. It will make everything go so much easier."

"Or I could tell you that I finished *Corsair's Run*."

I immediately fold in the stare down competition. I round the counter to get in his face, and he sits upright again. Thank goodness there isn't a rule about being quiet in a bookstore because I would break that rule every day.

"You finished it?" Confirmation is unnecessary, since I've never known Miles to lie. Exaggerate a bit maybe, but not about this. He's more likely to downplay anything to do with his writing—if he says he's done, he's done. "Why would you not lead with *that*? I've been waiting for this book for a literal year."

He drops hints about what he's working on sometimes, and once in a rare while, he'll talk out story ideas with me, but I'm running on scraps here. I need to know how my favorite space pirate's story ends.

"I could send it to you, but you'll probably be too busy vetting dates for me to read it."

I take him by the shoulders and growl like an angry puppy. "Are you really going to withhold Captain Aster from me? That's cruel and unusual punishment."

He finally breaks into a smile. "I already sent it to your e-reader."

I cough dramatically. "I have to go home. I'm ever so sick."

He lays a palm across my forehead. "I don't detect a fever."

"I'm sick in the head."

He smiles down at me. "Without a doubt."

And that's how we're standing when half my family walks into the bookstore.

We break apart, but all three Donnellys stare at us open-mouthed. My stepmother's look of shock quickly turns into a knowing smile—Ava adores gossip. Especially about me.

She can never seem to decide if she wants to be my "bonus mom" or my best friend. Since she's only ten years older than I am, she usually aims for trusty pal. Now and then, she tries to scold me for something, with uncomfortable results for everyone.

My half-siblings, Finn and Willa, just go on goggling at us. They're twelve and eight, so in their minds, the innocent way Miles and I were touching each other is probably even more scandalous than whatever Ava has in her head. Finn will let it go, but if I know my baby sister, I'm never going to hear the end of this one.

"Hey, guys." I throw on a big smile. "What are you doing here?"

She said oh-so innocently.

Ava greets us both with a little too much enthusiasm but then puts on a sad face. "Christopher forgot I had plans with friends this afternoon, and he won't be home to be with the children for another hour. Could I possibly leave the littles here with you?"

Sam and I gave them that collective nickname years ago, but our younger siblings are quickly becoming *bigs*.

"Nice of Dad to take the afternoon off," I say as Willa throws herself at me in a big hug. I squeeze her tight. However irritating I might find my dad and Ava, they made some adorable kids.

"He does a few times a month," Ava says. "You know how he is—he doesn't want to miss anything."

"Yeah, he sure would hate that." I can't put much life into my voice. When my older brother, Sam, and I were growing up, Dad missed entire birthdays for work. He's become rather more dedicated to his new family in his later years.

I'm glad he's around for them. Honestly, I am. But sometimes the proof of it stings like salt in an old wound I can't quite bandage over.

"We're going to have noodles!" Willa grins up at me, her dark hair straggling out of a complicated braid around her head.

"Dad never cooks." Finn runs his fingers through his hair, making it stand up in spiky bits that look suspiciously like Miles's unruly hair. "He says that's not his skillset."

At least some things haven't changed.

"I'm working today," I tell Ava. "Maybe I could have changed my shift around if I'd known about it, but—"

Her face crumples. "Oh, please. It's just for an hour. I need to make it to this luncheon."

Naturally, her luncheon is more important than my work. It's not the first time she's brought the littles to the bookstore at the last minute, but I'm terrible at saying no to her. Actually, I can tell *her* no any day, but it's more difficult to look into my little sister's eyes and tell her to get lost.

Because she's too stinking cute for words.

I turn to Miles, who gives a quick nod. What did I say about the man being the very best?

"Okay." I manage not to sigh, but I don't love that Ava uses me as free babysitting when I'm at the bookstore. At least we can all pretend I'm not busy working on book covers when I'm at home, but there's no excuse here. "They can hang out for a while."

Willa screeches her approval, and Finn flops onto one of the plush chairs.

"Thank you so much," Ava says. "Christopher will be here in an hour. Hour and a half tops."

By the time I register that tidbit she tacked on, she's already out the door.

"No school today, huh?" I look down at Willa, who hasn't stopped hugging me yet.

"Nope. It's a teacher learning day."

"I bet they need to stay smart to keep up with you."

She giggles. "I wish they learned every day."

"Can you play a game with me, Miles?" Finn's already opening the backgammon board next to his chair. Every time they drop into the store, it's the same thing: Finn wants to play a game, and Willa wants a sweet treat from the pastry case.

Now Miles is the one checking in with me, but I wave him on. "Willa and I can handle the front counter."

Miles takes the seat across from Finn and helps him set up the board, while Willa and I sit down on the stools behind the counter. She tells me about what's going on at school and all the hot gossip with her little friends. *Claire's been giving out friendship bracelets. Amina has the latest Nike Dunks that cost more than a car.* We greet customers who come into the shop, and she sits quietly whenever I need to get up to make an espresso or cash out a purchase.

I actually start to think she's entirely forgotten what she saw when she walked into the store, but her eight-year-old brain holds onto things longer than I'd hoped.

She leans over to whisper to me during a lull between customers. "I like Miles."

"So do I," I whisper back.

"Do you kiss him the way Sam kisses Harper?"

Nerves skate through my stomach. She's been innocently

fascinated by our oldest brother's relationship ever since it started two years ago. Mostly the parts that involve kissing and hugging. Incidentally, these are the same things that give Finn a case of the gags.

I look over at Miles, but thankfully, he's too focused on his game with Finn to have heard. I think. With him, it's hard to know for sure. He can be low-key sneaky.

"We're best friends," I tell her. "So we don't kiss."

"You could try."

Her goading remark shouldn't make my stomach flip, but there it goes anyway, getting distinctly wobbly. It's probably because I haven't kissed anybody in a million years, and my boss-slash-best friend is a crazy pick to break that streak. And anyway, having an eight-year-old give me dating tips is a sad statement on my life.

"Friends don't do that." I sound absolutely scandalized, as if I really care what the people wandering the stacks and eating cinnamon rolls in the café would think if they overheard.

"Why not? I kissed Jaxon, and he's my friend."

Hmm. Maybe I *should* be getting dating tips from Willa.

"You kissed him on the lips?" Is third grade really so different these days? I had my first kiss in middle school, and it was terrible. Isn't that still normal?

She makes a face. "On the cheek. Mouth kisses are for your really-real boyfriend."

"I see." I need to steer this conversation somewhere other than the best kissing locations, and quickly. "Did you do anything fun this weekend?"

"Daddy took us to breakfast on Saturday." Her happy smile grows brighter. "Grandpa Glen did magic tricks."

Our grandpa is still going strong at eighty-seven and is a total character. My only explanation for the one-eighty between him and Dad is that awesomeness must skip a generation. He's my biggest champion and most trusted advisor. When my parents blew up their marriage—and lied to Sam and me about it in the worst way—Grandpa was the one I turned to. He and Grandma were the reason I came back to Magnolia Ridge after college. He lives over at the retirement center now, but I visit him as often as I can.

I wrap Willa in a side hug. "Did he pull a coin out of your ear?"

She giggles. "Out of my nose."

That's our grandpa.

I let her go. "What are you going to do with Dad this afternoon?"

"Daddy said we'll have a movie date. With popcorn and blanket forts and candy!"

"That. Sounds. Awesome." I accentuate each word with a gentle poke to her side.

"Did Daddy watch movies with you when you were little?"

I look into her eager brown eyes and can't possibly tell her the truth. That our father didn't have quite as much time for Sam and me when we were growing up. That even when he did, he was more likely to use that time lecturing us than bonding over something as simple as a movie or a game. That I barely recognize the doting father he's become for Finn and Willa.

That I don't understand why he couldn't have been that kind of father for me.

"Sometimes," I tell her. She just beams.

Soon enough, the man himself arrives to pick up the littles. He's clearly come from work, dressed in a neat suit, his salt-and-pepper hair still perfectly combed away from his face. Willa darts straight into his arms, and he lifts her up into a huge hug.

"How's my baby girl?" he croons. "Ready for movies?"

"Ready for movies!"

He kisses her cheek with a big smack. "That's good. I'd hate to have to watch Jumanji all alone."

"Not Jumanji. Jungle Cruise."

Dad makes a silly face. "I knew it was something like that. With that guy with the little muscles?"

"He has big muscles, Daddy!"

He slides her back down to her feet. Then, his adoring expression shifts into something distinctly cooler. He surveys the store in the same detached way he does every time he comes in, like he's inspecting a sterile room instead of seeing a warm and cozy place where people love to shop and hang out.

Before he can pass judgment on Dogeared yet again, Finn joins him.

"I almost beat Miles at backgammon. He's good, but he's not as good as Grandpa Glen."

Grandpa ropes anybody he can into playing backgammon with him over at his retirement village. He's been delighted to find a real challenger in Miles, since Sam and I don't stand a chance against him.

"Nobody is, kiddo." Dad looks over at me. "If you ever change your mind and decide you want a real job, there's always room for you at Donnelly and Burke."

I urge my face not to do anything sarcastic. "I'm good."

He takes Willa's hand. "We've got movies to watch. Thanks for looking out for them."

Finn and Willa call out their goodbyes, and in a blink, they've disappeared down the sidewalk.

After a minute, Miles joins me behind the counter. He can probably hear me grinding my teeth down to dust.

"You could see it as your dad saying he'll always be there for you."

I can't help the bitter laugh that exhales out of me. Miles

likes to see the best in people, but when it comes to my dad, I just don't feel it. "Redirect your altruism elsewhere, please."

"In other news, Finn will be able to beat me at backgammon soon. I should probably retire from the game now to avoid the humiliation."

"You would sacrifice a young boy's triumph for the sake of your tattered pride?"

"In a heartbeat."

He wouldn't, though. I've seen him play enough board games with Willa to know he's not above throwing games to make a little kid happy.

"Where were we? Oh yeah, you were about to tell me what you're looking for in a woman."

He sighs. "Speaking of my tattered pride..."

I keep my voice low so people in the store don't overhear. "Maybe we should focus on physical preferences to narrow it down. Brunette? Short hair? Are you an elbow man?"

His bold eyebrows slash down, his concern morphing into confusion. "Elbows?"

"I'm being polite."

"I can honestly say I've never noticed a woman's elbows."

"You should pay more attention," I tease. "Elbows are sexy."

He moves to try to see mine, but I swing them awkwardly behind my back. Now I'm pushing out my chest—not that it makes much of a difference for me. But at least he can't see my un-sexy elbows.

"Someone shorter than you is a given, since you are a giant," I go on, still standing like a frozen chicken.

He's six-four and slender, which can make him seem even taller than he is.

He's also remarkably silent.

"Come on, you have to give me something to work with."

He levels me a flat look. "It'd be a shame if you had to give up the cause."

"Younger? Older?" I gasp. "Are you a gray hair chaser? Should I look for available ladies at Grandpa's retirement complex?"

That at least earns a laugh. "Might be inappropriate."

I raise my eyebrows at him, waiting for him to throw me a crumb.

"I don't really care about all that," he finally says. "It's a person's heart I like."

Aww. How is this man single?

"You're seriously the best man there ever was. And I am going to find someone who's absolutely perfect for you."

His half-smile makes me think he doesn't believe me, but I've made up my mind. I'm going to see him happily matched up for his awards ceremony, or my name isn't Georgia Donnelly.

Chapter 4

Miles

Georgia ends her shift singing a made-up song about dates, magic, and galas. Honestly, it kind of blurs together. The sultry wink she gives me as she nudges the door with her hip to leave stays vivid in my mind, though.

I'm a lunatic for letting her set me up. An absolute madman. But telling her the truth feels crazier.

Eventually, I close up Dogeared for the night and head out. New ideas for my next book have been simmering all day, and I'd like to hunker down on my couch with my laptop and a marginally healthy dinner so I can let them loose. But tonight, I have other responsibilities, and head in the opposite direction from my apartment.

It's still weird driving out to my mom's house. You'd think I'd get used to the changes, but they never quite sit right. Every time I come out here, I turn into an old man complaining about how things aren't what they used to be. *Youths*.

Ten years ago, my mom and aunt sold my grandparents' acreage on the south end of Magnolia Ridge, where green, sprawling farms dominate the landscape. It was tough to give up the land they'd loved for so long, but with my grandparents gone, we had to be realistic. None of the rest of us would ever farm it. I don't have that gene, and my cousins in Houston certainly don't either.

My mom and Aunt Cece each kept two acres for themselves and sold off the rest. We genuinely thought a rancher or a farmer would pick up the torch and keep the land just as it was. Maybe add a new barn.

Turns out we'd all been a little naive.

Today, that former farmland is Rivendell Acres, an upscale gated community featuring huge houses on tiny cement lots. Ironic that it's named for one of the most beautiful and pristine lands in Middle Earth.

I have to be grateful for the development—the sale of the land provided for my mom and me, and aunt and cousins. I wouldn't have been able to open Dogeared and dedicate myself to writing books without my share of the money.

But I've never seen anything uglier.

At Mom's house, the old elm trees blot out the wall and the McMansions, and I can breathe again. Inside, I forget it all when the scent of baked peaches envelops me. It's both deeply comforting and highly irritating.

"I thought you were going to wait for me." I cross the living room into the kitchen where Mom is setting the golden-brown pie out to cool. I arrived right on time to catch her red-handed.

She just shrugs. "It's a good day."

I try not to grumble. I'm always thankful for the good days. But she doesn't need to do anything to make it worse when she knows I'm nearby, ready to help her out.

Slipping off her orange plaid oven mitts, she turns to fully face me. "Turn off your worried face. I told you I won't do more than I feel I can, and I'm sticking to that."

"In hindsight, that's a pretty vague promise."

Especially from a woman who hates to admit there's anything she can't do.

"I stopped by Evans Orchards and had to get a few pounds of peaches. I can't help it if they demanded being turned into a delicious pie."

Can't blame her. Evans Orchards has the best peaches around. "Always listen to the peaches."

Her smile turns wistful. "Sometimes I miss it, you know."

My face probably mirrors hers. "I know."

Mom owned Butter & Batter for almost twenty years. Right up until her arthritis got so bad she couldn't bake anymore. Selling Grandma and Grandpa's land was hard on her, but it was worse for her to sell the bakery she'd built from the ground up and poured so much love into.

It's still going strong, though—the new owners didn't turn it into a condo or anything like that. I even stop in sometimes when I want a slice of pie with a debilitating wave of nostalgia.

"They're selling hand pies at the farmers market now. Did you know that?" She sits at the kitchen table, surreptitiously rubbing one of her wrists. Her hair is in a bun so messy, I can't tell if it's intentional or accidental. It might not be as good a day as she claims. "They've got a cute little display case and everything. I wish I'd thought of that."

"Marketing's tricky." It hurts to watch her knobby fingers massage the base of her thumb. I go to the sink and fill it with soapy water to take care of the dishes left over from her illicit baking.

"Are you doing anything at the market yet for the bookstore?"

"Not yet, but Georgia has ideas."

"Ooh, tell me about these ideas. That girl cracks me up."

"She found an old adult tricycle on *Found & Freebies* a few weeks ago. It's got a big wooden box mounted between the two front tires. She's dead set on converting it into a bookmobile and taking it to the farmers market in the spring."

Mom's laughter fills the kitchen. "I bet it will look good, too."

"It will. Georgia's got a vision for stuff like that."

"Are you helping her convert the bike?"

"The mechanics of that aren't really my strong suit. Her brother and grandpa will do that part." I just rode it from its previous owner's place to her apartment. With an afternoon of experience, I can safely say that thing is a beast. Can't imagine how it will handle filled with books, but I love her enthusiasm.

"She's a real nice girl." Mom's pause is a verbal shove in the back. No doubt she's waiting for a detailed confession.

I go on scrubbing bowls. I haven't expressed to her in words how I feel about Georgia, but it's clear I've said more than enough without them.

"Is she seeing anyone?" Mom's curiosity has a pushy lilt to it.

"Nope."

"That's a shame. Someone should snap her up."

I make a noncommittal sound, even though I would *very* much like to commit to snapping up Georgia.

I rinse the dishes and set them aside. Wiping my hands, I turn to face Mom. "What else can I do?"

There's always something. Her arthritis flareups can make even the simplest household chores excruciating. Her medications and herbal remedies only do so much.

"Just sit around and wait for the pie to cool."

Down the hall, the dryer chimes.

"I'm on it."

"You don't need to do all that."

But I've grabbed a laundry basket and started unloading

before she can finish admonishing me. I fold the towels, put them away in the linen closet, and return to the kitchen.

She looks distinctly unimpressed, but we go through this every time I visit. I do something to help her out, she claims she doesn't need the help, and she feeds me a delicious treat she swears she forgot how to bake. It's a never-ending cycle.

"I have news."

Her eyes go as wide as the pie plate in front of her. "About you and Georgia?"

I probably should have prefaced that better, given the direction of her thoughts.

"Not about me and Georgia." A knot works in my throat as my head fills with all sorts of announcements I'd love to make about the two of us. Maybe one day. "I've been nominated for an Andromeda Award."

She leaps out of her chair to attack me with a hug. "Oh, honey. I never would have guessed. An Andromeda Award. How wonderful."

Laughing softly, I hug her tight. "You don't know what that is, do you?"

She looks up into my face. "I've never heard of it before in my life, but it must be something special if you're up for one. Tell me all about it."

We sit and I explain about the awards and how they're voted on by my peers in the science fiction writing world. Really, they're not even my peers—most of the authors on the panel have been big names for decades. They're more like dukes and baronesses to my measly commoner.

I thought it was bad knowing regular people were reading my books, but that's nothing to having my author heroes reading them.

I mention the gala, but I don't tell Mom about Georgia's scheme to find me a date or my counter-scheme to make sure the date is her. She already jumps to enough conclusions. I don't need to drive her to the edge of the cliff.

Even if that cliff is the exact right conclusion.

"I'm so excited for you, honey. This is really special, isn't it?"

I'm trying to downplay it for my own sanity's sake, but I can't pretend it's not significant. The Rising Star nomination means people expect big things from my writing career. No pressure, or anything. My agent has called twice already this week to congratulate me, guess at the boost in sales numbers I've received, and check on the status of the last book in the series I'm revising. It's a lot, but none of it quite feels real.

"It's...something."

Mom reaches out to take my hand. "You're allowed to celebrate yourself. Enjoy this moment."

Sounds a lot like what Georgia said, except she specifically wanted me to celebrate with a date. Who isn't her. Which is the opposite of a celebration in my book.

"Your dad would be so proud." Mom's voice takes on the gentle tone it always does when she mentions him.

It's not a fresh wound. He's been gone fourteen years. But it still aches.

Unlike my more reserved nature, Dad had enthusiasm for everything. He would have loved Dogeared and found a way to work it into every conversation around town. He would have giddily bought my books in every possible format. And he would have seen through me a long time ago with Georgia.

"I've got a favor to ask of you," Mom says.

"Must be serious. Usually, you try to convince me you don't need any help."

Doesn't matter anyway—I'll handle whatever she asks of me.

Mom shakes her head. "It's really Cece's favor. I just said I'd be the messenger."

"Now I'm nervous." Mom's favors are usually things like yard work or errands she swears she can take care of herself. My aunt is more of a wild card. When she needs something, it could be anything from being a guinea pig for her latest hair dye experiments to helping her bathe her cat.

I'm never doing either one again.

"You know the Kissing Corn Maze?" Mom asks.

"Sure. The Mackay Farm's version of a bachelor auction." Every year at the end of October, they hide a bunch of men in their cornfield, and a crowd of women rush through trying to be the first to their chosen man. They have one where women wait in the cornfield for a swarm of men, too, but I wouldn't say it's a step forward for equality.

"They're finalizing this year's bachelors, and they're one short."

I'm waiting for more, but Mom's watching me so steadily, my gut twists. This is the favor?

"You want me to be the last bachelor?" I can't imagine anything worse. I guess standing on a stage and being auctioned off to the highest bidder would be up there, but waiting to be "picked" in the cornfield sounds humiliating any way you look at it.

"It's for a good cause. All the money they raise this year is going to the Cortez family. Their teen daughter has a long road of physical therapy in front of her after getting hit by that drunk driver over the summer."

I know she didn't say it to be manipulative, but that's all I needed to hear. Victims of drunk driving are a soft spot for all of us since we lost Dad the same way.

"How does this work? Am I supposed to go on a date with

whoever 'wins' me?" I don't know how that sentence could be any more awkward.

"I think it's tradition." Her eyes turn so gentle, it's like she's read the pages of my heart. "It doesn't have to mean forever."

No, it doesn't. But it'd be a whole lot easier if I weren't already in love with someone else.

It's ridiculous, and terrible timing, but obviously, I'm not going to turn her down.

"I'll do it."

Georgia's trying to set me up, and my mom and aunt are volunteering me for a bachelor auction. And here I thought I'd have a quiet, relaxed fall without any dating whatsoever.

Text Thread

Georgia: I've got some ideas of dates for you, but I need you to rank them

Miles: Feels wrong

Georgia: Would you rather go out with a teacher, an insurance agent, or a florist?

Miles: Don't matchmakers decide that?

Georgia: Matchmakers do a lot of research

Georgia: I'm researching

Miles: I won't be surprised to get a 100 question survey in the mail

Georgia: You're a genius! I'll do that

Miles: Do not do that

Georgia: Are you opposed to single moms?

Miles: I am opposed to questions

Georgia: Do you care about an income gap?

Miles: I wouldn't mind being a sugar baby

Georgia: OMG

Georgia: Do you want kids?

Miles: One day, yes

Georgia: Big family or small?

Miles: Hopefully more than one child

Georgia: You know I'm going to need you to drive me to pick up the bookshelf, right?

Georgia: It won't fit in my car

Miles: I figured

Miles: I'm at your disposal

Miles: Except for this set up thing

Georgia: You know you love me

Georgia: You'd be lost without me

Miles: Undeniably

Chapter 5

Miles

"You're doing what now?"

The incredulous look on Owen's face confirms that Georgia's plan to matchmake for me is just as bonkers as I imagine it to be. I see no need to mention the Kissing Corn Maze and sink his opinion of me even lower.

It's been days, and Georgia's talked almost nonstop about her goal to find me a date to the Andromeda Awards. After useless agonizing on my own, I enlisted my friend to join me at Lupe's Escape for dinner. We'd barely dug into our enchiladas before I blurted out what's bothering me.

Owen and I don't usually have heart-to-hearts, but I'm not usually this tormented by my best friend's "goodwill," either.

"I am reluctantly participating in Georgia's dating schemes," I confirm.

He's looking at me like I just revealed I'm secretly a cyborg here to spy on the human race. Which is probably something I should write down for brainstorming later. A secret cyborg spy could be good.

He scrapes a hand over his beard. "This is a terrible plan."

"I know."

Letting her set me up is a nightmare scenario. Like when I relive college in my dreams and show up to class completely unprepared, unsure if I'm in the right room, and wearing nothing but my underwear.

However, the alternative involves telling her things I don't know that she's ready to hear. She's turned down every guy who's asked her out for the last two years, possibly longer. She's comfortable with me now, but she might see me differently the minute I tell her how I feel about her. I'm not ready to lose our closeness.

If that means I have to go on a few dates with someone else, I'll do it.

I guess we're both bonkers.

"I don't have room to throw stones," Owen says. "But this… this is a truly terrible plan."

He shares my pain. For months now, he's been pining after Josie, an environmental scientist new to Magnolia Ridge. She joined a couple of the book clubs that meet at Dogeared, and I see her once in a while around town. She seems lost in her own thoughts half the time, but when she speaks up, it's clear she's brilliant.

Owen has managed to talk to her exactly never. We've only been friends for two years, but I've never seen him lack for confidence with a woman like this. He's a burly MMA instructor who owns every room he walks into.

Unless *she's* in the room. Then, he stares longingly for a few minutes, avoids all possibility of actually speaking with her, and turns right around and leaves. It's painful to watch, but so far, it seems I'm the only one who's noticed the pattern.

"I think you're wrong about Josie."

You can tell when people are judging you. It's in the way their eyes move over you or an inflection in their voice. They've seen something in you that doesn't measure up, and they write you off. But Josie's never given me those vibes.

He grunts. "What would a literal scientist want with a guy who teaches people how to throw punches for a living? She has a PhD."

"You're a lot more than just your fists."

He takes a drink of his margarita. "High praise."

"You have interests beyond the ring. I still say your gardening is a good place to start."

Another grunt. "I'd come away from any conversation with her sounding like an idiot."

"Unlikely." Our friendship sprang up from conversations in the bookshop. He can be gruff, and he's about as easy to get to know as I am, but he's an interesting guy when he gives himself space to talk.

"She's...soft and delicate. And crazy smart. We won't have anything in common."

"She could be a motorcycle aficionado, for all we know."

He has two. Despite his suggestions I should learn to ride, I've avoided that deathtrap so far.

"Don't even think it. She'd have me on my knees if she were."

"So give her a chance. Be honest with her. Try."

He glares. "Says the guy who's letting the woman he's in love with set him up with other women."

Yeah, that kind of springs a leak in my "be honest with her" advice. I've parroted those same words for a while now, but it's different when you're on the receiving end.

"In my defense, I created a loophole. If Georgia's set ups don't pan out, she'll be my date to the awards ceremony."

Owen nods over his enchiladas verdes. "So you're going to torpedo the dates."

I lay a hand over my heart. "With the utmost respect."

I had enough first dates explode on the launchpad in my twenties. It shouldn't be hard to get the same results on these setups.

"And then you'll tell her?"

Nerves plummet through my gut. I don't have a specific plan beyond taking her to the awards ceremony. Will I actually tell her how I feel afterward? I've been waiting for her to give some kind of indication she has feelings for me, too, before I confess anything.

I might end up waiting for the rest of my life.

"I don't know what I'll tell her. But the date is a start."

"Why wait? You two spend most of your days together as it is. You could just tell her how you feel any time."

"You could just come to one of the book clubs Josie's in and ask her out."

He splays a hand at me. "Take your time."

I chuckle. Neither of us is ready to risk breaking our own hearts. "Is Rumble Room doing something for the Harvest Festival?"

He grunts confirmation. "The gym owner seems to think I'll do well with the kids. I'll probably be in charge of bobbing for apples or something like that."

"Do they still let kids do that?"

"Can't be worse than anything else kids do."

He's got a point. Half of what I've seen Georgia's younger siblings touch with their bare hands makes me want to whip out some disinfecting spray.

"It's a good idea though."

Owen's eyebrows tug together. "The apple bobbing?"

"Sorry, no. My mind wandered there. I mean having businesses volunteer their time at the Harvest Festival." It encourages a sense of community involvement and reminds residents we're all in this together.

His mouth tugs into a smirk. "You say that because you're planning to have Georgia volunteer right along with you."

"Guilty." I have to subdue a smirk of my own. Of course, my volunteering together plan would have been a whole lot smoother without her matchmaking plan heaped on top of it.

"How's your arm doing?" I ask.

He lifts his short sleeve to reveal a new tattoo scene covering his left upper arm. The right is already covered shoulder to wrist. He's got more tattoos on his chest I've glimpsed when we spar at the gym where he teaches. Probably even more than that, but I haven't asked for a full inventory.

"All healed."

He twists his arm so I can see the design. It's an underwater image that includes everything from softly floating jellyfish to starfish along his elbow to the hammerhead shark centerpiece.

"That's good work." I don't know much about tattoos, but I know good art when I see it.

He replaces the shirt sleeve. "I'm happy with it. Hammerheads are the coolest."

"Maybe that's what I need. I'll get a tattoo to confess to Georgia. One of her drawings permanently inked on my skin would be a pretty good love declaration." I'm joking, but it's not the first time the thought's crossed my mind.

His dark look tells me he isn't impressed. "You're a writer. Seems like you could think of another way to confess to her."

"Possibly." Like possibly the drawer full of letters I've written and never given her. Once in a while, when my heart feels like it's going to overflow from longing, I write everything I'm feeling in a letter. It's a relief to get it off my chest, however short-lived. I've got a good thirty letters stashed away now.

A full-body tattoo would be less painful than sharing those.

Chapter 6

Georgia

It turns out the bookshelf I was so happy to score for free is haunted. It makes a terrible creaking noise every time the Lazy Susan base moves. Which is, sadly, the whole point of the bookshelf.

Miles drove me to its former residence, and we maneuvered it in and out of his station wagon, up three flights of stairs at my apartment complex, and finally onto my balcony. It's not very heavy, but it's awkward to carry, and we're both a little sweaty after all that wrestling.

With the bookshelf. Duh.

We get it situated on a tarp I set out here for it. I'm not dumb enough to strip the bookshelf's old paint in my apartment. I have no intention of passing out from toxic fumes.

Miles spins it again, prompting the terrible screech. I put my hand over his and pull him away slowly.

"Don't do that."

He chuckles. "Now we know why it was a freebie."

"WD-40 should do it." I hope. I can probably take the base apart and inspect it, but my handiness generally stops at the surface level. If paint can't fix it, I probably can't either.

"I'm looking forward to seeing what you do with it."

"Everyone's got high expectations today," I grumble as we go back inside.

"Wait." He stops me with a gentle hand on my arm. "I didn't mean that to sound critical."

His immediate and unnecessary apology makes my shoulders sag. He's not being the jerk—I am. "Sorry. It's not about you. My dad left me a very...detailed voicemail this afternoon."

Miles's gaze turns hard. "Do I want to know the subject?"

I'm sure he can guess by now.

"My negligible career ambitions, my reckless financial instability, how unrealistic it is to live off my art, how unwise I am to keep working for a business that's constantly courting bankruptcy." At least my dad's efficient. He hit all his favorite talking points in one message. "And that part's completely untrue. Dogeared is doing amazing."

"Slights against the bookstore are the least of my concerns." Miles tips his head closer until I meet his eyes. "He doesn't know what he's talking about."

I love the vehemence in his usually calm voice. It's a nice contrast to the condescension that rang out loud and clear in my dad's.

"He's not totally wrong, though. I don't have huge ambitions. I just want to make art and read books and be happy." I try for a laugh, but it comes out a snort. Like even I don't believe I can achieve that much.

"You should quit the bookstore."

My mouth drops open, but I snap it shut and squirm out of his grasp to walk across my living room. This again? "Miles Forrester, stop trying to fire me."

His mouth twitches into something like a smile. "I would never fire you. But you should quit so you can make covers full time."

My heart squeezes. That's the job description I've been working toward these last few years: *Georgia Donnelly, Illustrator*. But I can't pretend my dad doesn't know what he's talking about. He didn't build his seven-figure company without learning a few things about smart business choices.

Going totally out on my own *is* reckless. I want to...but I don't want it to fast-track me to debt and disappointment. And I've got this troubling fear that the second my art becomes my entire job, it will lose its magic.

And anyway, I've invested a lot of time and energy at Dogeared. I can't just abandon Miles to go do my own thing.

"Are you saying you don't need me?" I cock a hip against my kitchen counter because I know I have him. Not to brag, but he couldn't have breathed new life into that store without me.

His mouth flattens into a thin line. "I would never say that."

"See?" I toss a hand up at him. "As long as you need me, I'm staying."

He slowly approaches me across the room. "Okay. You're staying. But try to put your dad's opinions out of your head."

Some of my swagger fades. "It isn't easy."

"I know. I wish..." He moves one hand like he's going to touch my face or brush my hair out of my eyes—*something*—but stops himself. He balls his hand into a fist and drops it to his side. "Your father should support and encourage you. He should always have your back, no matter what. He should be defending you, not cutting you down."

"Maybe in a parallel universe." I try to exhale out all my frustration, but it doesn't work. I hate that Dad's low opinions still get to me even after years of telling myself I don't care. "I'm sorry. I shouldn't complain when you..."

It's unfair Miles had such a great dad but so little time with him. I sound like a brat whining "my daddy's not being nice to me" when Miles would do anything for one more minute with his.

Drunk drivers are the literal worst.

"We don't do that. We don't need to compare our past hurts."

"I know. You're right." He's told me that every time it comes up, but I still feel like a jerk. "Can I have a hug?"

This look comes across Miles's face as though *he's* the one who's being comforted—it's tender and sweet and just makes me want to hug him even more than usual.

He doesn't say anything, but he wraps me in his arms. I burrow in, sighing against him. Sometime in the last three years, I learned what a great hugger he is and developed a slight addiction. He holds me close like he'll never let go—none of this "loose hands, almost ready to pull away" nonsense some guys do. He goes all in for as long as I need.

I take slow breaths, safe in my cocoon, and try to forget Dad's message. Miles's heartbeat at my ear soothes me until I feel like myself again. I hold on even longer, soaking in the goodness. I have so few high-quality huggers in my life. I don't give up the experience easily.

But eventually, I let him go. I can't use my boss/best friend's hugs as free therapy forever.

Or can I?

No.

"Want to see my latest cover?"

His half-smile is a sparkler dancing around in my chest.

"Always."

I lead him into my living room, and he takes a seat on my couch. I grab my tablet from my bedroom, and when I return, he's glancing around at my decor he missed when we fumbled through with the bookshelf.

"You haven't seen the full autumn glory yet, have you?"

His eyebrows hitch up as he scans the room. "It might be even more glory than last year."

My living room looks like it should be on a fall candle label —cozy throw blankets, rich plaids in browns and reds, natural wreaths dotted with leaves faux and real. My orange Pyrex casserole dishes sit out on the kitchen counter next to a giant ceramic walnut cookie jar. And everything smells like apples and cinnamon from the secret surprise I baked earlier.

"You know me. I don't do understated."

I flop down next to him on the couch and pull up the cover I'm almost ready to send to the author for approval. It shows a couple holding hands on a gingham blanket next to a lakeside. I put a lot of detail into this one and probably spent more time perfecting the trees and the braid in her hair than I should have. But illustrating soothes me almost as well as hugging Miles does.

Dealing with authors doesn't always have the same result, but most of my clients are great.

"Your covers get better and better." He's carefully holding the tablet as though he could break it, his eyes roving over the illustration to take in every last blade of grass and blanket tassel. "I'm in awe of your talent."

My fingers brush his as I pull the tablet from him. "Says the guy who writes whole books."

He doesn't say anything because why would he? He'd never respond with, "Yeah, I'm pretty great, aren't I?" Even though he is. His brain is full of spaceships and pirates and renegades and the most wonderful space opera ever.

I set the tablet aside and take a deep breath. I've been as patient for as long as I possibly can in one afternoon. We had a job to do earlier, but now I can't avoid the elephant trampling around in the room.

"I'm trying to be normal about this, Miles, but...you're torturing me."

His eyebrows twitch in the center, drawing closer like they're seeking comfort in each other. He swallows hard. "I am?"

"You let Captain Aster get kidnapped?" I unleash the reader beast, practically launching myself at him, even though I can't get much closer. "Kidnapped! And his old commander surrendered to try to rescue him and threw himself in front of blaster fire and it *didn't even work?* Do you want to give me a heart attack?"

He looks unaccountably pleased with himself for putting one of my favorite characters ever into mortal peril. "So you're enjoying the book?"

"I'm miserable. I've had trouble sleeping. I can't think about anything else. *Obviously* I'm enjoying the book."

A huge grin breaks across his face. "Glad to hear I've got your approval."

"Five-star review to come." My enthusiasm fades somewhat. "But I'm getting nervous you're going to kill off Captain Aster as a full-circle, 'mercenary sacrifices himself for the greater good' plot point. And I do not endorse that. He needs to retire and live happily ever after with his second in command, even though it's going to take him another ten years to admit he loves her."

His expression doesn't change. "No spoilers."

"Please let him at least kiss his second. Just once, softly, before he dies saving his crew from an exploding nebula."

Laughter rumbles through him. "Maybe you should write the books. You're full of ideas."

"Nah. I just know my tropes. Want to stay for dinner?"

"Sure."

I drag myself off the couch and head for the kitchen. "How about ramen?"

"Sounds great. Just tell me what you want me to do."

Magnolia Ridge isn't exactly a hotbed of vegetarian dining

options, so when we discovered we both avoid eating meat, we immediately banded together. We share recipes and swap reviews of various faux meats, often making meals together when we're hanging out. With me in charge of the broth and Miles on veggie duty, we get the ramen whipped up in no time.

We take our bowls to my table and get comfortable. The miso soup and ramen are exactly what I needed on this cloudy fall day. It's not really *fall* in central Texas yet, and most days still creep into the mid-eighties, but I'll take it. We talk over dinner—a small thing really, but some days it feels like a gift.

Sam lived with me for a few months after he came back to town two years ago. Since he moved out to be with Harper, it's easy to forget just how comforting it can be to have someone else in the apartment with me. I don't mind my own company, but there's such a thing as getting bored with yourself.

"I read that getting nominated for an Andromeda Award can boost a book onto *The New York Times* Bestseller list." I try to sound casual, but I'm nothing close. Never am.

He blinks at me over his soup. "You've been doing a lot of research lately."

"I'm excited for you. I've never been so invested in characters in a series before." Even if now, I'm mildly terrified my favorite anti-hero will wind up dead by the end of it. His death had better be extra noble. And his second had better cry over his body in a big dramatic scene.

"Not even your romances? You get pretty caught up in them."

It's a polite way of saying I obsess over my couples. I accept that.

"I might love the characters, but there's usually less stress in those. I'm always guaranteed a happy ending." I stare hard at him.

He just stares back.

"Sure would be nice to know all the characters will wind up safe and sound in the end, right?" I add a wink as I get up to clear our bowls away.

That earns a short laugh. "I think you would eviscerate me if I actually spoiled the book for you."

"It would be so painful too." I come back from the kitchen with the Dutch apple pie I baked this morning. I set it in front of him like it's his birthday and we're ready to light the candles.

Shoot. I should have got candles.

"What's this?" he asks.

"I suspect you still have some celebrating to do. It's for Miles Forrester, Andromeda Award nominee, writer genius, best boss ever, esquire, and such and such, in perpetuity, yada yada."

He stares up at me, a slow smile spreading across his face like the brightest comet streaking across the night sky. "I'm honored. Thank you."

In typical Miles fashion, he's making *me* feel like the one who deserves the accolades and the celebratory pie. I curtsy like a goof and serve up slices for us.

He takes his first bite and groans his approval. "This is so good, Georgia."

I'm ready to do a happy dance in my chair. *Success!* His mom used to own a bakery in town—impressing him with pastries is a big deal.

"If you're not going to promise me that Captain Aster and his second fly off into the sunset, then I guess we'd better talk about *your* happily ever after."

Some of his pie delight fades. "Terrible transition."

"*Perfect* transition. I really do have a short-list of candidates and ideas for potential first dates. Do you want to go over them, or do you want to be surprised?"

His expression falls as though I offered to stab him in the heart. The hurt look in his eyes winks out my eagerness. Like a lot of things in my life, just because I'm excited about something doesn't mean anyone else shares my enthusiasm.

"I'm sorry," I say, easing off the pushiness. "Do you really not want to date anyone? Maybe you're...demisexual or something? I don't want to force you into a situation that would make you truly uncomfortable. The whole point was to try to bring more happiness into your life, not less."

I really do have good intentions, but none of that matters if I'm actually hurting him in the end. I would never do that.

"Sometimes I get over-excited and do my best impression of a steamroller." He knows that, but it bears repeating. I put my hand over his where it rests on the table. "I'll let it go if you're just not interested in dating."

He loops his thumb over my fingers, locking me in. His eyes never break from mine. Everything inside me stills as though I have more riding on his answer than a few names on my Notes app.

"I am interested in dating," he finally says.

Relief floods through me, and I bust out a stupid grin.

"I don't think I'm demisexual, but I haven't thought about it much. Sometimes sparks hit right away. Other times...it's a slow-burning ember that grows into an inferno as friendship develops into something deeper."

Oh. It's suddenly really warm in here. Why am I wearing a sweater when it's almost eighty-five degrees out? I let go of him and wipe my clammy hand on my jeans.

He flexes his fingers. Double *oh*. Did he feel the clamminess too? So gross.

I force a laugh. "See? You're a romantic at heart. You just need a little push."

"You're a romantic, too, but you don't date either. Maybe you need a push too."

I hitch a shoulder. "Classic trust issues, I guess. That's why I prefer my men fictional."

"Right," he says, his tone flat. "Your special ops guys."

"Aw, you remember." Of course he does. Miles remembers everything.

"You've mentioned them once or twice."

"That's what I like. A strong, capable hero ready to rescue me when I get kidnapped by my brother's drug gang friends."

He laughs softly. "I didn't know Sam had a dark side."

"There's always a reason for some light kidnapping and a guns-blazing rescue."

"That's what you're waiting for? A hero to sweep you off your feet?"

It sounds ridiculous when he says it straight out like that. Is it so wrong to want to be protected and cherished and loved so totally that all my broken little pieces fit back together? I'm not naive enough to think I could have that in real life. I just want a little slice of vicarious love to get me through.

"For now, I'll be happy enough to see *you* go on dates," I tell him.

"Your priorities confuse me."

Text Thread

Georgia: Phenomenal. Amazing. I'm in literal tears

Miles: I need more context

Georgia: I finished *Corsair's Run*

Georgia: I have no words for how good it is

Miles: The ending wasn't too much?

Georgia: The best amount

Georgia: Aster is a true hero. His arc is just...ugh

Georgia: So good

Miles: I'm glad my star rating didn't go down

Georgia: As if you read your reviews

Miles: I care about your review

Georgia: I'm on a book high right now

Georgia: It's probably going to lead to a reading slump

Georgia: But it's worth it

Miles: Thank you. I guess that means it's ready to go to my editor

Georgia: Thank you for leaving in a hint that his second in command is the person he sought out in that cantina in the epilogue

Miles: It's vague

Georgia: They'll be happy forever

Miles: Could have been anyone

Georgia: It's romantic

Georgia: You're romantic

Georgia: And now that I finished the book I can devote myself to finding *your* second in command

Miles: Yay?

Georgia: That's right, yay!!

Chapter 7

Miles

A battle raged in the café's small kitchen this morning. Rival pirates searching for the same lost spaceship pursued each other over a dead planet, unaware of the intrepid adventurer already looting the ship's riches below.

All imaginary, of course.

I never expected baking would be such a good brain-storming activity. There's something about the routine of mixing ingredients and rolling out dough that flips a switch in my creative brain. In my body, I'm pouring icing over scones, but in my mind, I'm creating something entirely different.

After I put the last tray of baked goods in Dogeared's display case, I grab my phone so I can dictate the chaos in my brain before I forget it. Tonight, I'll add the transcript to the loose outline of the book I'm working on. Eventually, I'll actually start writing, but I like to let the ideas percolate for a long while before I get words on the page.

I stifle a yawn as I unlock the front door and flip the sign to *Open*. Since Hannah quit, I've been in the store full time most days—baking by five and closing up at six. I need to hire someone new to fill in the gaps, but with everything going on in my writing world, dealing with interviews is low on my priority list.

Customers file through all morning. With our minimal selection and small dining area, we're not a hotspot for the morning rush. We have our regulars, though. Mostly other bookworms and a few people too impatient to wait in a larger coffee shop's line.

My aunt Cece waltzes in just before nine. She greets the couple in the café—it never ceases to amaze me how many people she knows—before wandering over to me.

"Miles, you're looking dapper, as always."

I glance down at my jeans and sport coat combo. Fashion has never been my thing, but I've found a few pieces that work for me.

Or...I think they do. It's not like I consult anyone. Maybe I should.

I run my palms over my pale blue button-down. "How are you, Cece?"

"Just awful. I'm halfway through a regency romance one of the book club gals recommended, and everything's fallen apart." She sighs like a heroine in a period drama. "I need a palate cleanse before I can go on and find out how they resolve it. Maybe some Stephen King?"

I have to laugh at her chaotic TBR. Most people have specific results they want to get out of reading and gravitate to certain genres that deliver it. Not Cece. She can swing from a dry non-fiction to an intense thriller to the funniest rom-com without flinching. She's the purest bookworm: she just loves *reading*.

"You know where to find the horror."

Waving a hand over her shoulder, she sashays down an aisle. She returns a few minutes later with a paperback of one of King's short story collections.

"Good choice. Those are some of his most frightening stories, in my opinion. I try not to think about them in the dark."

"I'll be prepared to be scared. And I'll take one of your vanilla scones, please."

I bag up a scone and the book and hand them to her. "On the house."

She manages to look shocked, even though we have this conversation every time she comes into the store. "You'll do no such thing, Miles Elliott. When I'm in here, I'm not your aunt. I'm a paying customer."

I fight back a smile and take the cash she pushes my way. "As you wish."

I well realize I'm in business here, but it's uncomfortable to charge friends and family. It's lucky I don't have many of either, or the bank would have foreclosed already.

"Lydia told me you agreed to the Kissing Corn Maze. It will mean so much to the Cortez family."

"I couldn't say no to that."

She smiles sweetly, fully understanding why. "And you never know. You might get picked by someone special in that corn maze."

I make a vague sound. I have zero expectations of finding my love match in a cornfield.

"She also told me about your nomination. Are you enjoying your moment in the sun?"

"I'd hardly call it that." Other than an uptick in conversations with my agent, it hasn't affected me in a tangible way yet. "I'm pleased, though."

I'm happy about the nomination. I just don't want to get my hopes up.

"Where are your books, anyway?" She cranes her neck to look around the shop, even though she knows exactly where my books are. Right where they belong, in the science fiction category. "They should be on a special display."

"Georgia says the same thing."

"As usual, Georgia's right. You need a big banner overhead that reads *Local Author*."

Georgia already ordered one. It's in the back room, rolled up next to our coffee supply. She put it out once, with a whole display of just my books, but the showiness of it sat so wrong in my gut, I'd had to stuff it all away.

"Better yet, let's get you a pin that says *Ask me about my book*." She steps behind the counter until we're practically toe to toe. Stretching, she runs her fingers through my messy hair. "You're overdue for a trim. You know I'll always make space for you in my chair."

"It hasn't been on my mind lately."

"My ladies all miss you over there."

I just bet. Every time I visit Cece's salon, Hair and Now, I'm shocked at how bold the older ladies in Magnolia Ridge can be. They're not quiet in their open admiration of men, whether locals or celebrities, and they don't get shy just because I'm around to listen in. Their commentary is incredibly...vivid.

"I'll set something up before the awards ceremony."

"Mm hmm." She sighs. "It's unfair for you to have such thick, gorgeous hair when I would commit so many crimes for locks like this. Genes are a fickle thing."

I don't think genes have much to do with Cece's current hair, but I would never say such a thing. She's too skilled with scissors for me to risk it.

Behind her, Georgia sweeps into the bookstore. She wears a bright yellow sweater with geometric stripes in brown and red, looking the very definition of fall cozy. Her wavy blond hair hangs loose over her shoulders, and she pushes the tangles away from her face. When she sees me, her smile lights up, hitting me in the chest like a thunderbolt.

She's sunshine and adrenaline and a warm hug on your worst day. She's a star chart mapping my way home. She's—

Aunt Cece makes a tiny sound of satisfaction, watching me too closely.

If the ladies at Hair and Now are bad gossips, my mom and her sister are their queens.

I wipe the dopey expression off my face and greet Georgia like a normal person. A normal, non-desperately in love person. Or as close as I can manage.

Honestly, it's not that close.

"Good morning." Georgia's cheeriness is a long-awaited sunbeam peeking through the clouds. "How are you, Cece?"

"If I had a tail, it'd be wagging." She rounds the counter, moving closer to Georgia. "I was just telling Miles we should make him a pin so everyone will know he's a famous author."

I shake my head at that. My books might be doing moderately well, but I'm not *famous*.

"I was thinking about making him wear a shirt with his face and book cover on it." Georgia's grin is a solar flare. "And he'd have to walk all through town, talking to everyone he meets."

I do my best to scowl at her. I'm not sure I'm physically capable. "Why not make me wear a crown, too?"

Her eyes practically throw sparks. "I know where to order all three."

Aunt Cece's laughter rings out. "You're in good hands with her, Miles. Come visit me sometime."

"I will." I wave as she walks out the door.

Georgia stalks closer, smiling like she has big plans for me. Unfortunately, I doubt they're the kind of plans I so rarely let myself imagine for us. The kind where we're alone in the shop, and she corners me in the stacks, leaning up on tiptoes to reach me. Her lips part, and...

Having a vivid imagination can be a curse.

In real life, she gets right up in my space, closer than a boss-employee relationship warrants, but nobody in the store is paying attention to us.

"I found contestant number one."

I didn't think "whispering triumphantly" was a thing, but she made it happen.

My heart sinks a touch. Just a small dip in my ribcage. In spite of her unaccountable excitement to pair me up, I'd still hoped it wouldn't come to anything. We could go to the awards together and cut out the middleman. Middle*women*.

"Are we really going to call them that?" I say. "Contestants?"

"I found potential life partner number one."

I frown. "Go back to contestant."

She settles on one of the wooden stools, resting her red sneakers on the foot bar. "Don't you want to hear about her?"

"I feel like I'm about to either way."

"So perceptive. Okay, her name is Kara. She's an admin I met at yoga class."

She pauses. I wait. Her eyebrows tip up. She wants a reaction shot from that?

"Yoga class. Got it."

"She's a vegetarian, loves *Firefly*, and she's super cute. Twenty-nine, no children or pets, but she's open to both with the right person. Recently ended a long-term relationship, but she's ready to move on."

The amount of information she has about this woman mildly horrifies me. "Just how long did you two talk about this?"

"A few minutes."

"And you got all that?"

A little line furrows her brow. "Sure. Don't guys talk about stuff like that?"

"Not remotely." I've known Owen two years and have no idea if he's a cat person or a dog person, his preferences on children, or even his exact age. Thirty-something sounds about right.

"Well, she's fabulous. I'm going to text her to meet you at Bella Italia Friday night for a casual dinner." She's already got her phone out, her thumbs tapping away.

My stomach twists over on itself, but I focus on my plan. Endure a couple of dates that *so sadly* don't work out, and then I'll be free to go to the gala with Georgia.

"Dinner feels excessive for a first meeting, don't you think?"

She runs a hand over my shoulder. "Just relax and be yourself. She's sure to love you."

If only it were that easy.

"But I'm sad that you have no faith in me," she adds.

"What do you mean? I agreed to it."

"Not that. This." She pulls a piece of paper from her purse and holds it up like she's presenting *Exhibit A*.

It's a bright orange flyer with *Kissing Corn Maze* written across the top. Eight male faces stare back at me, including my own.

"Where did you get this?" Are they all over town? I didn't think Mackay Farm would actually advertise the bachelors. But I guess you need to see what your motivation is before you willingly run through a corn maze to find it.

"Margaret Mackay stopped me at the grocery store this morning. She said we should put it in our front window. So..." She grabs some tape from behind the counter and moves to do exactly that.

"Maybe it'd be better back here behind the counter." Someplace out of anyone's direct line of sight. In a drawer would do.

"Nope. It's going right here in the corner of the window. It'll go perfect with our fall display."

"Great." The last thing I want is people coming in and thinking I might actually want to talk about this.

"Seriously, though." She returns the tape and centers herself right in front of me. "Why didn't you tell me you volunteered for this? It's a great idea. I mean, for you. I don't mix well with cornfields."

She gives a big, fake shudder.

"I didn't so much volunteer as I got thrown into the ring. It was Mom and Cece's idea. And it's for the Cortez girl's recovery."

Georgia's expression turns soft. "Oh, right."

She lightly runs a hand along my sleeve. Obviously, she understands why the cause means a lot to me.

"You're a good guy for doing this. The chance for a date with you is going to bring in so much money."

"That's not a thing I ever thought I'd hear."

"And I'm sure Kara will understand."

"Who's Kara?"

She grips my hand and giggles. "Your first setup, you goof."

"Right. It's hard to keep track of my dating opportunities these days."

"I bet. You're a real hot commodity. A bookshop owner, a writer, a guy who'd sacrifice his ego to help someone else out. You're every bookish girl's dream man."

I don't care about being every bookish girl's dream—I just want to be hers.

Chapter 8

Georgia

Does happiness normally make a person queasy?

Tonight's the night. In about an hour, Miles will meet up with Kara at Bella Italia. They'll chat, hit it off, she'll realize he's the hidden gem of Magnolia Ridge, and they'll set up date number two. They'll be happy. I *want* Miles to be happy.

So why does my stomach feel like I just ate bad tofu?

Maybe it's my brother and his wife. I came to their place so I wouldn't go to the restaurant to watch Miles on his date—which I would only do for *science* and not regular stalker-y reasons. I was so, so tempted. But ultimately, I decided even scientific stalking is too much, so here I am on Sam's couch.

Watching him cuddle up to his wife in their kitchen while they cook dinner.

And kiss her like his life depends on making her sigh "just one more time."

And trace his hands over her like he's desperate to reacquaint himself with the shape of her body.

I probably shouldn't have turned up unannounced on a reunion day.

Sam works as an outdoor guide and is often away leading

multi-day hikes and adventures and I don't know what else. He just got home after four days in the central Texas wilderness. He's been married to Harper for a year now, but they're obviously still in the honeymoon, "can't keep their hands to themselves" stage.

It's cute. And super, super awkward for any and all witnesses.

"Can you guys tone it down just a touch?" I call. "My innocent eyes can't handle the show."

Sam laughs but doesn't release Harper. "Your innocent eyes have seen worse."

True. He was still living with me when they first started dating again. I walked in on them making out so many times, I started coughing like mad every time I walked into the living room just to give them fair warning. I used it so much, my fake cough did real damage to my throat.

I'm glad he's so in love, but he's my brother. I don't need to see any of the details of that love.

Harper slips out of his arms and waves me closer. "Come in here and keep me company."

Sam nuzzles against her ear. "I'll keep you company."

She playfully pushes him away. "Focus on buttering the bread."

"I'll butter your bread."

"Ugh, no," I cut in. "Food euphemisms will spoil my appetite."

I sit down at their table. I'd help them in the kitchen, but we've already found out it's too small for three cooks. Next time, they can come to my place, and I'll cook for them. Probably while they make out on my couch, but such is life.

"I'll try to behave." Sam winks at Harper. Any effort he puts toward that goal has a very short time limit.

"I saw your latest cover reveal," Harper says to me. "That circus carousel is adorable. It must have taken forever."

"That was a fun one. I'm excited to read the book, even if I think carousels are kind of creepy."

Some scary books stick with you forever.

Sam looks at me over his shoulder while he follows instructions and butters thick slices of bread. "I thought it was scarecrows."

"Shush. I can be afraid of two things."

"Are you adding more covers to your monthly schedule?" Harper asks.

I lift my shoulders and let them slump again. "Not yet."

"Don't you still have a wait list?"

"I don't like to think about it." Calendars and planners exhaust me. I have to have them to keep on top of my business, but every time I open one, I get a tiny headache behind my eyes. I like the creative part of my job. The actual planning side? Not so much.

"How far out are you booked?"

"A year and a half."

"On part-time work?" Sam says. "I still don't get why you won't commit to illustrating full time. I thought you were going to do it months ago."

The long wait list stresses me out but relying solely on my art to survive stresses me out more. How long will it last? How long before I hate it, just because it's my job?

"Trends change. If my clients decide readers aren't into my stuff anymore, my work could dry up, and then I'd be totally out of work. I refuse to go to Dad and ask for a job."

He's constantly telling Sam and me we could come work for him at his financial consulting firm. I can't think of anything that would turn my soul into a shriveled husk quicker.

"I'm not one to judge, but your business strategy confuses me."

"It doesn't feel stable enough. Right?" Harper comes to my rescue, putting my jumbled career worries into one nice, neat sentence.

I'm not sensible about tons of things, but I'm trying to be about this. I need some security here. Following my dreams and hoping my art will sustain me full time and long term? Not especially secure.

"Exactly. And I love making covers, but I don't want to give up working at the bookstore. I need to interact with humans sometimes." As focused as I get on illustrating, I could easily become that person who only leaves her cave once a week to gather food and supplies. "And anyway, Miles would crumple without me."

Sam nods. "Truth."

"I'm even helping him find a girlfriend." Feels like a thing I should say, since his date will start any minute now. Not that I've been peeking at my phone to double check the time or anything.

Both of them stop their dinner prep and turn to face me.

"You're doing what?" Sam asks.

"Finding him a girlfriend. Well, helping him find a date first. The girlfriend part will come on its own."

He can be as humble as he wants, but I know he's awesome. Kara doesn't stand a chance.

Sam shares a look with Harper. Then he turns to me, staring blankly. "You...are setting your best friend up...on dates?"

"Yes. He's out on the first one right now."

That queasiness rises again in my stomach, but I shove it away. Sam and Harper aren't even putting on a disgusting show of togetherness. Aside from the mutual staring-at-me thing.

"You're doing this...why?"

"It takes him forever to get to know someone well enough to ask them out. I'm just helping him along." Perfectly normal and reasonable. "I'm his wingwoman."

I really need a little pair of wings to clip onto my shirt like they give kids on a plane. *Official Wingwoman.*

Sam gestures with the butter knife. "You don't feel that's a... conflict of interest?"

"Why are you putting so many pauses in your questions? And why would it be a conflict of interest?"

He sets the bread on the table and stares down at me where I'm sitting. "Georgia, you're a smart, talented woman. You are not one of the too-stupid-to-live heroines in a bad rom-com. You *know* the answer to this. Are you sure you're not interested in the position for yourself?"

"Sam, come on. You know I'm holding out for one of my book boyfriends to come to life."

He gives me a look like he's ultra-disappointed in me. "That's not more reasonable."

Harper perks up, though. "Which one?"

She sets down plates of roasted vegetables and chicken. They cooked them separately to accommodate me, which I appreciate. At Dad and Ava's, I have to pick the meat out of my meals like an irritable child.

"One of the 'former military turned private security' guys. They're strong, dedicated, protective, older, and quietly capable."

I adore this small-town series. Every single one of the guys is the dreamiest, sweetest, fluffiest cinnamon roll—wrapped in a muscular, take-charge package. *Thank you, U.S. Army.*

"Don't forget fictional," Sam says.

"That's the best part."

Harper sits down next to him across from me. "I'm behind on that series."

I looped her into my romance book group a couple of years ago. It's pretty vibrant now, even if we mostly sit around and fan ourselves over the heroes. We rotate through different tropes every month. Right now, we're on older brother's best friend.

"Catch up. The next book is about a quiet grump nobody knows very well who's secretly in love with the sassy heroine."

Sam groans. "Are you kidding me right now?"

Harper lightly smacks him. "It's romantic."

"I'm not disputing that. I know a thing or two about being secretly in love." He goes in for a kiss.

"Exactly," I say before their quick peck can get out of hand. "And since I set you two up, you shouldn't scoff about me setting up Miles."

Sam whips his head around to me. "You don't get credit for us."

"My work was important."

"I came back to town specifically to see Harper again."

"Rude." I know it's true, though. He loves me and the rest of our family, but I can't pretend it was anything but the hope of reuniting with his high school love that brought him back to Texas.

"If anyone gets credit for helping Harper and me along, it's Grandpa." Sam smiles softly at Harper. "His constant updates about you brought all the hopes I'd been pushing down back to the surface. I had to come see you again."

Harper works as a physical therapist at the retirement complex where Grandpa lives. Sam worked there, too, when he first came back, and according to Grandpa's stories, watched her like a lovesick puppy before he found his courage to ask for a second chance at love.

Which actually proves my point—waiting for romance book scenarios is totally realistic and normal.

"Okay, but my part helped things along too," I add. "I was

skilled at dropping special bits of gossip about you whenever Harper came into Dogeared. Getting you two together on the Christmas wagon ride just sealed the deal."

Sam frowns, but Harper nods. "It really did. Seeing you with Finn and Willa was a turning point for me."

I splay a hand at her. "See? I'm an excellent matchmaker. Just call me Emma."

Harper gives me a pitying look, like I'm sweet but also a teensy bit pathetic. "You know who Emma winds up with in the end, right?"

I refuse to take anyone's hints. Miles is across town on a date of my devising as we speak. My upset stomach is from my brother and sister-in-law and their PDA-fest, *not* my best friend out with a cute, remarkable woman who won't be able to help falling for him.

"I'd take Mr. Knightley, too," I tell her. "Kind, compassionate, humble, and down to earth."

And one hundred percent imaginary.

Chapter 9

Miles

I'm an author—I know how to create conflict. I constantly write my characters into uncomfortable, sometimes tortuous situations, all in the name of entertainment.

But in real life, here in this restaurant? I'm less skilled at drumming up conflict.

Honestly, I'm not trying very hard. Despite what I said to Owen about planning to sabotage my own dates, it's not as easy as I'd thought it might be. I can't just be mean to Kara. I don't have it in me. She's cute, funny, and nice to the waitstaff.

She's also obsessed with celebrity gossip.

"Have you heard the latest about Vance Vickers?" She leans forward over her pasta, ready to spill the juicy details. Dinner conversation has jumped from one rumor to the next, a steady stream of names I can't remember and events I'd rather not contemplate.

"I don't think so." The action movie star has been the subject of some tabloid story or another for the last twenty years. It would be hard to keep up even if I wanted to. Which, for the record, I don't.

She launches into the rumored cause of his recent divorce,

adding salacious speculation about who he might be dating now. Apparently, bets are on his much-younger nanny. It would be fitting, since Kara says that's how he met his most recent ex-wife.

It's enough to turn me off the pasta.

"If I could talk to these celebrity wives, I'd tell them to hire the oldest, crankiest nannies they can find," she goes on. "Mrs. Doubtfire it up. But they don't always cheat with the nannies. Sometimes it's the costars. Did you hear about…"

And she launches into a story about two actors who are very much married to other people but supposedly took their on-screen romance off-screen when they were filming overseas.

This is why I have limited apps on my phone. I want curated information only. I'd regress all the way to a flip phone if I didn't need to keep up with Georgia's texting habits.

"Of course, they haven't admitted they had an affair, but all signs point to yes." Kara smiles as she takes a sip of her soda. "It could have just been PR for the movie, but how disappointing would that be?"

"So disappointing for them to be faithful to their partners," I deadpan.

"I know, right? Be more interesting."

I honestly can't tell if this is a joke or a legitimate plea for more tantalizing gossip.

"Georgia said you two met at yoga class." I can only hear about so much infidelity before I break. "Do you do yoga often?"

She seems unfazed by the subject change, so that's good. Or bad, since I'm supposed to find a way to tank this date.

"I go at least once a week. Anjelica Desmond says it's the best exercise for longevity and heart health. Do you follow her lifestyle vlog?"

Conflict, Miles. Just be honest and tell her you would never take life advice from an actress-turned-influencer with zero health or psychological training, and questionable motivations and morals. Easy.

"I don't really keep up with celebrities."

So close.

Kara purses her lips and reaches into her handbag. Wait. Was that it? Is she done with our date? All I needed to do was admit I'm not interested in the daily lives of people I don't know and will never meet? I could have started with that and saved my ears some truly traumatizing information.

She pulls out her phone and calls something up, turning it around to me. "This is where I get all my news."

She scrolls through a neon green site filled with dozens of links to celebrity sightings, fashion statements, and relationship statuses. It's a dizzying array of intrusive articles and baseless rumors, covered in photos of people caught off guard and at their worst.

And Georgia wonders why I don't want people to know I wrote the Quantum Station series. I'm not egotistical enough to think actual paparazzi would care about me, but small towns can make anyone's life harder than it needs to be.

In Magnolia Ridge, this would probably look like all the ladies in Hair and Now discussing my personal life in excruciating detail, but that would be more than enough for me.

Kara holds her hand out. "Give me your phone, and I'll put the app on it for you. You'll never miss a thing!"

I lean deeper into the plush booth, protecting my phone that's safe in the back pocket of my jeans. "Thanks, but I don't need the app."

My phone's lock screen is a picture of Georgia and me the day we painted Dogeared. We're tired and sweaty but proud of our work and grinning like happy lunatics. As much as I would like to start a little conflict, showing Kara *that* could get messy.

She opens and closes her fingers. "Come on. It's fun."

"I don't have enough memory for a new app." Fudging the truth a little, but who knows how big those files are?

"What's clogging up your phone?"

"Duolingo. I'm learning Klingon."

She laughs. "You're funny."

I wasn't trying to be. It's an interesting exercise that helps me create alien languages in my own books.

The waiter comes to clear our table, and I take care of the bill. Kara just smiles at me while I scramble for something to say that will wrap this date up with a period instead of an ellipsis.

"I'm really glad Georgia set this up," she says. "I haven't been out since I broke up with Billy. If not for you, I probably would have just sat at home tonight watching cringey celebrity videos."

"How are those different from regular celebrity videos?"

She laughs again. "You know, like when they sing something really emotional, and they've just got no voice."

"Oh. Or when they create separate social media accounts for their pets."

Her laughter dries up. "You think that's cringe?"

"Kind of. Documenting their pets' daily lives as though they need their animals to be famous too? That counts, doesn't it?"

Kara's mouth flattens into a hard line. "Did Georgia tell you about Mr. Pickles?"

Mr. Pickles? I've lost the plot here. If he's a celebrity, I've never heard of him, but that's not saying much. "I don't know who that is."

But as her face twists, I figure it out. I wanted conflict, right? I think I just got it. The knot in my gut isn't very satisfying, though.

"I'll have you know, Mr. Pickles has a *very* popular Instagram account." She sits up straighter. "More than you, Mr. Doesn't Have Social Media."

"Kara, I didn't realize—"

"He has thousands of followers."

Thousands? "That many people follow a random cat?"

"*Dog,*" she says through gritted teeth.

"Right. Dog. I'm sure he's a...very interesting subject."

"And it's not cringe to post pictures of your dog with captions of celebrity quotes."

I go completely still. Must not move a muscle. Otherwise, I will break into laughter that just might result in a punch to the nose. But come on? Celebrity quotes with her dog?

Kara tilts her chin up. "Thank you for dinner, Miles, but I don't really see this going anywhere between us."

I nod, willing myself not to imagine photos of her dog alongside quotes from Vance Vickers about the importance of hiring the right nanny. "I understand."

She slides out of the booth and escapes into the night. Once she's gone, I exhale out all my tension. Not really the way I'd wanted that to go, but I can't be sorry about the end result.

I'll probably have an unflattering story go around town about me, but I'm one step closer to going to the Andromeda Awards with Georgia.

Text Thread

Georgia: I heard it didn't work out with Kara

Georgia: I'm sorry

Miles: What did she say?

Georgia: That you're a dog hater and know zero pop culture references

Miles: That's weird. She didn't recognize my Monty Python reference

Georgia: Which one?

Miles: Nobody expects the...

Georgia: Spanish Inquisition!

Georgia: That's too bad

Georgia: I'm not giving up

Miles: I didn't think I'd be that lucky

Georgia: Ha ha. I'm going to make the most of our time at the Harvest Festival tomorrow

Georgia: I'll give you some dating pointers

Miles: Based on?

Georgia: Un

Georgia: Called

Georgia: For

Miles: You're the one who set me up with the Vance Vickers fanatic

Georgia: All right, we'll call it a draw

Chapter 10

Georgia

Whoever is in charge of decorating Magnolia Ridge's Harvest Festival is the exact right amount of extra. Every booth is covered in hay bales and corn husks, pumpkins and mums. Even though it's in the high seventies today, it *looks* like a perfect autumn day, and in Texas, that's close enough.

Miles and I wander through the booths to our station for the afternoon, deftly avoiding the little children running up and down the aisles. There must be some kind of decoration scavenger hunt going on because most of them have paper and crayons, checking things off before they run away again.

In the center pavilion, men in variously colored flannel shirts file across the stage, vying for the day's trophy. It's basically a thinly veiled beefcake parade, although a few women are in the lineup, too.

"Aw. If I'd known about the flannel competition, I would have told you to wear one."

"I don't need to destroy their egos all at once." He tosses me the tiniest smirk.

I loop my hand around his arm. "You're right. Better to humiliate them individually."

"What's going on at the community center?"

I follow his gaze. A bunch of *Abandoned* signs are boarded up across the building's front doors.

"They make it look more run down every week in September, and by October, it will be a haunted house. Wait—you've never seen the progression of the Abandoned Manor?"

"I don't usually come to the Harvest Festival. I didn't realize the farmers market was this big."

"They get more vendors every year." Sam's sister-in-law, Eliza, is a big advocate for the market. "And next year, they'll finally add the bicycle bookmobile. Bookcycle?"

He chuckles. "The fabled Dogeared bookmobile. How are things going with that?"

"Really good. Grandpa and Sam worked through the hardest parts of putting the shelves in. Now we just need to add the doors and find a way to strap in the books when it's in transit. It'll be ready for the spring market, don't worry."

He smiles down at me. "I never doubted you."

I've had two bosses in my adult life: myself and Miles. And of those, Miles is the more supportive one. I can fret over my cover ideas until I'm practically ready to give up illustrating altogether. My negative self-talk game is strong. But Miles always acts like it would be impossible for me to fail.

Is it any surprise I've stayed at Dogeared this long?

I give us a wide berth past a stall with grinning scarecrows on either side, shuddering as I go.

"Still a no from you, huh?" he says.

"They're creepy."

"They're smiling."

"With *stitched-on mouths*. That's horror movie stuff. Scarecrows were literally created to be frightening, and now we've collectively decided they're benign good guys we should put all over our house and yard every fall? No, thank you."

He turns his head to get a better view of the ones I avoided. "They've got Raggedy Ann faces with cherry red cheeks."

"And straw stuffing falling out of their arms and legs. That's morbid. Haven't you seen the movies? Scarecrows are evil, the end."

His eyebrows hitch up like he can't possibly reconcile my *evil* brand with the cutesy versions we just passed. "I feel like you and I watched different movies growing up."

"Sam might have let me watch an especially scary show when I was little." I normally don't throw my brother under the bus, but the trauma is real. "I still sometimes have nightmares about getting chased through cornfields."

I know scarecrows are meant to scare away birds, but they've really done a number on *me*.

He puts his hand over mine on his arm. "I promise to protect you from any scarecrows we encounter, good or evil."

"You'd better."

As if there's even a way to defeat spooky possessed scarecrows, but I don't want to ruin the offer.

"Here we are. Stall seventeen." Miles stops short. "Huh. We actually got apple bobbing."

The morning volunteers give us a quick rundown of how the stall works before they leave us to it. Looks pretty easy: the apples go in the barrels. But in the name of good hygiene, instead of using their mouths to grab the apples, kids have to use sets of chopsticks.

"Kind of anti-climactic, isn't it?" Sure, this version eliminates kids running around with wet heads covered in shared germs, but where's the chipped teeth and near-drowning?

"I don't know." Miles watches the row of children fumbling around at the four big wooden barrels. "It might be harder than the original version."

We sit down on the closest hay bales so we can supervise.

There's not a lot more for us to do. We don't even get to give out cool prizes—the apples are the prizes. Kind of a *wah-wah* moment when the kids realize it, but we can't all be the cool booths that give out Jolly Ranchers.

Miles leans his shoulder against mine. "I like your sweater."

I beam at him. "Aww. Thanks for noticing."

It would be pretty impossible not to notice my sweater. It's covered in red, yellow, and gold appliqué leaves. Some of them, inexplicably, have faces on them. The eighties must have been wild times.

"The shimmery ones are an interesting addition."

He runs one finger along a gold lamé maple leaf on my forearm. It's a soft, almost-nothing touch, but it still spreads a flush of warmth across my skin.

I exhale a shaky laugh. "Its previous owner must have really wowed the other ladies at her Tupperware parties."

"She probably had matching leg warmers to go with it."

"Ooh. Now I kind want to make a pair."

"If anyone could pull it off, it'd be you."

I'm not even sure looking good in hideous leg warmers is a valid compliment, but it makes me stupidly happy.

We monitor apple bobbing—well, apple chopsticking—and replenish the fruit supplies whenever it looks like the barrels are running low. All in all, not a bad way to volunteer a little time for the community.

"Now," I say softly so none of the kids hear me. "About your date."

Miles blows out a breath. "It's not looking good for your matchmaking plans."

"I'm not worried. It's good data to help me narrow down my next pick."

He side-eyes me. "Since when do you care about data?"

"Since it's going to help me find the woman of your dreams."

His mouth pulls into a frown. "We were just going for *date*."

I wave off his concerns. "Sure, sure. But it would be nice if she was everything you're looking for, right?"

He goes on staring at me. "Yes. It would."

His voice hits an especially low note that makes my insides weirdly fluttery. He's got a really nice voice, steady and rich. You don't expect it when you first see him standing there in his fitted cardigan and dress shirt. He has the perfect voice for reading a book out loud to someone.

Which is definitely a thing I'll remember to mention to whoever I find for his next date.

"If I'm unsuccessful—and I *will* be successful—there's always the Kissing Corn Maze," I say before I get too distracted thinking about his voice. But the longer I think about it, the less I like that idea. I'd rather have a hand in choosing his dates than just leave it up to whoever races to him first.

One of the little girls at the barrels has given up trying to catch an apple between her chopsticks and is now attempting to skewer one with them. She brutally stabs at the water, completely soaking her arm and splashing half the kids.

"Whoa, whoa," I tell her. "We don't want to get everyone wet. It's best to do it gently."

She smacks her fist into the water again. "I don't like apples."

I lift my hands in front of my face to avoid as much of the spray as I can. "All we have here are apples."

"I like candy."

I'm trying to come up with a polite way to tell her she doesn't have to play the game if she doesn't want an apple when her father intervenes and pulls her away. The children who were splashed the most have already run off, leaving us momentarily on our own.

"I feel like there might be complaints about the lax supervision at the apple bobbing station," Miles says.

"Yeah, right. Mixing kids and huge barrels of water has one conclusion, and it's not staying dry."

Despite the inevitable splashing, more kids fill in the gaps left by the ones who just escaped and get to wrangling apples.

"At least we're not working the dunk tank." Miles coughs into his fist. "This week."

"Are we really doing that?"

"I didn't rule it out. But there are more stations than weeks we're volunteering, so you might get lucky."

"I might get real lucky and opt to let you and Arlo work the tank together."

"I can just imagine him and his morose face begging people to put him out of his misery and dunk him already."

I laugh at the image of our once-happy coworker languishing on the dunk tank bench like a sick Victorian child. "Poor Arlo. He's taking the breakup so hard."

I haven't witnessed the fallout of very many failed relationships, but they all seem to go out in spectacular fashion when they do.

"At least he's eating regularly again."

I pass out chopsticks to newcomers. "If you can call those cheese-filled beef jerky tubes food. I have to air out the bookstore whenever he's on shift so it doesn't smell like a meat market."

"He'll get through this stage, too."

"Is this a normal post-breakup stage? What's the vegetarian version of jerky tubes?"

"Doritos."

"Nothing says 'I miss you' like scarfing down tasty corn chips."

He looks at me like he's reevaluating something. "You haven't been through a breakup? Ever?"

I'm aware it's at least slightly unusual to be a twenty-eight-year-old woman who's never been in an actual relationship, but I'm fine with it. I dated a teensy bit in college, and no part of me has regrets that those relationships didn't work out. The longer my no-dating streak goes on, the easier it is to turn down the random guys who ask for my number at work. It's automatic now.

"Nope. Better safe than sorry, right?"

"You can't succeed if you don't try."

"But you can't fail if you don't try, either. It's a pretty solid system." I laugh, but he doesn't join in. "Not that I think *you're* going to fail on your dates. We're definitely going to find someone right for you."

Which is less reassuring than I thought it would be when I said it.

"I'm not worried about that."

Oh. "Don't worry about me. Someday, AI will advance so much I'll be able to order one of my special ops guys right off the pages of my favorite book."

He frowns harder. "I'm against AI for most uses, but especially that."

"Do you have a better solution for turning fiction into reality?"

"Does it have to be fiction?"

We're just joking around, but he sounds so serious, I go completely still. Sam likes to give me a hard time about my book boyfriend obsession, but this is something different. Like Miles genuinely wants to know if pretend is all I want.

Pretend is all I've ever let myself have.

"What if he's not a special ops guy?" he asks softly. My gaze drops to his mouth so I won't miss a word. "What if he's not out of the pages of a book? What if he's—"

"Hey, mister!"

I jolt so hard I almost fall off my hay bale. My heart's racing so fast, you'd think Miles and I were caught doing something naughty in front of the kids. But like I told Willa, we're just friends, and friends don't do that.

I don't think.

We turn to see an older boy leaning over one of the barrels with both arms inside while some of the other kids watch him warily. "My apple's stuck."

Miles tilts his head, examining the situation. "Stuck how?"

"I don't know, but it won't come out. Can you help me?"

He stands and leans over the barrel, obviously trying to figure out what the problem is. "I don't see—"

The boy does something with his hands under the water, and suddenly an apple launches out of the barrel into the air.

And hits Miles square in the face.

Chapter 11

Miles

If that's how things went at the apple bobbing stall, I hate to think what happened to the people running the horseshoe toss.

"It's not too bad." Georgia pulls the small bag of ice off my face and immediately winces at whatever she sees underneath.

"Very reassuring."

As soon as our volunteer time ended, we walked back to Dogeared, and she made an ice pack for me. She's been fussing over me in the back room, alternately telling me everything's fine and making sad little sounds whenever she peeks at the results of the apple beatdown.

If I wanted a way to prove to Georgia I can live up to her former military romance book heroes, getting assaulted by fruit wasn't it.

"At least it didn't hit your nose." She's said as much half a dozen times now. I think it's the only upside she can spin.

"Yes. My eyes are expendable, but my nose—that would have been a tragedy."

Frankly, I don't care much about either. I'm sitting on a barstool in Dogeared's small kitchen with Georgia standing between my knees. She's leaning in close so she can tend to my bruise, her face inches away from mine as she inspects me. She gently runs her fingers over my skin, one hand holding herself steady at my shoulder.

I would take a thousand apples to the face for more of this closeness with her.

"I guess you need your eyes, too." She presses the ice over my right eye and cheek again. It stings, but more from the cold than the bruise. "But your nose is perfect. I'd hate for you to break it."

"My nose is perfect?" It's a weird compliment to fixate on, but praise from Georgia hits different. I snatch up every one and hoard them like Gollum obsessing over the One Ring.

"It's got an ideal slope to it." She slowly runs a fingertip from the bridge of my nose down to the tip. She gently taps the end, all but saying *boop*. "I should know—I draw a lot of noses."

"I've never been told I have an ideal slope before." I haven't thought about the shape of my nose since middle school. It's... average? All I really want is for her to touch me again, even if it has to be on the nose.

She nods, gently holding the ice to my face. "I've used your nose as inspiration on some of my covers. Every hero with a straight, strong nose? That's yours."

I've suspected as much—not about the nose, but about her sources of inspiration. It's why I had a print made for the cover of one of her books. The couple looks exactly like the two of us. She's never said a word that it might actually be us, but when I look at it, that's all I can see.

"Anything else?" Barely a whisper because I can't manage more. It's taking a shocking amount of energy not to touch her in return, pull her to my chest, and hold her close.

"Eyebrows, sometimes."

She traces each of them with the same soft touch, making my chest constrict from want. Normally, I would put eyebrows at the bottom of the erogenous zone barrel. But this is Georgia—every touch is top of the line with her.

"How about my hair?"

She laughs, her breath ghosting across my skin. "Oh, yeah. You've got the best hair. Very inspirational."

She runs her fingers through my hair, messing it up more than it already was. I have to force myself not to close my eyes and lean into her hand like a touch-starved kitten. Each sweep of her fingers sends shockwaves through my body and down my limbs.

I want more. I crave it. This is a dangerous game, but I'm not ready to take my wins and fold.

"Mouth?" My suggestion is gasoline on a blazing wildfire. She'll either fan those flames...or douse them.

Her gaze drops there and holds. The muscles in her gorgeous throat work as she swallows. "Once. Just the hint of it."

When her fingertip grazes over my lips, I think I might be dead. I'm definitely not breathing. Then again, my heart is pounding fast enough to be a bigger medical concern than my injured face.

We've touched hundreds of times before. We hug. Snuggle. Hold hands. But that always has an air of innocence over it, like she's pasted the "friendly" label on those touches, and they barely even register to her as a point of connection.

But this...this is something new. This is curiosity and exploration. This is a borderline sensual touch that she's initiating like she can't help herself. This is standing on the edge of a cliff, trying to decide if we're ready to jump into the water below. Even if I'm not sure she's entirely aware of what she's doing.

She certainly doesn't know what she's doing to *me.*

Her finger stills on my lips. It would take nothing at all to kiss her fingertip and change the dynamic between us. Possibly change everything. But I need her to be clear about what she wants. I'll give her anything she needs. Including limitless space to make up her mind.

Right now, there's barely a breath of space between us.

Her gaze darts up to lock with mine. There's a question written there. I just can't be certain what it is.

"Do you..." she breathes.

I wait for the rest, ready to answer her truthfully, whatever she asks.

Then she blinks. And blinks again. The hazy look in her eyes disappears as if she just woke up, and she steps out from between my legs. She exhales an embarrassed laugh, smiling her not-quite-real customer service smile.

My pounding heart falls.

"What were you going to ask?" I have to say the words, even if I already know she won't tell me.

Her hesitation confirms it.

"I...was going to ask if you think that's enough ice for now. I'm pretty sure you're only supposed to do it fifteen minutes at a time. We don't want to freeze your face off."

"I can live without my face."

She pulls the ice pack away from my cheek, smiling sadly at what she sees there. "I think it's keeping the bruising down."

"That's something." Deep down, I'm disappointed, but I refuse to sound like I am. My sky-high hopes and dreams aren't her fault or her responsibility.

"Hey, boss?" Arlo leans past the back curtain.

I turn to him. "Yeah?"

Georgia takes a single step farther away from me. I should be grateful things worked out how they did. I wouldn't have wanted Arlo to interrupt...whatever might have happened between us otherwise.

For the record, I am not grateful.

"The receipts aren't printing. I tried restarting the thing, but it's not working."

I shift to get off the barstool, but Georgia puts a hand on my shoulder and presses me back down. "I'll take care of it. You rest for a bit."

"Thanks." I'm hardly injured in any way that requires rest or medical care, but I *do* need a minute to myself back here.

I take the ice pack she offers, and she disappears out front behind Arlo.

The ice won't do any good for the parts of me that are truly bruised, but I give it a go anyway. I put the pack right over my foolish, hopeful heart.

Chapter 12

Miles

I can't stand fighting. Arguments make me uncomfortable, and physical altercations are even worse. And yet, here I am, throwing punches at Owen like we do every week, pretending to fist fight as a means of exercise. I make no sense.

On so many levels.

As averse as I am to confrontation, I do try to keep an open mind, so I didn't immediately shut him down when he first invited me to the gym. It seemed like a big concession at the time. I've never been very athletic, and most team sports are beyond my interests or abilities. But eventually, he got me in here, and it turns out I kind of like throwing punches. In a fake, completely controlled way.

I wouldn't say I'm skilled at it, and I'd never want to have to translate this into an actual scuffle, but I enjoy our weekly training sessions. We've been doing this for over a year now, and I have enough muscle memory for the moves that most of my brain goes offline and my body reacts on instinct while we spar. It's a nice antidote to overthinking.

Usually.

Tonight, not even the threat of one of Owen's jabs can keep

me focused. I'm stuck on my afternoon with Georgia a few days ago. How close we were. Her soft little touches. The mystery of whatever she stopped herself from asking me.

The tantalizing question of whether she'd ever allow me to touch her the same way.

A sharp smack to the shoulder brings me back into the present.

"You're not paying attention," Owen barks. "Do you want me to drop the mitts and find your focus?"

That's the other thing that keeps our sparring enjoyable—the punches only fly in one direction.

I land a hit on his right mitt. "Your threats aren't as motivating as you think."

"You're concentrating again. My methods work."

We spar for a while longer, and I manage to keep my mind from zeroing back in on Georgia. More or less.

When we finish up, we take off our gear and sit on a bench along one wall of the gym. It's a bright, clean space that's found a mix of clientele. On any given night, you're just as likely to find a burly, tattooed man decimating a punching bag—ahem, Owen—as a mother of three moving in sync with a trainer.

"Do I need to ask what's distracting you tonight?" he asks. "Or should I say, *who?*"

I drain half my water bottle, breathing hard from the exertion. "You don't need to ask."

Owen nods. "What happened?"

A group class works through their moves in the center of the gym, but they're far enough away I'm not concerned about being overheard.

"We had a...moment."

He laughs. "That's nice and vague."

I don't want to be more specific. Those few minutes were mine alone. "It wasn't anything, but it was everything."

"Huh. You're sure you're a writer?"

I exhale a laugh, unsure how to explain. "It gave me a stunning amount of hope. That's all I can say."

A hope I've been clinging to for days now.

He runs one hand through his sweat-damp hair. "Can I ask exactly what you're waiting for? I mean, I get it, you don't want to ruin your friendship. It's hard to risk, all the rest. But do you ever think you're waiting for her to pass a test she doesn't know she's taking?"

"It's not like that." I don't like the implication I think Georgia's failing at something. I'm not testing her. If anything, I'm testing myself. "She has solid reasons for being wary of relationships. Family stuff. I can't force her to work through that on my timeline."

"And?"

Owen's quiet but perceptive. He sees a lot more than he lets on. Which can be surprisingly annoying when you're used to cruising under the radar like I am.

"And...I don't want to be that friend-zoned guy who's only waiting around for her to change her mind and date him. I value our friendship for what it is now. I love being around her even if nothing romantic ever develops between us. I don't want to make her question my motives or think our entire friendship was a lie because I was hoping for more."

It would rip me to shreds if she discounted the last few years because of my feelings for her.

"I get that. But you are hoping for more."

I sag against the brick wall. "It's kind of a Catch-22."

"I think she'll know the difference between you and the type of guy who abandons the friendship the minute he's rejected."

I would love to believe so. "Except proving that theory requires getting rejected."

"Right. That part's tricky."

We drink our waters, listening to the rhythmic thumping as the class moves through their strike routine. It's louder than I like, but it almost becomes white noise in my head.

"On the bright side, you took an apple for her. That's got to prove something." Owen smirks beneath his thick beard.

"All right. You already had your laugh about it." For a full five minutes when I showed up tonight. Such a good friend.

"When you inevitably tell the story about the apple around town, don't mention that I train you. I have a reputation to uphold."

"I'm sure that will be people's first question. 'But who's your trainer?'"

"Exactly my point. 'Shouldn't Owen have prepared you for fruit-related dangers?' I don't want to deal with the gossip."

I laugh, but it's not really a joke. People *will* ask about the fist-like bruise on my face. And if they don't ask me directly, they'll at least talk. Clearly, I can't go see my aunt at Hair and Now until it's completely healed.

"Will you be at Fiesta Village tomorrow night for games?" I ask.

He nods. "Wouldn't miss it. Grams says it's her favorite part of the week. That was a really good idea you had."

I shrug it off. It wasn't that difficult to find volunteers— spending a couple of hours every other week at one of the local retirement complexes playing board games isn't a hardship. I'm just glad they scheduled game nights during the evening after Dogeared is closed so I can join in.

Even if, lately, I don't have a whole lot of time to spare for games no matter the time of day.

"They like visitors and new activities. Maybe you could teach the residents how to kick box."

I'm teasing, but some of Fiesta Village's residents would

probably take him up on it. Feistiness is the name of the game over there.

"I don't know if I could handle them." He chugs the last of his water and gives me a look. "Any news on the setup front?"

"The first one was not a love connection. Georgia's still looking for date number two."

He shakes his head at me.

With all the apple-related excitement at the Harvest Festival, Georgia didn't have a chance to ask me more questions as my wingwoman. It's unlikely the reprieve will last, but I remain optimistic. "Maybe she won't come up with anyone and we'll coast through until the end of October. Then I'll just take her as my date."

A man can dream.

"That doesn't sound like the tenacious woman you've described to me."

No, it does not. "If I know Georgia, she'll have another date set up before the next week is out."

"This is a weird mess to be in, man."

I'm well aware.

Chapter 13

Georgia

Of all the things I'm confident wielding, an electric drill is not on the list. I like paintbrushes and tablet pencils, not things with motors that could seriously injure a person if used incorrectly.

I'm almost guaranteed to use it incorrectly.

"This feels like a mistake," I say, keeping my trigger finger at an angle so I can't accidentally turn the thing on.

Grandpa just chuckles. "You can do it, Georgie. Just go slowly and hit the places we marked."

He's sitting in a camp chair in the carport at my apartment complex. It's a pretty warm day, but he's still bundled in a flannel shirt and puffy coat. I thought Sam was going to come by to help us do all the hard parts on the bike bookmobile today, but Grandpa had other plans. He thinks *I* should do it.

This must be where I get my unfounded optimism.

We're gradually converting the wooden storage box on the adult tricycle into a cute little book display, complete with two rows of shelves and hinged doors on top and front for access. Sam already installed the bookshelves, and I painted the inside white and the outside the same hunter green as Dogeared's interior. But now we have to put all the doors on.

I move the dangerous-looking drill bit closer to the mark, but then pull it away again. "I don't want to ruin the wood. Are you sure you can't do it?"

"Oh, I'm much too feeble for that."

Hmm. Also a bit of a liar. He's remarkably spry for eighty-seven, and I *know* he could handle this project himself if he wanted to. "I think you're feeble when it's convenient."

"That's right, and it's convenient for me now." He makes himself more comfortable in the chair, and I get the message. He has no intention of moving. "You won't learn if you don't try."

I keep my grumbling to myself and turn back to the wood. Apparently, using a drill is an important life skill or something. I've gotten by pretty well these last twenty-eight years without it, but Grandpa's determined.

Finally, I put the drill to the wood and give it a go. It's...not that bad. I start and stop about as much as I did back when he taught me to drive a stick shift, but I get the holes made.

I start installing the hinges I bought, but with a normal handheld screwdriver. Not everything needs to be electric and supercharged today.

"See?" he says, gloating the same way he does after an epic backgammon battle. "It's not so bad when you get out of your own way and let yourself try."

That takes me straight back to my conversation with Miles at the Harvest Festival. *You can't succeed if you don't try.* I know this on a logical level, but on the heart level? It's all gibberish.

"That lesson's true of a lot of things," Grandpa adds.

"Do I have to learn how to use the power saw next?" I might give up the project entirely if he insisted on that.

"I'm thinking more like relationships."

There's way too much understanding in his eyes, so I refocus on the pretty brass hardware. I liked it better when he used his meddling to help Sam get back together with Harper. It's a little too much when he aims it my way. Like when you're relaxing at the beach, but then somebody's watch reflects the sun in your eyes and you're temporarily blinded.

"Are you going to teach me how to date boys, Grandpa?" I put a lilt of teasing into my question.

"Somebody needs to."

"Grandpa!"

He, of course, stares back at me with no shame. "You and Sam didn't have the best examples, Georgie. You might have learned some lessons your parents didn't mean to teach you."

I don't have anything to say to that. I tighten the next screw and hope he moves on to some other deficiency of mine. Time management. Organization. Planning for the future. He's got a wide selection to choose from.

As usual, he doesn't need me to engage him to keep talking when he's got a bee in his bonnet.

"But don't let their bad examples stop you from ever trying for yourself. You wouldn't make the same mistakes they did."

Mistake feels like such a small word for what they did. Dad cheated on Mom and had a whole baby on the way by the time he told her about it. Then Mom convinced him to keep it quiet for five more months so Sam and I could finish out the school year as a happy family. A big, deluded, happy family.

Who does any of that to people they're supposed to love?

"I'm not *not* trying. It's just not my top priority." It's not even *a* priority, but I doubt Grandpa would be happy to hear that little addition.

"I see. So if the right man came along, you'd give it a try with him?"

I snort. "I spend all my time in the bookstore, but sure. If the right man comes along, I'll give it a try."

Kind of a hypocritical thing to say, since I've had several

guys ask for my number while I'm on the clock. I think it's the customer service sphere of attraction—if you have a job where you have to smile and talk politely to men, some percentage of them will assume you're interested even if all you've done is hand them a book and a cup of coffee.

But obviously, none of those guys were "the right man." So it doesn't matter.

"Promise?"

I look up at him, ready to make a joke about my favorite imaginary special ops guy coming to life, but he's totally serious. I don't often see a lot of similarities between him and my dad, but right now, their intensity sure runs a bold line through the family tree.

"I promise."

He nods. "Good. Then let's get all this put away, and you can take me back over to the Village."

I survey the tiny amount of progress we made today. "But I didn't even get a whole door on."

"Now that you know how to use the drill, you'll go a lot quicker."

"Yeah, but I thought..." We've kind of turned our workdays into Grandpa-Georgia time, with takeout and hours of conversation. He's never opted out early like this. "You really want to go back already? Are you feeling okay?"

He smiles down at me, running a hand over his thin, gray hair. "There's something special going on over there, and I plumb forgot about it. You can come with me. How about that?"

Sure. Hanging out with my grandpa at his retirement complex is a great way to spend my evening. But at least I'm unlikely to meet a man who'll tempt me to live up to the ill-advised promise I made him. So there's that.

It doesn't take me long to lock the bike and tools away in my storage unit. Nothing's very far away in Magnolia Ridge, and we're in Fiesta Village's parking lot in no time.

"Come on," he says, waving me inside the big building. "It's in the activities room."

I follow him in, sure we're about to walk in on a Big Band music listening session or something similarly focused on life in the fifties, but the room is bustling. It's an odd mix of elderly men and women bundled up in scarves and sweaters talking and laughing with a group of surprisingly young men. They're spreading out at tables in twos and fours with an assortment of board games sprinkled among them.

I knew the Village had a regular game night, but I've never seen the *young men* part of the equation.

Then I spot Miles across the room. He's leaning on one hand over a table where two gray-haired women are listening intently to whatever he's saying. He gives them one of his small smiles as he talks, and from the way they're gazing at him, I can tell from here they're charmed.

He looks up and his gaze locks with mine as if he knew exactly where to find me. His small smile goes supernova, lighting up the whole room. My stomach turns gooey, and all I can think about is when I was with him in Dogeared's back room a few days ago.

I touched him. A lot. But that's normal, right? I'm sure plenty of friends touch each other's hair.

And lips. Probably.

Grandpa pats me on the back. "Don't forget about your promise."

He walks away to join one of the younger men with a cribbage board and deck of cards on his table.

Miles excuses himself from the ladies he's with, but I'm still standing in the doorway like a dork. He starts to cross the room, but before he can reach me, Owen steps in front of me.

"Are you joining us tonight, Georgia?" The Rumble Room instructor is decked out in a flannel, concealing his tattoos and muscles. It gives him a distinct loner lumberjack vibe.

Miles joins us with a downcast mouth, like he's been caught doing something he didn't want anyone to see. The slight black eye and bruise across his right cheek only add to the impression something here isn't on the up and up.

"Oh, um...sure. What exactly is going on?" I mean, it seems obvious. It's just that Fiesta Village doesn't normally have this resident-to-attractive-young-man ratio.

"The team over at All Aboard has started volunteering here for game night." Miles's explanation comes out a little too fast. He looks to Owen as if searching for back up. "A few of us over at Rumble Room and other shops on Center got in on it, too."

"That's really cool." I even spot Arlo setting up Battleship in the corner with one of the residents. "But why didn't you tell me about it?"

My own grandpa lives here. Seems like I'd be an obvious choice for a project like this.

His eyebrows lift, and his mouth drops open as if they're searching for answers in different places. "I just...it's a new thing. It's only been a few weeks. I'm sorry. I should have invited you right away."

I'm not *hurt* I wasn't invited to game night, just confused. I was kind of under the impression Miles involved me in every-thing in his life. Clearly, he keeps some things to himself.

"Harper would love it too. She's crazy about games."

He looks weirdly relieved. "I'll have to mention it to her."

"This is really great of All Aboard to do this for the resi-dents. I've never seen the activities room this full." They have a rotating list of games and events here to keep things interesting for the residents, but there's not usually quite this much enthu-siasm for them.

"Whoever put it together has a good heart." Owen stares hard at Miles.

"Yeah, well...it's a good cause," he says.

Miles is acting weird, but I can't quite put my finger on how exactly. The bizarre secret, for sure. But I don't understand the guilty vibes, either. Before I can come up with a good guess, one of the ladies from his table joins us.

"Miles?" she says. "We're ready to play."

"Of course." He looks to me. "I hope you'll join in for a while. Excuse me."

They return to their table, all set for a round of Scrabble. The ladies will be lucky if Miles doesn't absolutely dominate the game.

Owen steps closer to me. He's huge and doesn't give off the friendliest aura, but he's basically a big teddy bear. A grouchy one sometimes, but it's all bark.

"I don't know why he said that," he says low. "Miles came up with the idea. He's the one who invited the rest of us to join."

"He did?" I watch Miles across the room, chatting with the women as they pull tiles. "He doesn't even have anybody who lives here."

"No." Owen's like me—his grandma's a resident. I think that's her over at a Parcheesi table. "But he cares about the people here. More than he wants to admit."

He stares at me for ten whole seconds before he nods and slips away to join his grandma. After another minute of standing around like a dummy, I follow suit and take up an empty seat at a table getting ready to play Rummikub. I pull my tiles, still sneaking peeks at Miles like an amateur stalker.

Maybe I should have played Clue—I could sure use one right about now.

Chapter 14

Georgia

Romance book club is one of my favorite nights of the month. I've been excited all day, knowing my friends will start filing through the door soon, ready to talk about our latest rom-com pick. It's a fun time to just relax, hang out, and discuss imaginary men. But that's not the only thing that's got me slightly breathless.

Miles is wearing his glasses today.

He does sometimes when his eyes need a break from his contacts or after he's had a migraine. His black plastic frames are a rare sight, and it's throwing me completely off. There's something about him in his glasses that conjures up images of him relaxing at home after a long day, totally at ease and himself. Like the Miles Forrester equivalent of gray sweatpants.

No. I should not picture Miles in gray sweatpants and glasses. But I definitely already am.

He turns and catches me ogling him. His eyebrows hitch up in a silent *What?* but I obviously can't tell him I'm thinking about him hanging out in his apartment in sweatpants and an old, soft T-shirt, glasses on, hair a mess, while we read together on his couch, my legs crossed over his.

The cozy image fills my stomach with merciless butterflies.

His eyebrows dart higher, reminding me I'm still ogling. While making direct eye contact, which is the creepiest form of ogling. I shake it off and go back to rearranging Dogeared's seating to accommodate our book club.

We host a couple of groups each week, everything from mystery to self-help to fantasy. Miles participates in the science fiction group, but I guarantee Owen is the only one who knows he's actually *written* sci-fi books. His humility drives me crazy. Sometimes I want to barge into the group and shout his praise, yelling at everyone to buy his books and stand in awe of his fantastic mind. Or else.

I've resisted the temptation, but we're on a ticking clock. One day, I will explode.

The chime over the door rings, but it's not one of the book club members. Ava and Willa walk in. Well, Ava walks. Willa does more of a ballet move across the floor. She's wearing a sparkly tutu, and she's got something bright purple in her hands as she dances over to me.

She shoves a purple thing my way. "You're coming to my birthday party, right Georgia?"

I take the invitation from her. It looks like she wrote it herself on construction paper, which I adore. It's going in my special drawer of random cute stuff the littles have given me. "Of course, munchkin."

Ava smiles over us from the doorway. "I told her you wouldn't miss it, but she insisted you get an official invitation."

Willa dances her way to Miles and holds a second purple paper out to him. "Will you come, too?"

He stares down at her, seeming genuinely surprised to be included. He is too adorable for words.

"You want me at your party?"

Her head bobs in a vigorous nod. "But you can't do the piñata. Mama says that's just for kids, and you're an adult."

"Do I get to do the piñata?" I ask. Ava finds the most elaborate ones I've ever seen. Finn's was the Millennium Falcon last year. And while I would never steal the glory of breaking open the piñata, I'm not above indulging in the delicious treats hidden inside.

Willa laughs. "Of course, silly. You're a kid like me."

I smirk at Miles. "I'm still a kid."

"But you can't do the dress up party because you're too big for the dresses."

Kind of takes the wind out of my sails.

"Do I get to do the dress up?" Miles asks.

Willa bursts out laughing. "No way."

"No piñata and no dress up, I see." He glances my way, clearly asking for permission.

Doesn't he know he always has it? The littles adore him. I smile back, telegraphing my *yes*.

"It will be an honor to celebrate your birthday." He gives a little bow, which sends Willa into fresh delight.

Ava rounds her up, and they say their goodbyes, leaving right as Harper and her sister Eliza walk inside.

Most of the rest of the group wanders in for the evening meeting. Participation fluctuates, but we've got a good mix of women roughly my age, and older women like Miles's mom and aunt Cece. We've even got a man in our group. The combination always makes for interesting conversation about the books... assuming we get around to that.

Bailey walks in with a covered tray. She's one of Dogeared's more voracious regulars and claims the paperbacks she buys are "trophies" of her favorite books she's devoured on her e-reader.

She lifts the lid off the tray to reveal plump cookies. "Apple cider whoopee pies."

The golden-brown cream-filled treats are already calling my name. "These look incredible."

"I need some variety from the plain sheet cakes I make at the grocery store all day."

Eliza steps up to pile two plates with snacks. "Eden and June send their regards."

Both of them had babies pretty recently—Eden's second, June's first—and have understandably bowed out of book club for a while. Most of our larger group includes people who are related to Harper's family in one way or another. Sisters, cousins, aunts, and in-laws mingle through in any given month. They've all adopted me as generic "family," and treat me like part of their crew.

"Eden also suggested we try a monster romance next month." Eliza flops down on a couch next to Callie, who's married to her cousin. See the pattern? She offers one of the plates of snacks to the other quite pregnant woman.

"I'm sure it was Eden." Miguel winks at her. Eliza's been trying to work a monster romance into our rotation for months now, but she never gets the votes. "I've got a new recommendation for you. One's a human, one's a monster, but the other guy doesn't know..."

Josie widens her eyes as Miguel goes into detail about his book. She's a recent newcomer to Magnolia Ridge, and not in the wider family circle. She doesn't speak up during book club a lot, but when she does, it's always to make some interesting point or another about a character's deeper motivations or backstory. She pays more attention to the actual books than most of us do, and is an awesome addition to the group.

"He keeps it a secret?" she asks. "That he's a monster?"

"Well..." Miguel bobs his eyebrows scandalously. "He can't hide it for long."

"Wait, before we start dishing books, I want an update on

Grant." Nicole ties her long black braids into a knot at the top of her head, balancing our book of the month on her knees.

Grant is one of Eliza's brothers-in-law. Yeah. We're basically one big messy family tree in here. Small town life.

Eliza snorts. "Deliriously happy in Sunshine, Oregon."

Everyone coos over that cute town name, but the real *aww* is that he moved because he fell in love over the summer. He went on a hike and found love in the woods. Sounds about right for the outdoor store manager.

"That's the most romantic thing I've ever heard. If anybody deserves it, it's Grant. Surprisingly fast mover though."

That earns another chorus of confirmation.

"When you know, you know," Harper says.

Still kind of weird to me that she "knows" and is madly in love with my goofball brother, but I'm here for it.

Cece nods sagely. "When you meet the love of your life, you wake up and realize you're done waiting around."

My attention drifts to Miles at the counter, but he's already watching me. The force of his gaze hits me square in the chest, spreading warmth through me like red ink running on wet paper. I try to swallow, but my throat sticks. I'm staring too long. I am. But I can't look away. It's like I've caught fire and all I can do is sit here and burn.

The room goes strangely quiet. Miles breaks eye contact, glancing at the others in the group before returning his attention to the register and closing out for the day. I draw in a deep breath like I just had a close call.

I'm just not sure if I'm glad I avoided it...or if I regret missing out.

The others watch me with strange expressions. Like I'm the latest romance book cover, and they're scouring me for details about what's going on inside. I *really* don't want them to judge this book by its cover. Which is probably blushing like crazy.

"That just leaves his brother, Rhett, to fall in love." My voice is too loud in my effort to sound totally unbothered. Inwardly, I'm a tangled ball of yarn I can't loosen.

Eliza snorts. "He'd rather walk on broken glass."

"Commitment-phobes," Nicole says, wrinkling her nose. "Why are they always the cutest?"

"It's the hot-guy tax," Miguel says. Nicole holds out her hand, and they high-five.

"Sometimes the commitment-phobe has good reason to be wary," Callie pipes up. Her husband, Jed, was the same way, once upon a time. All the women in town pined after him, but he never looked in anyone's direction twice. Now? He only has eyes for her.

Josie nods. "People are more than the personas we assign to them. Maybe it's less a fear of commitment, and more a fear of not being the right person for the one they want."

"Or maybe he's seen too many relationships fail and doesn't want to risk the same thing," Bailey says.

Eliza pops a pretzel into her mouth. "I think y'all are giving Rhett too much credit. He just likes to date a lot."

Miles moves to the door and flips the sign over to *Closed*. He turns and flashes a small wave to our group. When his gaze meets mine, the *something* that was in it before isn't there anymore.

I refuse to worry about what it was. Or even think about why it's gone. Didn't I swear I'd find someone perfect for him? I need to stick to that promise.

Everyone calls out goodbyes as he walks through the door. The burning sensation in my chest lingers long after he's out of sight.

"That's the anti-commitment-phobe right there," Miguel says when he's gone. "The shy, reclusive nerd. Mmm mmm. I got myself one and never looked back."

"Miles is looking especially adorable tonight," Nicole says. "I can't put my finger on what looks different, but boy, do I want to."

"It's the glasses," I blurt out. Mostly to avoid any discussion of where Nicole might put her fingers on Miles.

"He always looks like he's busy writing books in the back room."

Cece laughs. "With good reason. He *does* write books in the back room."

That leads to a bunch of questions that are like sandpaper under my skin. Several of them have heard that he's a writer before, but they ask it again and it's always fresh and new. Like they can't possibly keep Miles in their heads beyond book club night. Which makes no sense, because he's literally the most memorable person I know.

"Wait," Eliza says. "He's not the actual Miles Forrester who wrote those space pirate books, is he? Dean's obsessed with those."

"The very same." Cece preens so hard, you'd think the praise is for herself and not her nephew.

"How do we not know this already?" Now Eliza's staring at me, as if *I'm* the one keeping it from everybody. "Why hasn't he done book signings here and big celebrations and put his face everywhere in town?"

"He's really humble. He likes to stay quiet about his achievements," I say. Doesn't sound like a good enough reason in the face of their excitement, but it's true.

"Ego that man up!"

"Now I kind of want to read his book," Bailey says. "What's it about?"

"Well..." How to sum up some of the best books I've ever read? "It's like pirates in space. It's funny, but there's a serious story going on, too, with this huge mystery and scheming bad guys and found family and an anti-hero captain who's secretly got a soft spot for his number two."

"Add to cart." Miguel's statement earns a round of applause.

Eventually, conversation circles around to our book of the month. We discuss tropes and storylines, but mostly we talk about how perfect the hero and heroine are for each other. Opposites, but ones who don't expect the other to change in order to be together. They support each other and encourage each other and basically make each other the best version of themselves possible.

Also hockey for some reason.

But as we discuss this sweet, bold love, the fire in my chest dies down to a dull ache. Because sometimes, way down deep where I rarely look, I wish love like that could be more than just make believe.

Chapter 15

Miles

I greet a shopper with a massive yawn for the third time this morning. Not exactly killing it at the customer service game today.

The woman just laughs. "You look like you could use one of your coffees."

"I probably should. What can I get for you?"

She orders an Americano and a cinnamon roll, and I get to work. By the time I hand both off to her and she's paid, I'm yawning again. Maybe I do need a coffee this morning. I was up late last night thinking about the new book and lost track of time. Five a.m. comes awful quickly when I'm running on a few hours of sleep.

"Thanks so much. Do you have a recommendation for a good sci-fi book? My husband's birthday is coming up, and I want to get him something I know he'll like."

"Er..." This is one downside to owning a bookshop and also selling books I wrote. It's an automatic conflict of interest. Obviously, I want to sell my books...but without feeling like I've unduly pushed customers toward them. I can't recommend my novels as though I'm an anonymous, unbiased bookseller passing along a hot tip. That's just shady.

But I'm also terrible at coming out and admitting I wrote the books. The last thing I want are pity sales because a customer felt pressured. Mostly, I avoid mentioning my books in any capacity. Unless I'm cornered.

Like right now.

Her smile slips the longer I hesitate. "He has a pretty big collection, but any advice would help."

"Sure." I lead her over to the science fiction section and point out a few books. A classic her husband might like in a special edition, and a couple of recent releases.

Inexplicably, she picks one of mine off the shelf. "How about this one?"

"I...yeah. That's good."

She looks up at me, apparently waiting for a lengthier endorsement.

"It's, ah..." How am I supposed to rhapsodize about my own book? You'd think after writing it I'd be able to summarize it in a sentence or two, but it's an impossible task. "It's pretty well-received. It has a nice character arc across the series. Funny."

Has anyone ever been swallowed alive by their own awkwardness? Am I the first?

"I'll go with this one."

We return to the front counter where Owen's waiting. I guess I was too busy tripping over my own tongue to hear him come in.

"That's a great choice," he says to the woman. "Kept me up at night to see what happened next."

"Oh. Thank you for that endorsement." Her gaze flicks to me, as if silently pointing out my terrible one.

Once she's left, Owen levels me a dubious look. "That's seriously the best you can do?"

"I'm not a used car salesman. I can't just launch into a spiel about how great my book is."

"Probably should."

All I can do is return his glare. Yes, I probably should. Marketing is huge for writers, and I'm not skilled at any of it. I don't have social media, I haven't done any signing events, and I don't even have a display of my books in my own store. All of that requires a level of social comfort I don't have.

"Are you here for your usual?"

He lifts a shoulder. "I could keep lecturing."

I get to work on his café mocha. He'll probably also want a cinnamon roll with extra icing. The MMA instructor has a terrible sweet tooth.

"You can't skimp out on marketing. That was the first thing I took over when I started at Rumble Room."

He's taken on a lot of their managerial responsibilities since he arrived. He could probably run his own gym at this point, but I'm not sure he wants that. He says he likes the freedom that comes with *not* being the owner.

"I realize that. It's just not my skillset." I slide the paper cup across the counter to him, wordlessly accepting his cash.

"No kidding." He looks around the store. "Where's your book display again?"

Marketing the store is easy. We have social media accounts and a newsletter that feature staff picks, book clubs, and special events. But marketing *my* books? Marketing *me*? I don't know where to begin.

"I'll work on it." Probably. Eventually. If I don't, whatever momentum my books have now could dry up faster than Vance Vickers's love for any woman he calls his wife.

"You've got to put yourself out there." His dark eyes narrow on me over his sip of mocha. "In lots of ways."

I ignore the hint. He doesn't take his own advice—I don't have to, either. "What are you up to today?"

"I've got an intro class this afternoon. Always fun to see a new crop of clients walk through the doors. Love seeing people respond to my marketing."

"Nice dig."

He chuckles over his drink. "First, I'm heading over to the nursery. I need something to plant in the cracks of the rock wall I installed over the weekend."

"You finished it?"

"It's looking pretty good. You should stop by and see it sometime."

I'm willing to bet it's looking a lot more than pretty good. Owen might be even more obsessed with plants than he is with fighting moves. His backyard is an oasis of native plants and natural landscaping that feels more like a botanical garden than a spot for a barbecue and a hammock. Even though it's excellent for both.

He wears one of his rare proud grins. "My baby's really filling out."

"You probably shouldn't refer to it that way."

The grin slips. "Yeah, I heard it."

Georgia bounces through the door, smiling so bright it's like the sun itself walked into my store. "Miles! I've got great news!"

She's got her cherry-printed tote bag over one shoulder. Seeing it plants a seed of satisfaction in my chest. It means she's got her tablet with her and plans to work in the store until her shift in a few hours. I love it when she's completely at home here. Love it even more when it means she's hanging out with me for no reason.

"Hi." She beams at Owen as she breezes by him and around the counter to me. "I decided who to set you up with for your next date."

I share a look with Owen. He seems sympathetic but also a touch annoyed. A common theme.

The smile freezes on her face as she glances between the two of us. "Oh. Did you not want anyone to know about the whole matchmaking thing? I've kind of mentioned it already."

There's no reason to conceal it, even if it's not my favorite. I'm not ashamed of the situation. I just don't know how to transform it into the outcome I want.

"He knows."

Behind her back, Owen slowly shakes his head at me. *He knows, and he's made his opinions clear.*

"Great. Well—I found her!"

I *know* I need to tell Georgia the truth, that I don't want to meet any of her set ups because I want *her*. But she's so happy right now, I can't just extinguish that. Even with Owen five feet away, giving me dirty looks.

"Who's the lucky victim this time?" I ask.

"It's Josie! From romance book club!"

My stomach folds over on itself like a crumpled receipt at the bottom of a trash can. I look to Owen again, but his gaze has dropped to the floor. Georgia means well, but this...this is bad.

"I realized after you left that I should be looking for your matches closer to home. She's in Dogeared all the time. We all know she's beautiful and sweet. She's a little on the shy side, but that could be a good fit for you. And we already know she likes books more than she likes Vance Vickers movies."

I knew her matchmaking scheme would be awkward, but I never imagined it could be painful for anyone besides me. The look on Owen's face...

"I don't think we're a good fit." It's all I can manage.

"What? Of course you are. She loves science. You love science fiction."

"That's not the same thing."

"I know, but come on. She's a whole *genius*. She's perfect for you and your awesome brain."

Behind her, Owen flinches like Georgia landed a cross hook to his face.

"It's not a good idea. Josie's..." I have no idea how to finish that sentence. *My friend's dream girl? Not you?*

Some of Georgia's enthusiasm fades. "You really don't like Josie?"

"I like her. It's just that she's not..." This conversation is loaded with dynamite, and every sentence is a match to the fuse. "I don't think we're right for each other."

Georgia turns to our friend. "Owen, you've met Josie. Isn't she great?"

He swallows, apparently at more of a loss for words than usual. "Yeah. She is."

"Tell Miles he should accept my help as wingwoman and go on a date with our resident scientist super-genius. Don't you agree we should get their big brains together?"

I guess I'm not the only one who can't tell Georgia no when she's grinning away at him. Owen's mouth drops open, and it takes him a second, but he turns his attention to me. "You should go for it."

I *know* how he feels about her. He doesn't want me to date her. This is tearing him up inside, even if nothing on his stoic face reveals it.

"This is a very bad idea. Josie's not for me. She should be with someone like—"

"No," Owen interrupts. "You should give it a try. Like Georgia said, she's a great woman. Smart. Well read. Any guy would be lucky to have the chance to be with her."

"Aww." Georgia turns back to me. "So can I call her and confirm?"

I look to Owen, pleading for him to...I don't know what.

Declare his undying love for Josie. Distract Georgia with a fake a heart attack. Something. He just nods once. Resolute. Resigned.

"Do it, Georgia," he says. "Miles needs to get out of his own way for a change."

"Yes! Exactly. You won't regret this, Miles." She darts into the back room, presumably to set up my date.

With my good friend's crush.

"I won't do this," I say to him low enough Georgia won't hear. The number of secret conversations I've had in this store lately is insane. "I can't go on a date with the woman you're interested in."

He winces but shakes it off like he's in the ring. "It's not like I've ever talked to her. No harm, no foul."

"It's a foul to me. You're my friend. I don't want to do this to you."

He shakes his head, throwing off my refusal. "It never would have worked out between us. What would we even have in common?"

"You know how I feel about..." I toss a hand toward the back room.

"I know. But she's right. Josie's a genius scientist. She deserves the best."

The fact that he thinks for a minute that's not him is hard to witness. "Owen, I can't—"

"It's all set up!" Georgia emerges from the back room, a victorious grin across her face. "You're going to the Harvest Festival tomorrow. I thought more low-key would be good this time. Keep the pressure off and give you a chance to talk. Arlo can dodge the apples this week, or whatever they give him to do. And I'll be here. Silently cheering you on."

She pumps her fists, miming a cheerleader's chant.

"I've got to head out," Owen says. "Good luck tomorrow."

His morose look and Georgia's happy one press in against me on both sides. I've written my characters into worse situations than this. I just have to find a way to write *myself* out.

Chapter 16

Georgia

I'm such a good friend. I not only set Miles up with a woman who's absolutely perfect for him in every way, now I'm helping him pick out what he's going to wear for his date. Because we're friends.

Even if, for a minute there during book club, I thought about abandoning the whole project. For a brief, agonizing moment, I considered keeping him to myself and not setting him up with anyone at all. But how selfish would that be? I made a promise to my best friend—and even if he's somewhat hesitant, it's clear he's interested in having a relationship. I can't just back out on it because I'm feeling *ways*. Ways I can't quite define and don't want to look at too closely.

Instead of examining my feelings about Miles, I'm examining his collection of books in his living room. Well, collection is the wrong word. *Hoard* is more like it. He's got a wall of bookshelves stuffed floor to ceiling with classics and contemporaries, hardbacks and paperbacks, new and very well used.

His apartment smells of this delicious mix of paperback books, flour, and coffee. It's like the bookstore, but with an undercurrent that's all Miles—something crisp and green. It's probably just a really nice soap, but romances have addled my brain, and all I can think about is wet clover and sun-warmed mint.

Most of his books fall into the science fiction and fantasy categories, but he's got a few here and there in other genres. I smile over a couple of my rom-com recommendations tucked away among the grittier works. Action figures from his favorite movies dot the shelves like they're doing their own exploring, and he's got a few mementos on display. A ticket stub from a truly terrible movie we saw together in the spring. A Hot Wheels version of the Muppets Electric Mayhem bus I gave him for Christmas. A couple of Rubik's cubes he's determined to figure out how to do.

A framed print of a cover I illustrated last year is propped on one shelf. I pick it up to get a better view of the couple— they're both holding books and gazing at each other like they just figured something out. It was supposed to be their "aha" moment. The author really loved it.

"Why this one?" I call. Miles is in his bedroom sorting through clothing options. He's grudgingly providing a fashion show for me, but I'm about five minutes away from going through his closet myself.

He joins me in the living room wearing a gray thermal henley and gray jeans. The shirt's not quite fitted to his lean frame, but it fits him well, casual without being "graphic tee" casual. I walk closer and run both my hands from his shoulders down his arms, loving the softness of his shirt and admiring the way it fits.

For *science*. Because that's what friends *do*.

"Why this one what?" he asks.

I tear my gaze from the way his shirt hugs his shoulders and gesture at the print. "Why that cover? It's not the first cover I did, and it's definitely not my best."

His gaze drifts to the shelf and back. Holds on me. "It reminds me of us."

"Us? It's not us."

"I think it looks like us." His voice is soft and low and ever so slightly amused.

Sure, Miles and I were sort of on my mind when I illustrated it, but it's not *us*, exactly. Just...our vibe together. The way we kind of matched the character descriptions and the close friendship they had as coworkers.

Oh, shoot. It's *us*.

I illustrated us as a couple who fall in love working together. That's...I'm not sure what to call that. Small step down from creepy, big step up from impartial friend.

"Well. You know. Art is up for interpretation." I give a weak laugh, and then, because I've lost my mind, I run my hand along his sleeve again. Indulge in tracing the softness of the fabric, and the shape of his muscles underneath. I could touch his shirt all day.

"What do you think of this one?" he asks, indicating his outfit.

Clearly, I love it. I can't stop touching it. But that might lead to *Josie* touching it.

"You shouldn't wear it. It's a little too..." I want to say *flattering*, but that makes no sense. Obviously, I want it to flatter him. Why else am I here? It just doesn't have to flatter him quite this much. "Too plain. I want you to knock Josie's socks off."

I wince, considering the context. "I mean, I don't think you should really take her socks off. Not that socks are the kind of thing that come off on a first date. I don't know when you typically take a woman's socks off. Her socks should definitely stay on the whole time."

Shut up, Georgia.

His mouth quirks. "So, should I or should I not remove her socks at the Harvest Festival?"

I lightly shove his shoulder. "Go change."

"Any suggestions?"

"Maybe your, uh...dark maroon sweater? That one looks really good on you."

His mouth tips into a smile. "Yeah?"

"Yeah." I swallow because my throat is suddenly Sahara dry. "It brings out the green in your eyes."

"I didn't know that."

We're standing so close, and he's speaking so low, you'd think we were talking about something even cozier than soft sweaters.

"It's my favorite of yours. It makes all the green flecks in your eyes brighter. Tiny emeralds in a sea of amber."

He looks immensely proud of that description. "That's poetic."

I'm close enough to see those flecks, and I swear they all grow brighter.

"It's because I'm in a writer's apartment."

"I didn't know it worked like that."

"The creativity is in the air here. Like pollen. Or pet dander."

I really need to stop talking. And looking. Talking and looking are a bad combination.

"I feel like I should vacuum." He inhales slowly. Probably to prove that his apartment is safe from pet dander. It's not like he's trying to smell *me*. "I'll go change."

Good. Great. He returns to his bedroom, and even though I'm tempted to follow him and supervise his selection, it's for the best if I stay out here. Things are weird between us today. I'm sure he can handle picking out a sweater for a date.

A date I set up. Because I'm just that good of a friend.

I slump onto his desk chair. He's got a simple writing desk with a wide drawer in the base and storage cubbies on the top. I run my fingers over the worn desktop as though I really can absorb his creative inspiration by touch. It's littered with sticky notes and pencils, with a small stack of writing craft books on one of the upper shelves.

I flip through the plain spiral notebook in the center of the desk. His neat handwriting fills the pages, becoming cramped and frantic in places as though he couldn't keep up with his own thoughts. I love how he can bring whole galaxies to life in his mind. His creativity just blows me away.

Something that looks like my name catches my eye, and I flip back to try to find it. Why would my name be in his idea notebook? Maybe I'm seeing things, but it looked exactly like—

"No spoilers."

I jolt and close the notebook. I stand to prove I'm not snooping, even though I totally was.

Miles isn't wearing the maroon sweater. It's possibly worse. He's got on jeans and a thin navy-blue cardigan buttoned over a white dress shirt. Both are rolled nearly to his elbows, exposing the white cuffs and—this is the part that's making my stomach squirm—his forearms.

Why is that so attractive? Romance novels always mention forearms like they're some universal aphrodisiac. Hands are obvious, and shoulders or biceps can be nice, but forearms? It sounds so ridiculous...until you're presented with two prime specimens.

I probably should not be objectifying my friend so shamelessly.

He endures my silent scrutiny, but then he decides to murder me. He slips his hands into his front jeans pockets. He's so cute it hurts. His shy professor look is a hundred tiny, adorable daggers piercing my heart.

My eyes skate up to his. If I open my mouth, I'll probably keep spouting nonsense about him, so I stay quiet and just enjoy looking.

"I decided to save the maroon one for a special occasion."

"You look great," I croak. I legitimately croak. Because now I want to know what would qualify as a special occasion between him and Josie. Second date? Third? Sock removal time? When he decides to tell her he loves her?

My stomach pitches. I think I need to sit down.

"Hey." He moves a step closer. "Are you feeling okay?"

He peers into my eyes for evidence of whatever ails me. That's no good. *I'm* not even sure what he'll find in there. I can't have him go digging around.

I paste on the biggest, brightest smile. "Yeah. I'm just so excited for you and Josie. I'm ready to be crowned Best Wing-woman of All Time. I think she's going to be the one."

He presses his lips together. "I thought you didn't believe in 'the one.'"

"For you? I definitely do."

This sweet, soft look shines in his eyes. "And for you?"

"Outlook is less clear." A pre-date pre-game is not the time to discuss my bleak romantic hopes. "Now come on."

I take him by the shoulder and arm and push. He chuckles softly but lets me steer him through his apartment.

"You don't want to be late, do you?" I say, ignoring the heat of his bare skin where my left hand landed on his forearm. Because of course it did.

He stops in front of the door and gazes down at me. "I want a great many things, Georgia."

My heart stutters in my chest. Why does everything he says today feel so strangely charged? It's like our wires are crossed, and we're having two different conversations. His is innocent and normal, but mine is full of this bizarre, unbearable tension. Obviously, I'm the one being a weirdo in this situation.

Case in point: the way I'm clinging to his arm with both hands.

I let go of him and make shooing motions. "Go. Have a great time with Josie. Stay away from the apple bobbing station."

I'm so upside down, I could swear he looks at me with longing in those beautiful hazel eyes. In spite of all my declarations that I only want to help him out and find the right woman for him, I've got a terrible urge to pull him back into his apartment and tell him I resign as wingwoman.

But I don't do that. Because that would make me a terrible friend.

Chapter 17

Miles

I'm a terrible friend. I'm on a date with Owen's crush at the urging of the woman I'm secretly in love with. Who does something like that?

It's not a horrible afternoon. Josie's on the shy side, but she's engaging and conversation is reasonably smooth. I do, however, steer us clear of Rumble Room's booth where Owen is trying to recruit new gym members. The last time I was at the festival, I came away bruised—I don't think I'd be that lucky if it came down to it with Owen.

He's fully aware of my feelings for Georgia, but flaunting my date in his face would test our friendship in dangerous ways.

"This really is the quintessential small town fall festival, isn't it?" Josie hasn't stopped smiling at everything.

We're slowly strolling the aisles, stopping to check out interesting vendors or watch kids play some of the games. Incidentally, I'm also avoiding Arlo, who actually *is* in the dunk tank this week. Georgia will be thrilled she dodged that dip in cold water.

"Except for that." She points at the boarded-up community

center. They've added to the spooky aura, with more *Keep Out* signs and blacked-out windows.

"I guess it's going to be a haunted house soon. You didn't have anything like this back home?"

"Seattle had fall markets, but I was too obsessed with finishing my degree to enjoy it. This is Hallmark Channel cute."

"How long have you been in Magnolia Ridge?"

She pushes her dark curly hair behind one ear. "Just about a year."

"I didn't realize it's been that long."

She lingers by a stall selling handmade scarfs and shawls. "I mostly holed up in my apartment for the first few months. But I realized I didn't want to hide out forever and started doing more things in town."

"Like the book clubs." She's in three of them at Dogeared, which is a lot for most people.

"God's designated way for introverts to make friends."

We dodge kids tossing balls at a collection of milk pails. I have no intention of getting in the line of fire.

"Is it working?"

"I think so. Georgia's been inviting me out with some of the other women. I've joined in a few times, but her social battery has a lot more power than mine does."

"That's Georgia. When she's got something in her head, there's no stopping her. She can be a little overzealous, but her heart's in the right place. She just wants the best for everyone."

I wish she'd be as ready to fight for the best for herself, too, but she doesn't respond well to nudges in that direction.

"On my own, I'd just be that weird plant lady who rescues dying ferns from home improvement garden centers. Now at least I have a few friends to say, 'Do you *really* have room for another plant?'"

"You garden too?"

"My backyard is my baby. My expensive, leafy, green baby."

I stare at her. It couldn't be as simple as this, could it?

She glances away, no doubt taking my obnoxious stare the wrong way.

"I know it's weird," she says softly.

"It's not weird at all." I match her pace, wanting to ask more but totally at a loss. I've never tried to be anybody's wingman before. "Do you like barbecue?"

Her mouth twists, and her eyebrows tug down. "I thought Georgia said you're a vegetarian."

"I am. I'm just curious about you."

"Yeah, I like barbecue."

"What are your opinions on seventies rock?"

She stops just out of the way of foot traffic down the main festival thoroughfare. "Generally positive?"

"Have you ever tried kickboxing?"

Her incredulity seems to turn into amusement. "I've always wanted to give it a try but haven't worked up the nerve. Are we speed dating now?"

"Something like that. How do you feel about tattoos?"

"I have one, but I might consider more." She lifts her sweater sleeve to reveal a botanical tattoo on the inside of her forearm. It's an ornate picture frame full of delicate, leafy plants I can't possibly name surrounding something I can—a hammerhead shark. "I originally wanted to be a marine biologist, but environmental science was a better fit. So I chose something that incorporates both."

I can't help my laughter. My mother always talks about kismet, but I've never seen it in action like this.

Josie's smile disappears, and she tugs her sleeve back down. "I like it."

She walks away from me, her arms crossed tight around her. Crap. My timing with the laugh could have been better.

I jog to catch up to her and lightly touch her arm. "Wait. I wasn't laughing at your tattoo. It's just...do you believe in fate?"

Now she looks confused. She's probably having second thoughts about Georgia's set up scheme right about now. Good. She should be—because I have a much better person in mind for her.

"I've never thought about it. Why?"

"I would really like to introduce you to someone I think you share interests with. Is that okay with you?"

She frowns up at me. "I'm not comfortable leaving."

"We don't have to leave the Harvest Festival. I'd just like to introduce you to a new friend. That's all. No expectations."

"Okay."

Her skepticism remains, and I've definitely ruined this date. That's fine, too.

I lead her to the part of the market I've avoided. This is quite possibly a terrible idea, but too many signs are pointing this direction for me to ignore. Owen's standing beneath a black Rumble Room awning, wearing a similarly branded black shirt, his arms crossed over his big chest while he talks with someone. Thankfully, the person walks away before we reach him.

He sees us coming, and for just a second, hurt and surprise light his eyes. Then he locks it down into something more detached. He gives a curt nod but clearly doesn't expect us to stop at his booth. When we do, all he does is stare.

"Josie, I'd like you to meet my friend Owen. Owen, this is Josie." I probably sound a little too proud of myself, but I don't know how these things are supposed to go. No wonder Georgia doesn't play it cool with people. I want to shout, "You two are perfect for each other!" like a crazy man.

He gives me a brief look, and I suspect I'm going to hear about this later. But he turns his attention to Josie and holds out a hand. "Nice to meet you."

His greeting is softer than he normally speaks, but I'm just grateful he's speaking.

She slips her hand into his, and I swear she gasps. Maybe it's just wishful thinking or Georgia's romance books getting to me, but I'm pretty sure her little intake of breath isn't entirely in the realm of normal.

"Hi."

They shake hands in slow motion. This is either a great start or a bad one. I'm not the best judge there.

"Josie and I were just talking about backyard gardens, and I thought, 'You know who knows a lot about backyard gardens? Owen.'"

Owen blinks hard, like he just realized he's still shaking her hand and releases her.

"What did you just plant in your yard, Owen? Some kind of fern?" I am a lawyer carefully leading the defendant to incriminate himself.

"Silver cloak fern," he says. "And some autumn ferns."

"Autumn ferns are so pretty," Josie says. "You must get a lot of shade in your yard."

"There's a big ash in one corner. I've got some clerodendrums back there. Of course, the blooms are gone, and they've just got seed pods now." He winces as though maybe he's revealed too much. For whatever reason, his gardening obsession isn't something he often brings up.

"But the seed pods add interest."

He settles into a smile, seemingly relieved she understands. "Exactly."

"I've seen you at Dogeared."

Pretty sure Josie hasn't taken her eyes off of him since we came over here, but I'm good with that.

"I like books." He cringes, and a touch of pink hits his cheeks beneath his beard.

It's truly adorable to see this mountain of a man crumbling before my very eyes. I could be wrong, but I think Josie's crumbling just as fast.

"I like books too."

"Maybe we could talk about books sometime," Owen says.

"And plants," she adds with a smile.

"And hammerhead sharks," I put in.

"They're the coolest sharks," they both say at the same time. Their surprised grins are mirror images, kindred spirits recognizing each other. Sparks might as well dance in their eyes like cartoon characters come to life.

Yup. Fate. Kismet. Whatever it is, they've been hit by it.

"Josie, I've had a lovely time. Do you mind if I head out?"

She turns to me like she just remembered I'm still here. "Oh, Miles. Should we finish our...?"

Guilt mars her features as though I didn't just introduce them with the full intention of this happening. I couldn't have predicted it would go so well, but I'm not disappointed to end our date early.

"Believe me, nothing would make me happier than for you two to stay and talk."

Relief shines in her smile. "Okay. Thanks."

I point to my friend. "Owen. We'll talk later."

He shoots me a look that speaks volumes. *Thank you. I owe you one.* Also, a bit of *Help me*, but he'll sort it out.

I'm exceptionally pleased with myself as I leave them behind on my way back to Dogeared. I guess there's something to Georgia's matchmaking schemes after all.

"You set Josie up with Owen?"

Georgia's high-pitched shriek indicates she's less pleased with my attempt at matchmaking. She's been glaring at me ever since I walked through Dogeared's door earlier than expected, and my explanation clearly hasn't helped things.

"I didn't set them up. I just introduced them." With the hope that they will work out a date all on their own, but still. Semantics.

I take a seat on the stool next to her behind the counter. This late in the afternoon, the pastry case is mostly empty, but the shop still smells like the apple fritters I made this morning.

"Did it hurt Josie's feelings when you left?"

That's my Georgia—always thinking about someone else.

"Trust me, she was more worried about hurting mine."

Her lip juts out in a little frown. "It's going that well over there?"

I dip my head closer to hers. "The result of good matchmaking."

She crosses her arms and rolls her eyes, but she's fighting a smile, too. "It's like you don't even want these dates to work out."

"I plead guilty, Your Honor."

"But you said you wanted to date."

Seeing Owen blush and trip over himself but *finally* have a conversation with the woman he's crushing on made up my mind. It's time to take action with Georgia. No more pretending to be okay with her set ups.

I can be my own wingman.

I never take my eyes off her and speak with intention. "I do want to date."

Her breathing stutters the way it did in my apartment when she was admiring my sweater. Her newfound awkwardness gives me hope she's not completely unaffected by me. I won't push her past where she's comfortable, but I can encourage her. Just a little.

I extend one finger to loop beneath her pinky, where it rests on her leg. She sucks in a breath.

Maybe innocent hand touches that feel anything but innocent should go on my list of things I've learned from romance novels.

"What do we do now?" I ask low.

Her gaze drops to my mouth, making my stomach dip. My afternoon at the Harvest Festival was all about kismet, but it's hard to believe my winning streak would continue like this.

"We should probably have a practice date," she says to my lips. "So I can figure out where you're going wrong."

"It's that bad, is it?"

Her gaze darts back up to mine. "Your date is probably giving her number to another guy as we speak."

"I'm okay with that."

"Well, you definitely need some pointers. Think of it as remedial dating."

I can't help my grin. "Sign me up."

I'm ready learn whatever she wants to teach me.

Chapter 18

Georgia

I need some clarity. I need to get my head on straight. I need a little self-care.

I need some girls' time.

When Harper texted with an invite to Slice of Delight with her sister, I said please and thank you and counted down the hours. Five minutes ago, I closed up Dogeared for the night and headed out into the crisp fall evening.

I lie. It's still plenty warm here. September and October usually bring a couple of *fake falls* to trick us with chilly temperatures, swiftly followed by oppressive warmth. Actual cool weather will hit sometime around November.

Most of the shops on Center Street are decked out for autumn despite the balmy weather. A couple of them are getting ready to switch over to Halloween, and one very impatient thrift store already has a Christmas window up. Thanksgiving, of course, is completely forgotten.

Eliza flags me down as I dash across Center Street. "Jaywalking is a crime, you know."

I laugh at her cheeky greeting. "Then everyone in Magnolia Ridge should be behind bars."

"That's our town slogan." She wraps an arm around me in a quick hug.

"Did you have business down here tonight?" I ask.

Eliza owns a handmade soap company. She sells them in boutique stores all over the area, and a couple of the independent lodges. She's basically a one-woman success story.

"Nah. I just wanted to harass my husband before he finished up in the office." She leans closer. "And by *harass*, I mean *make out on his desk*."

One thing to know about Eliza—she has zero shame. I love that about her.

"Hey, look who it is." She gestures at the floor-to-ceiling shop window next to us.

I look up and stumble over my own feet. It's Rumble Room, the MMA and kickboxing studio where Sam and Harper sometimes take classes. Owen's sparring on the other side of the glass.

With *Miles*.

My Miles. He's throwing jabs and punches at the beefy bearded trainer like he's Captain America gearing up to save the world. And—holy cow. He does a perfect roundhouse kick right before my eyes.

Words fail me. My brain is stuck on my best friend in workout clothes, his athletic tee plastered to his chest from sweat, tossing out punches so gracefully. And from the way Owen braces himself, maybe even brutally.

Miles is the bookish guy. The writer guy. He is *not* the kickboxing until he's ready to drop a dude...guy.

Except, clearly he is. He's *good* at this. Like, film it and watch it on replay good. Which I have enough respect, both self- and Miles-centric, not to do. Even though I so, so want to because tomorrow I will not believe I witnessed this.

Owen nods at him, and it looks like they've called it a night.

They're winded and sweaty but grinning hard. Miles is having the time of his life in there.

Then, in a move I'll be replaying in my dreams, he swiftly pulls his shirt over his head. He wipes it down his chest, shifts to the side like he's about to leave the sparring area, and looks up.

Right. At. Me.

My stomach rolls so hard, I might be having an out-of-body experience. Now I know how Elizabeth Bennett felt when she was caught snooping around Pemberley by Mr. Darcy. Except nobody actually told me, *Hey, there's definitely no chance you'll see your best friend half naked tonight.*

I have nowhere to hide, no way to play this off with a *Ha ha, didn't see you there.* I can't find the will to break this horrible eye contact with him, like he's an exotic fish and I'm the weirdo tapping on the aquarium glass. Running away isn't even an option.

Inexplicably, his mouth tips up into a grin, like he doesn't mind that I'm shamelessly ogling him. Before I can process exactly what's happening, he moves to the door and is out on the sidewalk in front of me.

Shirtless.

Is hyperventilating the one where you breathe too fast or too slow? I'm not getting enough oxygen. That's all I know.

We've been friends for a while now, but we've never been shirtless friends. I have every intention of keeping my gaze above his neck. Collar bone at the lowest. But my eyes opt to do their own thing.

Which makes my heart rate do its own thing. Obviously, I knew he had a body beneath his clothes, but the difference between knowing it and seeing it is really dang wide. He's slim, with nicely rounded shoulders and biceps and a flat stomach. There's no defined six-pack, or eight-pack, or whatever the latest romance hero ideal is...but he still looks highly touchable.

I snap my gaze back up to his. I need to focus. This is just Miles.

Shirtless, shirtless Miles.

"Hey." Simple and casual, but he sounds happy to see me. "Everything okay?"

"Yeah. Yup. I'm just going to dinner with—" I look around, only to realize Eliza left me high and dry. Naturally. "I'm meeting Harper and Eliza for pizza. What, um? What about you?"

He laughs. It's pretty obvious what he's up to. "Just working out."

"I didn't know you did all this."

I gesture at him and almost graze his chest with my fingers. I don't know what to do with myself here.

He has the grace to look sheepish. "Owen can be pretty persuasive."

"You never told me you started doing kickboxing."

He lifts a shoulder, but I don't take the bait. I keep my gaze trained on his eyes and nothing else.

"Didn't I?"

"No. I'm pretty sure I would have remembered that. I definitely would have remembered it if I'd ever seen you—" And that is enough of that sentence.

"I didn't think it was all that interesting."

"Um, yes, it is. Everything about you is interesting." Wait. That sounds creepy. "I mean, you learning to kick box is very interesting. And watching it—"

Nope. Move along.

"The point is, I thought we told each other everything, and now I find out you've got all these secrets." Kickboxing, game night, that stupid corn maze I'm trying not to think about.

I mean, really? Running through a corn maze to pick your man? Have some dignity.

His smile makes my stomach flip. That's new, too. Does everything lately have to be so unexpected and unfamiliar?

"You're right. No more secrets between us."

Why, why is he doing the low voice thing again? And why does it have to make me so jittery?

"Good. Well." I need to cut this short or my eyes are going to rebel and wander down his chest again, and this interaction has already been embarrassing enough. "I should catch up to the girls."

"Have fun."

I almost go in for a hug but I remember he's shirtless and sweaty, and I stop myself. I end up sort of half-heartedly lurching at him without making contact. But I recover with a quick "See you tomorrow!" and dash off down the street.

I do *not* look back at him, even though everything inside me is dying to. If I start staring again, I might never stop.

I find Harper and Eliza in a booth at Slice of Delight, both looking especially smug. Eliza's always kind of got that look on her face, but it's a rare one for Harper. I slip in across from them and open the menu as if I've been right here with them the whole time.

"Everything good?" Eliza croons.

"Yes." I don't look up. *Now* my eyes are perfectly well behaved. Great timing.

"Are you sure?" Harper says. "You're a little red in the face."

I probably blush even harder.

"Need to dunk your head in an ice bath?" Eliza offers.

I drop the menu and stare at her. "How much did you tell Harper?"

"Hardly anything. Just that you saw your boss working out in the gym and kind of slipped into a trance staring at him."

"Miles and I are just friends."

They both nod, but their eyes are bright as if they're waiting for more. Or like they *know* more. Which I don't like at all.

"And I've been setting him up on dates," I add.

"What? Why?" Eliza looks ready to go on a rampage through the pizza place.

I sink against the booth. "Because it sounded like a good idea when I thought of it. But now…"

Now the idea of finding someone perfect for him makes me a little sick inside. Sending him off for his date with Josie was hard enough. I don't know if I can do it again. I don't *want* to do it again.

"Now it's not such a good idea?" Harper finishes gently.

I can only shake my head. Too many emotions are battling it out behind my ribs right now. If I try to explain how I feel about Miles dating someone else to them in actual human words, I'll wind up crying over my pizza.

"Does he really want you to set him up?" Eliza asks.

"No. I was steamrolling him into it." Because I'm such a good friend.

I kind of want to strangle that sentence.

"And he doesn't know how you feel?" Harper asks.

I shake my head again. "I don't even know how I feel."

Except, I think I do. It's like I'd kept all my emotions behind this dirty, smudged glass, and little by little, I've been washing the gunk away. Maybe I don't quite see everything clearly yet, but it's taking a very particular shape.

"I don't know how to do relationships. My parents killed theirs so spectacularly, I don't know how a healthy one even works."

"You've seen us." Harper's smile turns just a touch self-conscious.

Yeah, I've seen them.

"We can be your good examples."

I wrinkle my nose. "My brother? Yuck."

"Your brother is my biggest fan and loudest cheerleader. He looks out for me when I'm too tired or too distracted to do it myself. He takes care of me in big and small ways." She gets this wistful look on her face I recognize all too well. "He's my champion. So yes, he can be your good example."

She's not wrong. They are stupidly in love. Sometimes it makes my chest ache to see that play out in words and actions. Even in my earliest memories, Mom and Dad were never like that. Sam would walk through fire to get to Harper—and she would do exactly the same for him.

Ugh. Fine. Maybe Sam is a good example after all.

"And look, I was a mess when Dean fell in love with me." Eliza grins at me, unashamed. "And he still decided to come alongside me and fight for me and encourage me and love the heck out of me. You don't have to know how to do it to love somebody. You just do."

I want to tell her that's terrible advice, but it actually kind of makes me feel better. *Just do.*

"And let me tell you." She leans forward like she's ready to spill all the juicy bits. "Being friends doesn't mean you can't get together. It's basically the number one requirement to becoming anything more."

My heart squeezes so hard, I can't tell if I'm comforted or terrified.

Chapter 19

Miles

My brain is trying to kill me. It's honestly doing a pretty good job. Kudos.

I should have known when I had trouble sleeping last night. Definitely should have suspected when I struggled to keep track of the ingredients when I made pumpkin cinnamon rolls this morning. But I couldn't avoid it when half my vision turned blurry.

I don't get migraines often, maybe every other month. More when I'm stressed out over writing deadlines, tax time for the bookshop, or if my mom's health has hit an especially bad patch. Maybe later I'll examine my mindset to hunt for a cause for this one, but right now, all I can do is sit here and die slowly.

It's like my brain is ballooning, pressing against a skull lined with broken glass. The pain makes a detour straight through my right eye socket like I've been hit across the face with a two-by-four. My medication kicked in, but now I've got the headache, nausea, *and* caffeine jitters.

Not a great day.

"Do you mind putting on something else?" I ask Arlo. "I'm struggling with the country today."

It feels like there's a steel guitar playing in my brainpan, and I need it to stop.

"Sure thing." He messes with the old music player, and something classical fills the room. "Better?"

"Yes. Thank you."

He finally pauses to take a look at me. Our morning customers have kept him pretty busy since he came in. I've spent most of my time in the back room finishing the baking and clean up, my headache worsening every hour.

"Are you okay?"

"Migraine."

"You could go home. I can cover the afternoon shift."

"I don't want to drive when I'm this out of it." Impaired driving is still impaired driving. I won't risk it.

He gives me another once-over and pulls out his phone.

"You don't have to call anyone. I'm not that bad." I would really love to crawl into the back room and lie down in the dark for a few hours, though.

"Don't need to wait for it to get worse." He turns away from me to make his call. "Hey, it's Arlo. Yeah, Miles is in a pretty bad way with a migraine today. Do you think you could— Great. Thank you."

I don't have to ask who he called. "It's Georgia's day off."

"She's not coming in to work. She's coming to take care of you."

Nothing has ever sounded so perfect.

"You didn't have to call her."

He hitches a shoulder. "My sister gets bad migraines too. I know what they can do. Why don't you go in the back and turn the lights out while you wait?"

This is my store, my responsibility. I should be out here. But currently, it feels like a sadist is trying to scoop my right eyeball out with a spoon. So I go into the back room.

I flick off the lights, sink to the ground against the wall, and lay my head on my forearms draped across my knees. The dark and quiet help. Not nearly enough, but one layer of the throbbing in my head eases.

Ages later, a cool hand brushes over my forehead. I peel my eyes open to see Georgia crouched next to me, hazy in the darkness. She's a vision, even in this mangled state.

"Hey, sweetie," she says softly. "Let's get you home."

I can't protest. I let her help me up, and she slips one arm around my waist, the other on the center of my chest as if she thinks I might fall. I've never passed out from a migraine. The litany of things I *have* done from one pushes me to accept her help without argument.

She carefully takes us into the shop and thanks Arlo for calling her about me.

"Are you sure?" I ask him, even as I let her lead me to the door.

"Go, man." He waves us away. "You don't need to be here."

I don't have time or the mental capacity to say anything before we're out on the sidewalk.

"I parked right out front."

Normally, I'd know Georgia's car anywhere, but today it doesn't even register. Migraines scramble my brain's wiring like an old PC with half the cables ripped out.

She opens the passenger door to her little sedan and helps me inside. I press a hand over my eyes and rest the side of my face against the cool glass window. I cannot throw up in Georgia's car.

She climbs in and pulls away from the curb. "What else do you need?"

"I just need to sleep it off. I have medication at home that will help knock me out."

"You could have called me right away."

In this state, I can't process her inflection. Is she hurt? Scolding? Both at once?

I didn't avoid the call because I thought she wouldn't respond. I just have too much to do in any given day to walk away from it at the earliest sign of trouble.

"I was cautiously optimistic."

She takes one hand off the steering wheel and runs it over my leg. So soothing. I can't properly appreciate that gentle touch right now, but I'm grateful for it.

"Let's get you home to bed."

In another life, that sentence would have me on my knees. As it is, I might still drop to my knees, but not for any fun reasons.

When we reach my apartment, she comes over to help me out of the car. I want to tell her that I can handle it, but that would be a lie. My head swims and my stomach roils, and although the migraine blind spot cleared up hours ago, my vision's still off. I hold onto her and pass her my keys when we get to my door.

Inside, I head straight for the bathroom. I take more meds, remove my contacts, and slip into my sleep pants and T-shirt. I rub an essential oil blend on my temples and the back of my neck for good measure. When I emerge, I stumble to my bed and pull the covers up.

Georgia's already closed the blinds, the sweetheart. She sets a glass of water on my nightstand. "Do you need anything else?"

"There's a cooling eye mask in the fridge."

She disappears and returns a minute later with the mask full of green gel beads. I take off my glasses and slip it over my eyes. I have just enough sense to regret the ridiculous situations she's seen me in these last few weeks.

"I bet your special ops guys don't look this good."

She gently runs her fingers through my hair. "That would

be impossible. How about I come back later with dinner? Will that be okay?"

That leaves me a good eight hours to sleep this off. Might not be enough to completely drown it, but it should douse it a little. "Thank you."

Then, the softest, sweetest lips press against my forehead.

At least if this migraine kills me, I'll die happy.

When I wake up, it takes a while to shake off the grogginess from the medication. Also, I fell asleep with the eye mask on, and I need a minute to figure out where I am. But I no longer feel like I've got a harpoon stuck in my eye socket, so all in all, it's an improvement.

Another benefit is that the nausea has subsided enough for me to recognize that I need to eat. I shouldn't take all those meds on an empty stomach, but sometimes the thought of food is so unsettling it makes it impossible to dose properly. I put on my glasses and pad out to the kitchen, ready to rummage around in my kitchen for the most filling thing I can find, when I stop short.

Georgia's on my couch. She's curled up in one corner wearing black sweatpants and a rust-colored long-sleeve T-shirt, working on her tablet with her stylus. The sight of her here, fully at home in my space, makes me forget every last thought of food. How many times have I imagined her exactly like this? A different me would wrap myself around her and find a hundred ways to thank her for taking care of me this morning.

She looks up and catches me daydreaming. She immediately sets her tablet aside and rushes straight to me, her arms out like she expects me to tumble into them.

Maybe I should.

"How are you feeling?" She gazes up at me as if she's a nurse scanning my vitals.

"Better. Not a hundred percent, but it's manageable."

She runs her hand over my forehead as if she can smooth away the lingering headache. I'm willing to give it a solid effort to see if it works. Her hand slides down to cup my jaw, and her fond smile squeezes at something in my chest.

This is all I want. Georgia here with me. Georgia looking out for me. Me looking out for her. Us together, making sure the other is safe and well and happy.

"Good. You look better." She runs her hand down to rest on my shoulder and leans in. "You smell like lavender and mint, too."

"It's essential oils that are supposed to help migraines."

"That explains it. I've wondered what that was." She slips her hand away from me. "Do you feel like eating?"

"I was just coming in here to find something."

"I've got it covered." She lets me go and beelines for my stove. "I made chili with the fake beef crumbles you like. I cooked it at my place. I figured all those strong smells might not help your headache."

Past her, a pot I don't recognize sits on the stove, and there's a fresh loaf of bread on the table. She grabs a green bag off the counter and holds it up.

"I also found this herbal tea that's supposed to help, too. The guy at the apothecary said he swears by it, but who knows?"

"You went to the apothecary for me?" Sacred Roots sells crystals, beads, and incense, as well as a variety of over-the-counter herbal remedies. I haven't explored their more unusual offerings, but I love their tea blends.

"One of the ingredients is catnip, so…" She shrugs. "Don't go in for a drug test anytime soon."

Georgia fixes a mug of the tea and sets it in front of me. I don't know about catnip, but the scent of peppermint and cinnamon swirls through the air. She dishes up the chili and slices the bread. As I fill my stomach, even more of the headache ebbs away, and I don't feel quite so weighed down as I did this morning in the throes of it.

"This is exactly what I needed. Thank you."

"The protein and fiber seemed like a good choice."

I can't help my smile. "You've been doing a lot of research lately."

"You haven't had a migraine for a while. I figured it might be worse than usual."

"You were right. I didn't have any of my food triggers yesterday, though."

A little line forms between her eyebrows. "It was probably from stress. You're working too much."

I focus on the food in front of me. "It's the same amount of work I always do."

"It isn't, though. With Hannah gone, you're in the store all day, every day. Baking, working the register, hanging out for half of the book clubs. If we weren't closed on Sundays, you might as well live there." She watches me like she's trying to calculate something. "Now that I think about it, you've never had a vacation."

"That's pretty normal for a small business owner."

"Plus, you're volunteering at Fiesta Village." The smile that peeks out ruins her scolding.

"It's playing games for a couple of hours every week. I'm not sure it counts as stress."

"You're at the Harvest Festival most Saturdays helping out there. I know you do a lot for your mom. And somewhere in between, you have to find time to work on your books."

Okay, so maybe it *was* a stress migraine.

"I'll admit, there are a lot of things on my plate—"

"Your plate is heaped buffet-style."

I pause, accepting that assessment. I do take on a lot. And yes, lately it's been harder to focus on my next book for long periods of time, with a hundred other things pressing on my thoughts. But I can't just "go to my writing cave" and shut the world out. I can't pretend my needs outweigh everyone else's.

She runs her hand over mine. "You're going to burn out if you're not careful. Your body's telling you that today. You can't do everything."

It's like my mother telling me a few weeks ago that it's okay to take time for myself. Even if I know it's true on paper, some habits are hard to break.

"There's this quote that says the best way to honor someone who's passed away is to carry on the qualities you loved most about them. My dad was always there for people. Family, neighbors, strangers—he was always the first to step up and help. To really be present. He had a way of making everyone feel like the most important person in the world. After he was gone, I guess I took that on, in some small way."

Working in my own store and doing a bit of volunteer work a couple of times a week is such a drop in the bucket compared to the man he was.

"That's really sweet," she says softly. She holds my hand tighter and drops her voice. "I love that you're carrying on his legacy. But don't forget, while you're helping everyone else out, you're allowed to receive some of that back. You deserve to feel like the most important person in the world sometimes, too."

In this small, quiet moment, I do.

Chapter 20

Georgia

Despite the turmoil raging in my confused little brain, Dogeared remains my happy place. I love the coziness of being surrounded by books, coffee, and delicious treats, even when my heart's on a never-ending rollercoaster. I come to work or just hang out and let it soothe me.

I don't so much fight the butterflies that threaten to overtake me whenever I'm in the same room with Miles now as just...let them do their thing. Flutter on, you crazy butterflies. I'll figure out what to do about you eventually.

Unfortunately, a few days after my big confessional to my sister-in-law, Sam shows up at my happy place. Not unusual, but still a tiny bit suspicious. I want to believe Harper didn't blab everything I said to Sam, but it entirely slipped my mind to make her swear she wouldn't.

I should have gotten it in writing.

Sam walks through the door with another man right behind him. He's got the biggest, most self-satisfied "Sam grin" on his face. That right there tells me he means to kick up a little trouble.

"Good afternoon, baby sister."

"Sam." I am wary, like an explorer wandering a jungle filled with stinging, annoying pests.

"This is my friend, Maverick." He gestures at the other man, who smiles and gives me a nod. "We're getting ready to head out on a hike for a couple of days, but he was thinking about picking up something to read first."

Maverick reaches across the counter to shake my hand. His generous smile is totally the stuff of romance novels. "Sam's talked about you a lot. It's good to finally meet you."

"Maverick was in the Army for fifteen years and now works for a private security company down in Austin." Sam's smile, on the other hand, is a virtual poke in the eye. "Isn't that something?"

"That's...yeah. That's very interesting."

If I had a button I could push and go back in time so I could just *never* talk to my brother, I would push it so hard right now.

Maverick laughs. "It's not all that interesting. We mostly do security for boring tech guys, but it pays the bills."

"Who did you say makes up the rest of your team?" Sam asks with perfected innocence.

"A couple of guys from the unit I was with back in the day. We already know how to work together, so it seemed like a good fit."

I just go on staring. This is a thing people really do, and not just in romance book scenarios? Get the unit back together to take on civilian baddies?

"He's still pretty new to the area. Meeting new people." Sam ticks his eyebrows at me.

I paste on my customer service smile even though my organs all seize up like they just got doused in ice water. He is *not* doing what I think he's doing. "That's really great for you."

"Isn't it?" Sam goes on smiling at me. Waiting for me to crack.

"I'm going to take a look around, if you don't mind." Maverick nods at me again and steps away into the stacks.

I plant my hands on the front counter and lean toward my awful, scheming, no-good brother. "What are you doing?"

It's a seething whisper I don't want Maverick or the people sitting in the café area to hear. If the place were empty, I'd have no problem going full volume, but I'm not going to make a scene. Even though I'd be well within my rights as a disgruntled sister.

"I'm introducing you to your dream man."

If Sam doesn't stop smiling soon, I'm going to smack him.

"Why would you do that?" I hiss. "I don't want that."

"Isn't he everything you said you wanted?" Sam at least pitches his voice low, but it's not nearly whispery enough for me. "He's former military, older than you, protective, skilled with his hands."

"Shh—I never said skilled with his hands."

Sam manages to look solemn. "It should be on the list, George."

I glance over at Maverick browsing the stacks. He really does look like one of my special ops guys come to life. Tall and broad, with a long-sleeve shirt that hugs his muscular upper body. Hair just shy of close-cropped so he can joke about "civilian haircuts." A couple of days' worth of stubble across his jaw.

He probably leans in doorways and growls at guys who look at his woman the wrong way too.

"Are you messing with me? Is he even any of that stuff you just said? There's no way that's his name. Nobody's named *Maverick.*"

That's squarely a romance book hero name, like Knox or Ransom. It's not the name of an actual human man.

"Oh, it's his name. And it's all true. I wouldn't lie to you."

Sam's grin reappears, which kind of puts a damper on his whole "wouldn't lie to you" declaration.

Even though I know deep down he wouldn't. Mercilessly tease, yes. Flat-out lie, no.

That's almost worse. Because that means that the man in the stacks really is a former military private bodyguard with a heart of gold named Maverick. I'm guessing at the heart of gold part, but all those kinds of heroes have them. Tragic backstories, found family, ready to move heaven and earth for their love interest. The works.

Behind Sam, outside the café window, I spot Miles on the sidewalk. He's talking with one of the elderly women I met at game night at Fiesta Village. He's been taking it easy these last couple of days since the migraine, but today he looks like himself again.

Hello, butterflies.

But, no. I can't have Miles walk in here when Sam is doing the absolute most to ruin my day with his good buddy Maverick. I want to crawl into a hole and then commit physical violence against my brother. Or maybe violence first, then get in the hole.

"So?" Sam goads. "Is this love at first sight?"

My gaze darts back to Miles. He's smiling at the older woman, listening attentively while she tells him about who knows what. Because of course he's going to stop and be a good person no matter what else he has to do in his busy day. That's just who Miles is. He's thoughtful, generous, and patient to the core. He's the sweetest ever.

Sam follows my gaze, looking over his shoulder. When his attention returns to me, his smile is even smugger than it was before. "That's what I figured."

I think I'm going to be sick.

Sam can't figure anything out. *I've* barely figured anything out.

Maverick joins us at the counter with a thriller in his hands. "Found one."

"That's a good option." I honestly don't even know what he's holding. I barely pay attention, working on autopilot to punch in the purchase price and tap his credit card.

Miles walks into Dogeared, and my mouth goes too dry to speak. All I can do is trust Sam not to make this a thousand times worse than he already has. Trouble is, I'm not sure that I do, in fact, trust that.

"Hi, Sam." Miles rounds the front counter to join me. "What brings you in?"

"Oh, just harassing my little sister. The usual." He flashes his million-dollar smile at us. Right now, I really want to knock his teeth out. "You're coming to Willa's birthday party this weekend, right?"

That reminder just gives me another reason to be disgruntled. It's one more thing Miles has agreed to instead of taking time for himself. As delighted as I am that Willa would invite him, and even more that he would accept, it's supposed to be his day off.

At least I know Ava's party planning will make it worthwhile, but it's the principle of the thing.

"I'm planning on it. But she wrote on the back of my invitation *No books*. I feel called out."

Miles grins at me, and my heart melts.

"She hasn't forgotten your Christmas present," Sam says. Then he winks at me. "Okay, we're heading out."

"It was nice to meet you, Georgia." The man who may or may not actually be named Maverick raises his hand as he walks out the door.

"You, too." I give him a feeble wave, and finally, they're gone.

I need to eighty-six my brother from Dogeared. Banned for life.

"Is everything okay?" Miles asks. "You look a little shaken."

"Everything's fine. Sam just knows how to get under my skin. He's like a tick."

Miles's soft laughter is a warm hug, ready to banish every last bit of discomfort brought on by Sam's pushiness.

"I've been meaning to talk to you about Willa's party," he says. "Obviously, I'm not the best at picking out presents for little girls."

"*The Secret Garden* was a really good choice. Willa's just not as into books that don't have fairies and unicorns in them right now."

"Do you have any suggestions?"

"Get her the biggest, fluffiest stuffed animal you can find, and she'll love you forever."

"Good tip. She also drew a stick figure in a party dress. Formal wear, I take it?"

I laugh. "Oh, yeah. You'd better be in a tux or no admittance."

We work through the afternoon, and once my shift ends, I move to the closest cozy chair and get out my tablet to get started on a new cover. It's another sports romance, which requires a lot of sketching football uniforms and padding to be sure I get the look exactly right.

I'm absorbed with trying to convey *big* without crossing over into *bulky* when the back of my neck prickles. I look up and find Miles watching me. A smile curls along his mouth, and he seems amused. Happy. Something...else.

"What?" I ask.

"I just like to see you relaxing in the store. Like you belong here."

It's a sweet compliment and especially reassuring since I'm

here practically all the time. But the wobbly sensation that washes through me makes me want to argue a little. Just enough to keep from turning to complete mush over a few simple words.

"Then why do you keep trying to fire me?"

"I don't try to fire you." He walks around the counter and comes closer, ultimately leaning against the doorframe that leads into the back room.

I'm a fan of the lean.

"I simply encourage you to spread your wings and fly, little bird."

I laugh. "Same thing."

He shrugs against the door. "I don't ever want to hold you back."

"That is the sweetest, most misguided thing. This is where I want to be."

He nods, gaze stuck on me. "We should talk about our date."

A shiver skates down my spine. "What date?"

"The one we talked about the other day."

"Oh. You mean our practice date?" The clarification is for me. As topsy-turvy as I've been this last week, it'd be too easy for me to think it's anything else.

"Mmm. Do you want to go to dinner, or should I cook for us?"

That straightforward question makes me strangely giddy. It's not the first time he's asked me that, but the context is new. It's not just hanging out as friends for the evening. It's a date.

Practice date, I rush to add. Which I should probably repeat to myself a hundred times slowly.

"What would you do on a real date?" I don't like how eager my voice sounds, and I try again. "Since I'm doing this to evaluate your skills."

His mouth quirks. "That's an interesting way to put it."

I look away. My face probably has flames dancing over it. "You know what I'm saying."

"If it were a date with someone I've known for a while, I'd probably invite her to my place and cook dinner for her. Maybe watch a movie and keep it low-key." Miles pauses, and I glance back at him. "But if it's a date with someone I don't know well, a public place would be better. Someplace neutral so she'll feel comfortable and safe."

I really want to go for the first option, but since this is supposed to be a "dating skills evaluation," I need to opt for the second. I won't get a feel for what he's been doing on his set ups if we just hang out at his place and watch a movie on his couch.

Even if that's basically my dream date now.

And I've lost my zeal for setting him up with anyone ever again.

"How about a restaurant? Maybe Thai?"

If he's disappointed—which he's not, obviously, why would he be?—he doesn't show it. "Thai sounds great. Are you free on Saturday?"

"That soon?"

"I don't see a need to wait."

Everything he says lately threatens to turn me to goo. I'm sure in his mind there's really no reason to delay—we're buddies embarking on a practice date so I can help him find somebody else. Just because I'm suddenly conflicted about the possibility of *us*, doesn't mean he's feeling the same way.

Great. I think I just hurt my own feelings.

I smile anyway. "Saturday it is."

Text Thread

Georgia: I'm really sorry, but we'll have to postpone our practice date

Georgia: I forgot I told Ava she could bring the littles to my place while she prepares for the birthday party

Miles: She needs a whole night to get ready for a birthday party?

Georgia: You haven't been to their house. She goes all out for everything

Miles: Sounds familiar

Georgia: Don't you dare

Georgia: Ava and I are not the same

Miles: Apologies

Miles: She sounds over the top while you are understated and subtle

Georgia: You'll think so once you see Willa's party

Georgia: Point is—I have two little terrors heading my way in a few hours

Miles: Do you want help wrangling them?

Georgia: You don't want to do that. It's the opposite of a night off

Miles: What else am I going to do? I'll even bring Willa's favorite thing

Miles: A huge pile of books

Georgia: Aw. Nothing like a man who knows how to entertain kids

Miles: After, we can do some math and clean

Georgia: Best babysitter ever

Chapter 21

Miles

I don't regret that I'm not out with Georgia on a "practice" date right now. She made a commitment to her family and she's following through. I respect that. And I'm glad she let me join in the craziness that is an evening with her younger brother and sister. I don't have siblings or even younger cousins, so I've rarely had a night like this. We're making personal pizzas, and then we'll settle in for popcorn and a movie.

I *do* regret letting Willa commandeer a ladle full of marinara sauce. Especially when she gestures wildly at me while she's telling an exciting story about her classmates, leaving a zesty red splatter all over my pale gray shirt.

"Oops." Her eyes go huge, and she tosses the ladle into the bowl of marinara. Sauce goes flying again, but it stays on the kitchen counter this time. "I didn't mean it."

"It's okay." I lift the fabric from my skin to try to escape the wet chill of sauce spreading down my front.

"All right, let's put a pause on our pizza making." Georgia presents two old dishtowels to the kids. "You two wipe your hands and go sit in the living room while I help Miles get cleaned up."

"Can we watch Netflix?" Finn asks. He's already made his personal pizza, complete with symmetrical olive placement. Maybe he actually would have enjoyed an evening of math and cleaning.

"As long as it's kid appropriate." Georgia swipes at Willa's hands with one of the dishtowels and gets her face for good measure. "We'll be right back."

She scoots the kids into the living room and turns apologetic eyes on me. "I am so sorry. That's never going to come out."

"Can we call it tie-dye?"

"I wouldn't." She takes my elbow and drags me into the hallway next to her washer and dryer. "I have stain removal stuff we can try, but we need to act fast."

She takes the bottom hem of my shirt and starts to lift as if she's going to strip it off me. Her gaze meets mine, and she sucks in a breath as pink washes over her cheeks. Glancing away, she takes half a step back. "Sorry. You go ahead."

I'm not sorry. Images of what it would have been like if she'd followed through fill my head. I should probably get my thoughts in check, though. There are kids in the next room.

Oh, and she still doesn't know how I feel about her. Can't forget that one.

I peel off the ruined shirt, careful not to let cold sauce drip on my skin or the floor. She takes it from me and lays it across the open washer, stain side up.

"Come with me."

She leads me into her bedroom. For all the times I've been in her apartment, I've never been in her room. Maybe it was a line I knew I shouldn't cross, or maybe there's just never been a need. But I'm here now, and it does not disappoint.

It's colorful, like I knew it would be, filled with favorite thrift store finds. A vibrant painting of a wildflower field scattered with pink-and-red blooms dominates one wall. A bright orange-and-yellow block quilt is across her bed, with a solid teal throw at the bottom. A red lamp with a vintage style floral shade sits on her nightstand, along with a stack of her next reads.

It's just shy of being too much, but that somehow makes it all the more inviting. Like the woman herself.

She pulls a couple of shirts out of one of her dresser drawers and holds them up. "Death Valley or Strawberry Shortcake?"

"How about Death Valley?"

She tosses the shirt at me. "It's one of my sleep shirts, so it's nice and oversized. I think it will work for you."

"It's great, thanks." I can't stop and think about her actually *sleeping in this shirt* or my brain will explode in a mess worse than Willa's marinara catastrophe.

"It's a good thing she didn't get any on your pants. I don't have anything long enough for you."

"You don't sleep in XL sweatpants, too?" I tease. Nothing she'd have would ever be long enough for me.

"Usually just the shirt. In the summer, I wear even less." Her smile disappears. "I mean a tank top and shorts, not like... never mind."

This is a great example of why I never came in here before. Now that I know what her bed looks like and what she wears when she's in it, I may never sleep again.

"I'll give you a minute..." She moves to scoot by me where I'm still standing in the doorway. "If you need to clean up, you can use the bathroom."

She gestures over her shoulder at the door just cracked open.

"Thank you."

Her eyes skate down my chest and back up to lock with mine. She blushes again, which is highly adorable. I don't want something just physical with her, but the fact that she's noticing the physical at all gives me hope.

"Yeah, of course. I'll just, um...go take care of your shirt."

With that, she slips out the door, closing it behind her to allow me privacy I don't really need. But I don't mind being closed up in her bedroom.

I pull the shirt on, stupidly pleased to know she sleeps in it. Next time, I want to see her wearing *my* clothes.

I debate the wisdom of lingering in her room but decide I'm too much of a gentleman for that. Actually, it's more like I'm not up for that much torture. I take one last lungful of the scent in here—it brings to mind the caramel apple booth at the Harvest Festival—which probably only proves I'm not a gentleman at all.

In the hallway, Georgia's scrubbing a stain stick over the red splotches on my shirt.

"You don't have to do that."

She shoots me a glare without any real fire in it. "Yeah, I do. I came up with the great 'build our own pizzas' plan. I should have been more on the ball with Willa."

"I'm the one who was standing right by her. If anyone fell down in their supervisory duties, it was me."

She frowns but seems to accept that. "I'll let this soak in and wash it tonight. Keep your fingers crossed it's some kind of space-age, no-stain marinara."

"I should find a way to work that into one of my books. What will technology accomplish next?"

"Credit me in the acknowledgements, please."

Pizza prep has no further setbacks, and after a while, we're all sitting around Georgia's dining table eating our specialty meals. Willa digs into hers like it's the best pizza she's ever had, getting sauce smeared across her cheeks. Georgia and I encourage her to at least dab at the damage with a napkin, but she refuses to lose her focus.

Finn shoots annoyed side-eyes at her. I'm not sure how

much of it is the natural difference in their dispositions, and how much is generic older brother disdain.

"You could at least chew with your mouth closed," he says to her.

Willa makes a face at him. "Do you want a closer look?"

"That's enough," Georgia says gently. "We don't need to show anybody what's in our mouths, please."

"She doesn't even have to try." Finn scowls at his sister, who looks ready to take the argument to a physical level.

She's also got a piece of crust hanging out of her mouth.

"Have you downloaded any new games, Finn?" Usually when we're playing backgammon, he spends the whole time telling me about hit points or world building in whatever video game he's currently into.

He abandons the argument with his sister and describes some demolition simulator where the only goal is to destroy all the buildings in-world using ridiculous weapons.

"I'll show you at Willa's party tomorrow," he tells me. "When she's busy with her girl stuff."

"Sounds good."

"I bet Ava's getting your house so pretty for your party," Georgia says to Willa.

"She did," Willa announces. "But I can't see it yet because it's a surprise for tomorrow."

"She already did?"

"Dad says it looks like a unicorn fairyland," Finn says. "I think it looks like puke on a stick."

Willa jams out her tongue.

"Then what are they doing tonight?" Georgia asks.

Willa shrugs, focused on her pizza. "Mommy and Daddy are on a date."

Georgia blinks at her. This obviously isn't the same information she was given by her dad and stepmom.

"Miles, did you know friends can kiss?"

Willa's question has me staring like a deer that just stumbled onto an interstate. I look to Georgia for help, but she's watching Willa with the same alarmed expression I must be wearing.

"I guess they can, yeah." I have no idea where this conversation is going. Frankly, I'd rather she show me all the chewed up pizza in her mouth.

She scoops a long piece of cheese dangling off the slice into her mouth. "But you and Georgia don't kiss?"

Next to me, Finn groans like his stomach's troubling him. "Would you please not talk about kissing?"

"There's nothing wrong with kissing!" She manages to work the cheese into her mouth and look vaguely threatening at the same time. "It's a nice thing to do."

"So gross."

"Miles and Georgia can kiss if they want to! You're not their boss!"

Love to hear that she's on my side, even if this is a wildly inappropriate conversation to have.

"We don't need to talk about kissing in front of other people like this." Georgia's remarkably calm, given the context.

"But we did before, and you didn't mind. You said you wanted to kiss Miles."

I think the pizza I ate is now wedged right behind my sternum. I take a drink of water before I can start sputtering like a madman.

"I didn't say that," Georgia says, eyes on me. "I said we *don't* kiss."

Not the relief I was looking for, to be honest.

"Oh." Willa considers this. "I think you should."

Finn's long-suffering sigh fills the kitchen. "Not everybody likes each other that way. You're obsessed with kissing."

"What's wrong with that?"

"Please shut up."

"You shut up," Willa tosses back.

"Okay!" Georgia says loud enough to snap them out of their squabble. "Let's wash our hands and get ready to watch a movie."

The kids scramble out of the kitchen so fast I'm surprised they don't upend the chairs. In another few seconds, a muffled argument over who gets the soap first drifts through the wall. Georgia and I lock gazes. Pause. And burst into laughter.

"Will you ever forgive me for tonight?" she says, getting up to clear the plates.

I start putting away all the leftover pizza ingredients. "The night could go a whole lot worse. Aren't uncomfortably inappropriate conversations par for the course with kids?"

She laughs, filling up her dishwasher. "You're not wrong. It's probably best to stay on Willa's good side if you can. She's a master at zeroing in on the worst things to bring up."

"She likes me." I'm maybe a touch overconfident in my assessment, but she's never told me to shut up or declared me a stupid-face the way she sometimes does with her brother. I'll count it as a win.

"Let's wait and see how things go at her birthday party tomorrow before you start bragging."

By the time we're finished cleaning up in the kitchen, the kids have made blanket nests on the floor in front of Georgia's television. They've even cued up a Muppet Halloween movie, one of my favorites. All Georgia and I have to do is collapse onto the couch together.

We don't leave much space between us, but we never do on movie night.

The movie gets rolling, and the kids settle in, lying on their stomachs and propped on their elbows. It's homey and comfortable in a way I don't usually experience.

I tilt my head a little closer to Georgia's so I can whisper to her. "Owen and Josie are on their second date tonight."

"I know. Josie called me." She nudges me with her shoulder, moving slightly nearer to me in the process. "Seems unfair that the guy against matchmaking has so much luck with it."

"It was pretty easy. I just saw two people who were meant to be together." I decide not to mention Owen's long-standing crush. Depending on how things progress with Josie, maybe one day he won't mind if it's shared.

"How did you know, though?" Her voice is soft, just for us. "That they were meant to be?"

I get the feeling she's asking about more than just Owen and Josie. As much as she loves imaginary romance, she doesn't have a lot of trust in the real version.

"Sometimes two people just fit, and all they're waiting for is a little nudge to get them to see it."

She never breaks eye contact with me, just goes on staring like she can find answers to other questions there. Daring more than I thought I might tonight, I slip my hand beneath hers where it rests on her leg and twine our fingers together.

The softest, smallest smile touches her mouth, and her hand tightens in mine.

It's more than enough.

A minute or two later, I turn my attention back to the movie and find Willa grinning at us.

So. That's going to be fun.

When Christopher and Ava Donnelly show up to collect their children, Willa is nearly zonked out. Finn's been quiet for a while, either getting sleepy or really missing his video game systems. Georgia helps them collect all their things, and I just sort of stand around superfluous.

"Miles," Ava says, as though we have secrets between us. "It's so good of you to help Georgia with the kids."

"I'm always happy to have pizza and watch a Muppet movie," I joke. Incidentally, the joke is true.

Christopher's thin smile doesn't carry much warmth. "How is the bookstore doing this quarter?"

"Dad!" Georgia calls from where she's stuffing Willa's sweater into a backpack. "You don't need to ask about that."

"It's a valid question I'd ask of any small business owner."

She glares, herding the kids to the door. "Then you should rethink your small talk."

Ava laughs as though they're always like this. From what I've seen, they mostly are. "Kids, say thank you to Georgia and *Miles.*"

The emphasis makes me think that seeing romance everywhere runs in this family.

The kids do as they're told, and Willa throws her arms around each of us. Finn is somewhat less affectionate but no less grateful.

"See you both tomorrow," Ava calls as Christopher ushers the family out of the apartment.

Once they're gone, Georgia closes the door and leans against it, facing me, her hands behind her back. "Scale from one to ten, how bad was it? One is the worst night ever. Ten is practically tolerable."

I shrug. "I'd say an eight. Minus a point for the marinara incident, and one for how much of Willa's food I saw while she ate it."

"Feral animals have better table manners. And you're way too generous with your points system."

"I had a good time." Aside from all the distance between us right now.

"I'm sorry we didn't do the practice date like I said we would."

"I really don't think I'm as hopeless as you seem to imagine I am."

Her mouth curls just a touch. "Maybe not."

Normally, at the end of an evening together, we just go our separate ways. Say thank you for dinner or the movie or whatever and carry on. Tonight, we stare like we don't know how to close out our time together. Or, wishful thinking, maybe neither of us wants it to end?

"We could still go through the end of date stuff," she says. "Since we're basically here now."

That's an intriguing possibility. "What do you have in mind?"

"You know. Do you ask to see her again? Do you play it cool? Do you kiss her?"

The word "kiss" on her lips sends a spark of adrenaline through my system. I take a step closer. "In this case, I ask to see her again."

She nods as though mentally ticking a box somewhere. "And, um...the kiss?"

I take another step. I'm in her space, but she just goes on looking up at me, hands still behind her back. "Are we imagining the date went well then?"

She swallows and presses her lips together. "I think we should, yes. Is a kiss part of your goodnight routine?"

This conversation is going to kill me.

"You have a misguided idea of what my dating life is like if you think I have a 'goodnight routine.'"

"I think it is." She ignores my protest. "I think you probably do kiss her goodnight."

I gaze from one green eye to the other, trying to hear her with no misunderstandings. "Do you want me to kiss you?"

She smooths her lips between her teeth and back. "Do you think you need the practice?"

"Maybe. It's been a while."

She nods again, staring up at me with mountains of trust in her eyes. "For me, too."

The writer in me wants to freeze this moment so I can write a poem about Georgia's exact eye color as she stares at my mouth. Take down every nuance of the blush that warms her cheeks. Immortalize her soft pink lips that are finally, inexplicably, waiting for me.

The man in me just wants to kiss the hell out of her already.

I lean down agonizingly slowly. I have never felt my height quite so keenly. My mouth is called to hers on an inevitable journey, but before I reach my destination, she whispers to me.

"We can kiss as friends."

The lava coursing through my veins turns into glacial ice. Whether her caveat is a warning for her or for me, it stops my momentum entirely. I won't kiss Georgia as friends. Not when it would be so much more than that for me.

I angle my face to one side and press a kiss to the corner of her mouth. The smallest touch of heat, and then gone. If I kiss her skin anywhere for longer than that, I just might forget all my noble intentions.

I straighten in time to watch Georgia blink herself out of a daze.

"I think on the first date, I'd just kiss her on the cheek."

She nods, darting away from the door and out of my reach. "That's smart. Always keep them wanting more."

Her shaky laugh doesn't reassure me. The trouble is, I do want more. But I need to be sure she truly wants *me*.

Chapter 22

Georgia

Have you ever seen a guy really whiff it in baseball? He's at bat, he's focused on the ball, and he throws everything he has behind his swing—only to miss the ball entirely and stumble to the side from all that wasted momentum?

That was me last night. I whiffed it with Miles. We were standing so close and he smelled so good, and he was leaning in to *kiss me on my mouth*, when...I panicked. What if he truly only thought of us as friends? What if he really was only practicing? I didn't want to kiss him and think it meant something when it really didn't.

But how do you just say that? "Um, hey, Miles, before we get down to it, is this a really-real kiss or just a friend kiss?" It'd seemed like a stroke of genius to follow Willa's lead and call it a friend kiss before he could. I hadn't expected him to skip it entirely.

I probably shouldn't take relationship advice from eight-year-olds.

But that's okay. It makes sense. We don't need to kiss. We *are* friends.

And now, we're friends who almost kissed but didn't, sitting in Miles's car as he drives us to my dad's house.

I thought I could use his behavior when he showed up to gauge where we're at. But he's acting perfectly normal—a few smiles, a little teasing, nothing out of the ordinary. Which probably means he didn't really care about the kiss that almost was. So it's probably a good thing I whiffed it.

Doesn't feel like a good thing, but I can't be sad when I'm on my way to an eight-year-old's birthday party.

"You really took my advice," I say. There's a huge gift bag spilling bright pink tissue paper in the back seat.

"I don't want another note about gifts next year."

"Fun fact: you'll get the note anyway. Willa is very demanding."

He chuckles softly. "As long as it's not just me."

"Turn left up here. It's about a mile down this road."

Miles makes a face I can't read at this angle. "They live in Rivendell Acres?"

"You know it?"

His eyes flash my way but don't reach me. "Yeah. I know it."

"You sound like that's a bad thing."

We near the big gated community, and Miles points to two houses just outside the brick wall. "My mom and aunt live right there."

It's a testament to how little I talk about my dad and Ava that it took us this long to realize our parents are sort of neighbors.

"They must hate having that development right in their backyard." While the two yards outside the wall are lush with old-growth trees and flower beds, most of the trees on the other side are barely over ten feet tall, absolutely dwarfed by the gigantic houses.

"Yes and no." Miles winces and stops the car outside the

automated gate. He turns to face me. "We do hate it. It's not what we were hoping for when we sold the land. But we're grateful for the comfort it's afforded us."

I suck in a slow breath as the puzzle pieces he laid down click together. "Your family used to own all this?"

"Back when it wasn't all this." He looks through the windshield at the fancy brick wall as if he can see the giant houses behind it. "Back when it was land my grandpa worked."

"I had no idea." I've always lightly hated my dad's McMansion, but for my own selfish reasons. The house he bought for Ava more than doubled the size of the house Sam and I grew up in, with a pool in the backyard and walk-in closets in every bedroom. Its luxury is a stark contrast to the more average home we used to have.

I don't want to care about those superficial things, but it's one more reminder that he never viewed our two families the same way.

Also, it's ugly as sin.

"Grandpa loved this land. Sometimes I think it'd break his heart to see this." Miles turns to me again. "But he'd be glad his daughters and grandchildren are taken care of. We were more important to him than any field."

I slip my hand around his and hold tight. "I'm so sorry."

He squeezes my hand back but shakes his head. "I'm making this sound sadder than it is. It wasn't sold out from under us—we made the decision. We just weren't expecting this."

"It's pretty obnoxious, right?"

His mouth tugs into a small smile. "So hideous."

"It's got to be weird for your mom and aunt to live right next to this."

"Occasionally, the residents petition to have the two houses knocked down to preserve the beauty of the development, but other than that, they don't really interact."

"That makes me want to punch that stupid wall. Or...toilet paper all the houses in there." That would show those snobs.

"Don't punch the wall." Miles lifts my hand to his mouth and presses a kiss to my knuckles. "You need your hands for art."

It's suddenly desperately hot in this car. My stomach flips and flutters like it doesn't know what to do with itself. Meanwhile, I can't take my eyes off his lips that just *kissed* me. Doesn't matter that it was my hand—it was a kiss. He kissed me. It counts.

Maybe my screw up last night wasn't irredeemable?

"But toilet papering is on the table?" I ask. Mostly to stop myself from begging him to kiss me again.

He flashes a grin. "The less I know, the better."

He releases me, and I give him the code to lift the gate. I direct him to the heart of the development, and we pull up in front of a stucco and brick behemoth. Three-foot-high letters spell out *Happy birthday Willa* in the yard, with approximately five hundred pink-and-purple balloons tied in bunches along the walkway and by the door.

"Are we sure this is it?" he asks drily.

"I told you."

We grab our gifts and head inside. I've never felt at home enough in their house to just walk in, but the fancy script sign on the door says we should. We're immediately accosted by the brightest, sparkliest party decor in the history of ever. Clusters of balloons sway in bundles throughout the house. Parents mingle in the living room drinking elaborate cocktails. The gift table is already piled high with bags, boxes, and bows. We set ours on the floor next to it and explore further.

Their dining table has not one, not two, but three rainbow

birthday cakes on it. There's a tray of pink cupcakes just in case the hankering hits, and crystal vases full of gigantic lollipops. Pink urns hold huge pink-and-white peony blooms, while others display pale pink cake pops.

Miles takes in all the excess. "I'm getting a sugar rush just from breathing the air in here."

"We're not done yet." I take his hand and lead him through the rest of the house, where more parents talk business over their drinks. I go through the French doors and into the backyard.

Pink unicorn floats fill the pool. Three piñatas hang from the trees—a birthday crown that says "Willa," a unicorn head, and a butterfly. A row of little girls in multi-colored fairy skirts are lined up to get their faces painted. The entire scene is excessively pink and ridiculous.

I spot my family beneath the covered porch and lead Miles their way. Grandpa sits in a padded wicker chair, and Sam and Harper are on a sofa next to him. Dad is talking to them with his back to us, but Sam spots me. Even from here, I can see his gaze drop to Miles's hand in mine.

I let go when we close in on them. I can only deal with so much today.

I go straight to Grandpa and drop a kiss on his cheek. "How are you feeling?"

His eyes are a little watery these days, but they still sparkle. "As fine as always. Just basking in the glow of the pinkest birthday party I've ever seen."

"I'm surprised you didn't hire mermaids to swim in the pool," Sam says.

Dad looks at the inflatable floats gently bobbing over the surface. "We considered it but ultimately went with face painting and the fairy godmother."

Sam and I share a look.

"Fairy godmother?" he asks Dad.

"She's outfitting the girls with skirts and doing their hair in the den."

That explains the surprising number of girls with elaborately curled hair today. I hadn't considered it was part of the theme.

"You're right. Much more practical than mermaids."

"Good to see you, Miles." Grandpa grins up at the man by my side.

"Thank you, sir. It's not every day I get invited to a party like this."

Grandpa chuckles. "No, I'd imagine not."

"I know it seems like a lot." The concession is a rare show of self-awareness by my father. "But there's nothing I wouldn't do for my baby girl."

My smile feels off, but I'm sure Dad would never notice. He's always been like this with Finn and Willa, as if parenting is something he just discovered twelve years ago, even though he's got children who are thirty and twenty-eight.

"Colleagues told me the children you have later in life are something special," he goes on. "I never knew how right they'd be."

It kind of feels like he expects us to applaud that.

Miles shifts closer to rest one hand on my back. Comforting me. Supporting me. His warm hand just became the most important thing at this party.

"I guess I missed out on one of those special late-in-life babies." Grandpa shoots a pointed look at my dad.

"Sam and Georgia know what I mean." Dad glances to us to back him up.

"I don't know if I do," Sam says. "Could you dumb it down a little?"

Dad scowls as if Sam is the one who's out of line. "I'm going to check on Ava."

He leaves us, pushing through the crowded back yard.

Sam tracks Dad's progress into the house. "He'll never get it, will he?"

"I expect he won't," Grandpa says. "It's probably easier to keep his head in the sand and pretend he's in the right than to accept how much he's hurt you kids."

Harper runs a hand over Sam's back, and Miles moves his on mine. Soothing in a way I can appreciate but really don't want to sink into right now.

"Okay, but is nobody going to talk about the fact that they at least considered hiring mermaids?" I say.

"I chose the wrong profession," Harper says. "I could have swam around in other people's pools wearing a bikini and a tail."

Sam nuzzles closer to her. "We can still make it happen."

"I take back everything I said about you and Ava being similar," Miles says to me.

"Thank you." I nod like a queen accepting a formal apology. "I'm over the top, but even I have limits."

He grins. "To be fair, your limits are pretty high up there."

I nudge him with my hip. "That's what makes me fun."

"I never argued that."

It takes me at least thirty seconds to realize we're staring at each other with goofy smiles on our faces. I snap out of it, but from the way the rest of my family is watching us, the damage has already been done.

Grandpa takes my hand and shakes it back and forth. "Are you keeping your promises?"

The air squeezes from my lungs. He narrows his eyes on me as if willing me to remember exactly what he's talking about. Of course I know.

Is Miles the right man? Maybe the harder question: am I trying?

"I think I am." It's about as honest as I can be. I don't know how to do this with Miles. I don't know how to move past these fears that still sit right below the surface.

But I want to try.

"Good to hear it. Now," he says, clapping his hands, "does anybody know if there's any cake around here?"

Chapter 23

Georgia

The party is a rousing success, as they always are. Willa and her friends get transformed into fairies, they play a few games in the yard, and make friendship bracelets at a craft station. As promised, Willa lets me try to smash the heck out of the piñatas, but I catch nothing but air.

That doesn't stop me from stuffing candies into my pockets for later.

I am uncomfortably full from eating two generous slices of rainbow cake. Most of the guests have left, leaving the house especially cavernous without all the tipsy parents wandering around. Sam and Harper left to take Grandpa back to Fiesta Village a few minutes ago, and now I'm lounging in the family room while Miles lets Finn show him his demolition game upstairs.

It's almost peaceful. Until Dad joins me. He sits down on a couch across from me.

"Ava always throws a good party."

I nod. "Kids had fun." Understatement of the year, but we all witnessed their berserk reactions.

"How are things going with your design work?"

Two sentences of conversation before he circled around to my job. Is that a record?

"It's going really well. I'm happy with it."

I love making covers, and I take on just enough that when I add it to my hours at the bookstore, I'm making a living wage. Even better than average, if I'm being honest.

"Sometimes I regret how I failed you."

Dad looks...apologetic? Sincere? It's not a look I see on him often. Maybe he actually took Grandpa's comments to heart.

"Thank you," I say softly.

"I didn't do a good enough job of teaching you to be ambitious and plan for the future. And now look." He tosses a hand my way. "You're stringing together part-time jobs making art nobody's going to see, and thinking you've made it to the top working retail."

I freeze, letting all that wash past me like water sliding off a downy duck. He really had me going there for a minute. A thread of anger with myself stitches through me for ever thinking he might apologize for being a disinterested father. For blowing up our family. For never caring how his affection for his four children is grossly imbalanced.

"I wish I'd taught you better. I want to be proud of you, Georgia."

It's like he's pleading with me to do something worthy of him. I'm halfway formulating a response I'll most likely regret when I spot Miles in the entryway. From the stormy look on his face, he heard most of that fun conversation.

He crosses the room and holds a hand out to me. "Georgia, I think it's time for us to leave."

I let him pull me up. "See you later, Dad."

"Thanks for coming to celebrate Willa," Dad says. "You, too, Miles. I hope you enjoyed yourself."

"Yeah, thank you. I had a nice time." Miles takes a few long strides across the living room, his hand almost too tight around mine, but he stops. He closes his eyes and takes a deep breath, then turns back to my father. "Actually, that's a lie. I didn't have a nice time."

Dad looks up at him like he can't conceive of such a thing. They didn't shell out a ton of money for people to *not* have a nice time.

"The party was great, the cakes amazing if a few too many, but I'm glad Willa enjoyed herself. All of that was nice. But this?" he says, gesturing between Dad and me. "Hearing the way you disregard Georgia? That wasn't nice."

Dad's mouth twists into a sour frown. "I'm not sure that's your place."

"No. It's yours. You're her father. You should be in her corner, not talking down to her and wishing she was somebody else. She's an incredible woman exactly how she is."

Dad's glaring as if he'd like to kick Miles out of the house, but he also seems to be speechless.

"I won't defend her working at Dogeared. I agree, she could do better. Any day. But thinking nobody sees her art? Do you have any idea what she actually does?"

Dad frowns harder.

"Her illustrated covers are some of the most sought-after in her genre right now. Do you want to know why? Because authors know that when they put her *colorful, evocative* art on their covers, they'll sell more books. Because readers *love* them. She's got a wait list over a year long."

Dad's eyebrows twitch at that. I guess he really didn't know.

"And you can't bother to be proud of her?" Miles takes another step toward the door but turns back again. "Actually, I will say something about her working at Dogeared. I'm lucky to have her on my team. Everyone loves her. We have customers who come in just to talk to her about books she recommended.

People who know that if they're having a bad day, they can come into our shop, and Georgia's right there with a smile and an encouraging word. She's singlehandedly turned my somewhat bleak early version of a bookstore into a thriving place people feel connected to. She is *vital* to its success. And I'm proud as hell of her. You should be, too."

It wasn't a growl, but *man*. I am swooning hard.

With that, Miles leads us out the front door, one hand still gripping mine. We make it past all the balloons and the gigantic yard sign, finally rounding the corner to where we had to park a few hours ago. He stops at his car and gets out his keys, clicking the door unlocked.

I'm still warming myself in his praise when he turns a look on me so full of regret, my joy wavers.

"Did I just make things better or worse?"

He seriously doesn't realize how much his support means to me? I don't even care anymore that my dad doesn't feel those things about me, but to know that *Miles* does? That he'll stand up for me and talk me up and encourage me? That he always sees the best in me, even when I feel one lane short of a full highway?

Harper's words echo around in my head: *he's my champion.*

I throw my arms around him and hold on tight. "So much better," I say against his chest.

He secures me to him and rests his chin on top of my head, nuzzling in. Miles's hugs are always perfect, but this one feels significant. I've never felt so cared for as I do in this moment—like no matter what else happens, he has me.

We stay like this for a long time, neither of us caring that we're putting on a hugging show for the McMansion residents. Miles runs one hand over my back, calming me as if he's spreading good endorphins into my skin. I soak it up.

After a while, I tilt my chin to gaze up, up, up into his eyes.

The affection shining there leaves me breathless. It's over-whelming, like I can't possibly hold this much tenderness inside me.

This is not the look of one friend comforting another. This is more.

This is everything.

Eliza's advice comes back to me, too: *Just do.*

"Miles," I whisper. "Will you kiss me?"

He takes a deep, slow breath. "As friends?"

He puts no judgment in his tone. No sarcasm. No pressure. He's asking me what I want.

I could still pretend practice kissing is a thing friends do. Avoid admitting the truth and stay in this safe zone where I'm not risking anything. But that's not what I want to do.

"Not as friends."

His fingertips dance along my hairline, smoothing strokes from my temples to my jaw. His gaze roams over my face, warming my skin like a caress. His focus finally lands on my mouth. I am nothing but nerve endings lit up to spell one word: *Miles.*

He bends down and brushes his lips to the corner of my mouth, right where he kissed me last night. Then the other side. Now one cheekbone followed by the other. My eyebrows. The tip of my nose. Each kiss is an achingly soft touch, unraveling me piece by piece as he cherishes every part of my face.

Except my lips. I don't know if this is a reward or a punish-ment, but he's saving the best for last. By the time he pauses his slow journey, I'm a tangle of longing and can barely open my eyes. All I can do is twist my fists into his shirt and pull him closer.

He presses a gentle kiss to my lips, then draws back.

Is that it? Confused, I open my eyes again and am startled by the wall of fire staring back at me. He's watching me like a starving man looking at his last meal. Like he wants to devour me and only a thin thread of control is holding him back.

"Miles." It's plea and demand, praise and rebuke. And he fully answers the call.

He kisses me, and it's like he's a new man. Or maybe he's finally showing me the man he always has been. He slides his fingers into my hair, tilting my head to a better angle as I open up to him. A soft groan rattles out of him as we taste each other, and I know he's as lost as I am.

I've been living vicariously through romance book kisses for years, but this is better than any words on a page. I've never had a kiss feel so right. Like we were always meant for this. For each other.

Did I seriously think this man needed kissing practice? He expertly slows our frenzied kiss to something languid, torturing me with achingly soft touches. One hand comes to the small of my back, locking me in place against him.

This is *my* Miles. We've been friends so long, I thought I knew everything about him. But in this moment, he's a mystery again. I want nothing more than to investigate, research, and uncover all the sides of him I haven't seen yet. There is so much left of him to explore, and I want to know it all.

Starting with: how do I get him to groan again?

The very loud, very annoyed sound of a throat clearing reminds us that we're not, in fact, alone in the world. We're standing on the street in a community where they have a gate specifically to keep these kinds of shenanigans out. Probably. I don't know exactly why they need the gate.

We release each other and turn to see a man standing on a walkway in front of the house behind us. I don't know him, but he seems like a man who's very familiar with passing judgment on people.

"Sorry," I call, wrapping one arm around Miles's waist. "We're with the Donnelly party around the corner."

It's petty, but I don't mind dinging Dad's reputation just a touch.

The man grumbles but must think he made his point because he walks back into his house.

I turn back to Miles. While I would love to continue making out like fools and figuring out this new side of our relationship, I also wouldn't put it past my dad's neighbors to call the cops on us for indecent behavior or something.

"What do we do now?" I ask. It's a little too open-ended, but I'll take any answer.

"I want to do some matchmaking of my own." He pulls his phone from his pocket and thumbs around for a minute.

His eyes sparkle at me, and a buzzing sound comes from my purse.

I fish my phone out of my bag. "I'm sorry, I have to take this."

Miles: Will you go to the gala with me?
Georgia: What took you so long?

Chapter 24

Miles

Full disclosure: I don't even like coffee. I stopped drinking it years ago in an effort to prevent migraines. But I don't have to like something to sell it in the store. Just like stocking books I have no interest in reading, adding coffee to our offerings was a business decision. One I question every time I'm elbow-deep in a dozen-drink order for an office down the street, and the café's crowded with impatient customers.

Owen walks in while I'm scrambling from drink to drink and leans against the front wall to watch the chaos. I don't know how long he's been standing there when I finally catch up with the orders and catch a break.

"Living the dream, right?" he says, approaching the counter.

I know he's only joking, but it's a good reminder that this *is* what I want. I can't be short-sighted enough to actually regret good business.

"Mocha?" I ask.

"I was going to, but after seeing all that, I feel like I should get you a pillow and a nap."

I ignore him and make the mocha. No sense breaking the

momentum I've got going. I pass the coffee to him and take a seat for the first time this morning.

"Some days, everything hits all at once."

He nods over his coffee. "Sure is easier when you spread the work around."

Replacing Hannah is still on my never-ending list of things to do.

"Thank you, sensei."

His laugh is a low rumble. "I'm here to thank *you*. I haven't had a good chance to swing by and say it to your face."

"You've thanked me plenty." Embarrassingly so, if I'm being honest. I played the tiniest role of everyone involved.

"Yeah, well. I need to apologize, too. I was jealous when Georgia set you up with Josie." He raises a hand before I can dive into all the reasons that was unnecessary. "I know. But part of me still thought you might go for it. A lot of guys I know would have. I'm sorry for doubting you."

"There's no need."

He hitches a shoulder. "Well...I roughed you up pretty good in my imagination. Feels like a thing I shouldn't do to a friend."

"Then I guess I'd better accept your apology. How are things going with you two?"

I don't think I've ever seen him smile so wide. It's a bright sunbeam on this giant of a man's face.

"She's incredible. Brilliant and so kind. Funny when you least expect it. I'm...happy."

He sounds like he's in awe—of the feeling, of her, all of it. I can relate. I've been on the same high since Georgia and I kissed over the weekend.

"I'm glad for you both. It's always—"

The woman herself walks in, and my brain flips off. She radiates openness and joy, like she carries her own circle of sparkling energy everywhere she goes. Even when she's wearing a black sweater with a bright orange jack-o'-lantern on it that looks like it was hand-knitted by monkeys.

For the record, I love her ridiculous sweaters.

Owen chuckles. "I guess I don't need to ask how things are going for you."

Her smile washes over me like I'm stepping into the sun. I should probably care that I'm openly staring at her like a love-sick fool, but now that I can, I'll indulge.

"Hi, Owen." She stops next to him in front of the counter.

Those last two feet between us might as well be a galaxy.

"Having a good day?" she asks.

He nods. "I've been observing Miles. It's very entertaining."

She turns that gorgeous smile on me. "What's he doing now?"

Nothing, just losing my mind over you, as always.

"He was running around like a chicken with its head cut off this morning, filling coffee orders." Owen shakes his head as if to say, "this fool."

"Aww. Was it the title and escrow place again?" she asks me.

"I think so."

"Prepare yourself. It's become their weekly office treat." She turns back to Owen. "So? Everything good in your world? Any brand-new girlfriends to share with us?"

He doesn't smile like he did before, but I swear he blushes. "Everything is good in my world."

"Mmm hmm." Georgia goes on gloating as if she knows all his secrets.

Now I'm dying to know what she's heard from Josie.

"I was going to ask Miles the same thing," he says. "I haven't heard about any more setups."

"Yeah. I've put a pause on my matchmaking."

"Really?" That does get a trace of a smile from Owen. "Last I heard, he was lost without you."

I shoot him a glare, but he ignores it. I don't need both of them ganging up on me.

"Oh, he is. Utterly lost. So I'm taking a more hands-on approach with his dating life."

All right, now *I'm* probably blushing.

He laughs and raises his coffee cup to me in a toast. "Sounds like a good plan for him. I'm heading out."

We say quick goodbyes, and a couple of customers walk in to browse the bookshop as Owen walks out. Georgia and I have worked together the last few days like we always have—but with a little more unnecessary touching when we slide past each other behind the counter, and a lot more watching each other across the store.

"I've been thinking," I say when the shop has cleared out again sometime later. "I'd like to take you to dinner this weekend."

She leans against one of the big wooden bookshelves. "Oh. Like a date?"

"Yes."

"A practice date?"

"No. This would be completely real." We're not going to have any more confusion between us.

"Are you sure you don't want more practice? That kiss the other day was lacking a little something."

I'd be panicked if she wasn't wearing the most wicked look I've ever seen on her.

"Really?" I stalk closer. "Where did I go wrong?"

"I wanted more."

That sentence does something visceral to me. It's a tangible thing coursing through my veins, followed swiftly by the sentence *I'd be happy to give you more.*

"Wasn't that part of your lesson? Always leave them wanting more?"

"I regret that I've taught you so well."

I nod sagely. "The student has become the master."

She laughs. "Don't get cocky on me."

"If I aced your remedial lessons, are there advanced courses I could take?"

Her laughter fades out, and her gaze zeroes in on my mouth. "We could probably figure something out."

With truly impeccable timing, a family with two little kids walks in. Georgia dashes over to them, eager to help out wherever needed. Logically, I know it's for the best, but emotionally, I'd love to usher the family out, bolt the door, turn the sign to *Closed*, and take Georgia up on her offer.

For my own sanity, I should probably institute some kind of *No PDA* rule in the store.

One day.

Eventually, the family leaves with their book selections tucked safely in their arms. But before Georgia and I can get back to her hands-on approach to my dating life, my mother walks into the store.

"Mom. I thought you said you weren't up for driving this week."

She shoots me a sour look and turns her attention on Georgia. "How are you, sweetheart?"

She beams at my mom. "I'm just great. It's good to see you."

It's been a while since Mom has felt up for a trip into town. Thus, my well-meaning but poorly phrased greeting.

"Cece brought me to town to do my hair." She pats her messy bun. "I'm thinking about going shorter, so I don't have as much to brush."

"I bet that will look cute on you. Do you want to come sit down?"

Georgia's being so sweet to my mom, and I'm still standing around like a stranger.

"We've got a few pumpkin cream cheese muffins left," I offer.

"Oh, no. I can't stay long. I just wanted to stop by and say hello." Mom turns back to Georgia. "And to tell you I saw that cute cover you did with that couple by the lake. It's beautiful."

I love the way Georgia glows from that brief praise. She needs to hear how impressive her art is every day.

"Thank you," she says. "I really enjoyed that one."

"But all your covers are so adorable. I'm sure the authors you work with are pleased."

"They seem to be."

"You could do even more with your art if you wanted. Digital prints, stickers, licensed work. You could have an entire online store." It's pretty clear Mom's been thinking about this a lot. Her entrepreneurial spirit tends to rub off on everyone around her.

Georgia stands a little taller, like Mom's encouragement is a grow light and she's a sunflower who can't get enough. "I've thought about some of that but haven't tried to pursue anything yet."

"Well, you've got plenty of time. Your art has a very distinct style. I can see why you have such a big following."

"You follow Georgia on Instagram?" I ask.

"Of course. I have to keep up with her cover reveals some-how." Mom turns to me. "I'd follow you if you had social media, honey. But alas."

Georgia laughs, light and bright. "I'm wearing him down."

"I'm sure you are." Mom flashes a small smirk at me. "Now, where is your sandwich board? I walk up and down Center, and every store has a sandwich board to draw people in."

"We don't have a sandwich board," I tell her.

"But I'm working on something better than a sandwich board," Georgia says.

Mom cocks her head closer. "I'm listening."

"A bookmobile bike to go out front. It will have a small selection of books on it, and we can add our pastry menu of the day to the inside of one of the doors."

"I heard something about that idea. I love it. Can't wait to see it." Mom turns back to me. "You'd better hold onto her, Miles."

I have every intention of doing exactly that—just as soon as my mother leaves.

Chapter 25

Miles

I'm surprisingly calm for my first official date with Georgia. Maybe I used up all my nervousness in the years it took me to get here. Or maybe that soul-searing kiss last week burned it out of my system. I'm at ease, ready to take our relationship to a new level.

Georgia, unfortunately, is *not* calm. Her smiles are a little too forced, her conversation a little too rushed for me to believe she's as relaxed as I am. I can't tell if her jitteriness is from an eagerness to make sure everything goes right tonight or from a fear that it won't.

We've already placed our orders at the Thai restaurant she'd opted for last week. Despite everything I said to her then, bringing her to my place seemed like too little effort for something that feels this significant. Now I'm thinking it might have helped us avoid the pressure of a "real" first date.

She gestures at me. "You wore the maroon sweater."

"I told you I was saving it for a special occasion."

She smiles even wider but then juts out her lower lip. "You didn't roll the sleeves, though."

Maintaining eye contact with her, I slowly push my sleeves to the elbows. "Better?"

"Yup. That's the stuff." She swallows hard, then winces. "Sorry. Is this weird?"

"Which part?" I don't think any of it is weird, but I need to know what's bothering her.

"I can't...you know...think you're sexy to your face."

My grin is probably the dopiest it's ever been. "I give you permission to think I'm sexy."

"That's not helping."

"Will it be better if I tell you that I think you're sexy?"

She hides her face behind her hands for a second, shaking her head. "That's it. This date is a bust. We need to start over another time without all the weirdness."

"Hey." I lay my hand on the table, palm up, and she slips hers into it without hesitation. "It's just us. Bringing more into our friendship isn't supposed to be stressful. We can open the door to possibility and see what happens. Okay?"

"Open the door to possibility." Her shoulders relax, and the smile returns to her face. "Okay."

Despite her nerves, she keeps her grip on my hand. That's good enough for me.

"I'm curious what would have been on the itinerary for our practice date." Not that the idea was stuck in my head for days or anything.

She laughs. "Rule number one, don't make fun of her favorite hobby."

"I had no idea about Mr. Pickles." A serendipitous mistake.

"Rule number two, don't set her up with other guys." She flashes me a loaded glare, even though we both know that worked out for everyone.

I run my thumb over the back of her hand. "Not a problem tonight."

She shakes her head at me, but I like her smug smile. I don't want other men to even look at her tonight. She's all mine.

"Third...I'll just watch what you do and point out any issues as they arise."

"Sounds about right."

Our dinner arrives, and we serve up our shared rice and noodle dishes.

"You still haven't heard anything from your dad?" I don't regret defending Georgia against her father's slights. Making sure he knows how extraordinary she is came as naturally to me as breathing, and I'll do it again if I need to.

That doesn't mean I want the man to hate me.

"Not yet, but that's pretty normal. He'll be in touch when it fits into his schedule."

At least he's not doing anything to make me feel bad about telling him off.

"Don't point those big sad eyes at me," she says. "He's always been this way. Well. With Sam and me."

"Georgia. That's not better."

His contrasting displays of affection between them has always rubbed me the wrong way. Maybe worse is the way Georgia just takes it because she's never known anything else. She pretends she doesn't care, but she can't tell me she feels nothing when he showers his younger children with tenderness he intentionally withholds from her and Sam.

"I know, but I can't be sad about his conditional love anymore. And I don't want you to feel bad for a second about what you said at their house. Nobody's ever stood up for me like that."

"Anyone with any sense would stand up for you. I hate that he can't see the successful woman you are." He's got this idea that there's only one version of success, and anyone who deviates from that is failing by default. It's not just his children—I suspect he thinks the same of me, Dogeared, and any other Magnolia Ridge business that doesn't fit his model.

"I can't do anything about it. And he wouldn't change even if I quit illustrating to take a job at his company—he'd still find things to criticize." She shrugs. "He's not cruel. He's just a really crappy dad. Selectively."

"You're making me want to tell him off again."

"I'm sure you'll have the opportunity one day." She groans and rolls her eyes. "This is so not first date conversation. I'm ruining the vibes."

"You're sharing with me. I like those vibes."

She laughs as though I wouldn't sit here for hours just to listen to her tell me anything she's willing to say. Something serious she needs to get off her chest? Something ridiculous and random that popped into her head? I want to know it all.

"It was good to see your mom in the store the other day," she says.

It's a rare sight lately. "I was happy to see her out, too. I don't like how much time she spends alone in her house."

Georgia puts her hand back in mine. A sweet, soft gesture I'm ready to eat up with a spoon.

"Maybe she'd like to play games at Fiesta Village."

I stare at her. Then stare a little more. "You're brilliant. I hadn't thought to ask her."

"Why did you keep that secret, by the way? You looked so guilty when I showed up."

In hindsight, it was silly not to mention it to her immediately. But the fear of being perceived as that "transactional nice guy" kept me from sharing the idea right away.

"I suppose I didn't want you to feel any pressure. As though I expected something in return for doing something nice for your grandpa and the other residents."

"Like... 'I was nice to your grandpa. Now you should date me?'"

"I never said I'm always rational."

She squeezes my hand tighter. "I never thought that about you. You're not that kind of guy. And I like that you're not always rational."

I lift an eyebrow. "Really?"

She leans closer. "You're fun when you're irrational."

I laugh, feeling exactly the same way about her.

She takes a big bite but hides her mouth behind her hand while she finishes chewing. "Did I tell you Keith is thinking about taking a transfer to Alaska?"

"That's a huge change." Her mom and stepdad live in the Houston suburbs, and he does something for the oil industry. As far as I know, she's never been back to Magnolia Ridge for a visit. Georgia always goes to see them.

"Mom wants him to take it. She's barely been out of Texas, and living up there would be a great way to explore. Can you imagine all the mountains and forests and wild animals? The snow?"

She gets a dreamy look on her face as if she's envisioning snow-capped mountains and frolicking moose.

"Do you think you'd want to join them sometime?" The idea of Georgia being thousands of miles away makes a spot behind my ribs ache. But Sam spent a decade exploring the world. Maybe she wants to do the same.

"I'll visit for sure, but I don't think I want to live in Alaska. Magnolia Ridge is my home. Everybody I love is right here." She cringes, and a hint of pink touches her cheeks.

"Good. Everybody I love is right here, too."

She smiles but shakes her head again. "Rule number three: don't imply you love each other on the first date."

I notice her teasing warning goes both ways. I also notice myself grinning like a fool.

"You're right. That would be so cringe."

"Right? Like having an Instagram for your dog."

I lay my hand over my thrumming heart. "I would never say that. That's in direct violation of rule number one."

She starts giggling. "Okay, but I looked it up, and Mr. Pickles is so cute. He's a chihuahua mix of some kind, and I just want to kiss him on his little snoot."

"Rule number four: don't make your date jealous of tiny dogs with huge social media followings."

"Aww. Do you want a snoot smooch?"

"Yes." Dead serious.

"Okay." She stands just enough to lean over the table. "Bring it in."

I do, and she carefully zeroes in to place a kiss on my nose. Mr. Pickles should be so lucky.

"Ideal slope," she says softly.

What a ridiculous phrase to make my heart beat this fast.

"Now," she says, settling back down, "if you're jealous of Mr. Pickles's huge social media following, I have some ideas about that."

"You don't have to run ideas for Dogeared's socials by me. I trust you." She hasn't checked in since she made a video using a trending sound and wanted me to be in the background standing perfectly still. Not to brag, but I nailed it.

"Aww, that's sweet, but my ideas aren't for Dogeared. They're for Miles Forrester, science fiction writer, esquire, first of his name, etcetera etcetera."

"I don't have social media."

She shoots me a "duh" look. "They're ideas to help you get started."

"Engaging with strangers on social media is not my wheelhouse." I have a small Discord of sci-fi writers that I participate in, but that's not remotely the same thing. Putting myself out there, shilling my books, trying to turn browsers into readers and readers into fans—I wouldn't know where to start.

She takes my hand like she's comforting a small child. "That's the point, sweetie."

I can't control the smile on my face. Don't want to.

Georgia closes her eyes. "Rule number five: don't give nicknames on the first date."

"Rule number six: give *all* the nicknames on the first date, darling pumpkin."

She opens her eyes again but breaks down into a fit of giggles. "Seriously, this date is over. We can try again some other day. Maybe I'll be more normal then."

"I don't want normal."

She laughs even harder. "Is the rest of that sentence '...I just want you?' Because that's kinda iffy as a compliment."

"'I just want you' is a complete sentence all on its own."

Her cheeks blaze red, but she can't stop smiling. "I feel like we're going to need a lot more rules."

"That's okay. I like being a rebel."

That seems to be the funniest joke of all, and it takes her a minute to recover. "Do you want to go to the Abandoned Manor?"

"Why not? Be prepared for rule number seven: don't scream like a banshee on the first date."

Chapter 26

Georgia

I just want you.

I can't get that thought out of my head. A few weeks ago, we were best friends who spent a ton of time together but didn't think about each other that way. Now, we're sneaking kisses in Dogeared's back room and openly flirting with each other. It's exciting.

Also terrifying. It's a leap of faith, and part of me wants to take that jump—the other part of me wants to give in to my panic and run away to find safer ground. I'm not even exactly sure what I'm afraid of. I just know it's right behind me, indistinct and ominous.

So why not combat those vague fears with more tangible ones?

We wander downtown's streets hand in hand. We've finally entered our first fake fall, and it's cool enough out that I need my sweater—a bold geometric pattern in burnt oranges and yellows. It whispers "fall," where my more unusual sweater collection tends to scream it.

Speaking of screaming, the community center has reached maximum haunted house vibes. Doors are boarded up, tattered sheets hang from a second-story window as though someone tried to escape, and the occasional moan echoes from speakers in the eaves.

I want to high-five whoever's behind the decor.

We get in line, putting us close enough to hear the *real* shrieks as groups move through the haunted house. My heart's racing, but this way I can blame it all on my fight-or-flight instinct and not my very big, very unwieldy feelings for Miles.

"Have you been through the haunted house before?" he asks.

"I have, but they change it up each year. There's the usual stuff, like creepy dolls and alien autopsies, but there's always something new, too." I squeeze his hand tighter. "Are you nervous?"

"No. I just haven't been to one in forever."

"Not a fan?"

He shrugs as we shuffle forward in line. "I used to go to the ones we had at school when we were little. Really amateur stuff. And I guess I went through a few in college. But not since then."

"Then prepare yourself to be scared, sweetie." I freeze, cringing inwardly. Also, probably outwardly.

Miles just grins down at me, his face illuminated in the streetlight behind me. "Never stop breaking rule number five."

We move forward again and reach the ticket booth. The ticket taker's in character just like everyone will be inside—he's a freakishly gray corpse whose dialogue is littered with puns.

"Stay with your group, or you'll face a grave situation," he drones. "We accept cash, cards, and *crypto*currency."

Groans and chuckles move through the line.

"I'm not funny," he says in monotone. "I'm dead serious."

Miles leans close to whisper. "If he's the opening act, it's reassuring me that the main event won't be too bad."

"That's exactly what they want you to think. They lull you

into a false sense of security, and then—" I bring my free hand up to his chest to scare him. I get a fistful of pec, which I don't regret, but he doesn't even flinch. He just stares down at me. "It's better when they do it."

"Not to me."

After a while, we're finally allowed through the doors. They keep us in small groups of about ten, probably so we feel more isolated. Really drive home the spookiness.

The first room is a parlor filled with—I called it—creepy dolls. Some have heads that turn to watch us pass, some have red eyes that light up. One is telling us the history of the Abandoned Manor, and I'm focused on the menacing marionette when a full-sized doll lunges at us from the shadows.

I scream, plastering myself to Miles. Handholding won't be enough for the rest of the evening. Jump-scares always get me. I'm laughing between shrieks, though. That doll's makeup is really believable.

The next room is decked out like a fancy lounge, with drinks and plates of food set out as though it was just packed with people who have mysteriously disappeared. In the back, a man dressed in black hunches over an old piano, playing a tune that's just off-key enough to jangle my nerves. When he turns and smiles, revealing fangs, we all scream and rush out.

The spooky factor ramps up with each room we explore, revealing the "manor's" sordid history. The deteriorating furniture and deepening dark is almost creepier than the monsters that pop out of every corner. The ghouls become more supernatural the deeper we get into the haunted house, and I've lost the storyline entirely—I'm going from one scream to the next, laughing at myself in between.

Every step of the way, I cling tight to Miles. It's for self-preservation, I tell myself. A horde of vampires open their coffins, and I press my face to his chest. Self-preservation. We escape a particularly evil set of clowns with my arm wrapped around his waist and my hand on his very nice stomach? That, too, is self-preservation.

We reach a hallway that's in near-total darkness. Our group stumbles along, everyone alternately laughing and startling at nothing. Sometimes the suspense alone is enough to get a scream going. We're funneled through a long hallway, and by the time the light of a fake moon shines on us, we're deep in a pretend cornfield.

My breathing stalls. Then speeds. A logical voice tries to argue that this cornfield is just as fake as every other scene in the haunted house, but it's drowned out by my brain's fear center. And that part's telling me to run.

I guess I make some kind of sound because Miles nuzzles his face against my ear.

"I've got you."

I can barely hear him over the spooky soundtrack of crows and owls they've got washing over us.

"Maybe that's all that will be in here—crows and owls?" My voice is thin and shaky, but I have to talk it out. Otherwise, I'll start remembering all my worst, most vivid nightmares of running scared through fields just like this. "I could beat up a bird if it came down to it. Maybe not a guy in a bird suit, but I think if—"

Every last thought in my head shatters. There's a scarecrow in here. He's hanging limp from a stake, and *obviously* his fabric face and straw hair aren't real. His lopsided hat is genuinely stupid. It doesn't matter. It's my childhood nightmares made real.

He lifts his head.

"I can't do this." I spin out of Miles's arms and try to back-track the way we came, but "ghouls" block the path.

"Can I please get out?"

They don't say anything, just lift their hands and point behind me. This ride only goes one way.

My breathing's coming too quickly now, my heart lodged in my throat as I pat down the fake cornstalks all around us. This is the community center. There's got to be another exit somewhere. Or a way past this scene and into the regular activities rooms that must still be here.

A scarecrow springs out of the cornstalks right next to me, and I scream. It's only a dummy, but that doesn't soften the jagged edge of fear that's slicing me in half.

This time, no self-conscious laughter follows the fright. I'm running on nothing but terror. I spin straight into someone's arms and scream again.

It's Miles. He's holding me, soothing me, but it's too late for that. Just past him, the scarecrow has climbed down from his stake. He's moving toward us.

I need to get *out*.

Miles pulls me away, urging me through the room so we can complete the maze of haunts and be done already. I turn away from the scarecrow and follow Miles's lead—I don't need more nightmare fuel.

Something runs along my arm. I glance down, and my stomach turns to ice.

It's the scarecrow's burlap hand. The thing's right next to me, laughing behind his sewn-on grin. I scream again, batting at it, but it doesn't move.

Suddenly, Miles is between us. "Back off."

The scarecrow gestures with its arms as if to say "Make me," and lunges for me.

Miles stiff-arms him like Iron Man blasting away bad guys, making the scarecrow take a step back to avoid getting hit. "Get out of her face. Now."

I've never heard him threaten anyone before, but it's seriously effective. The scarecrow mumbles, "Take a joke, man," and turns his attention to the people behind us.

Miles pulls me close into his side and leads us through the cornstalks. When we reach the next "ghoul" between rooms, he takes charge. "Let us out."

The person lights up a glow wand and leads us to a side door. "No refunds, no returns," he says, opening it out onto the small garden area next to the community center.

It's disorienting to go from a fear-filled room back to the real world so suddenly. Lamps in the garden illuminate us, and people wander around just half a block away on the main street. No ghouls, no frights, no cornfields.

That doesn't stop me from throwing myself the rest of the way into the safety of Miles's arms. I burrow in close, letting his reassuring words and gentle hands on my back soothe away the fear.

"I've got you," he says over and over again. "I've got you."

Once my heart rate's down to normal and my brain's no longer telling me to *Run, run, run!* embarrassment worms its way in. I mean, I just very thoroughly freaked out during an event *I* suggested and essentially dragged *him* to.

I pull back enough to see his face. "We can all agree this date was a total disaster, right?"

He laughs, but traces soft touches along my hairline, his other arm still tight around my back. "I wouldn't go for the haunted house again, but I wouldn't call it a disaster."

"Name one good thing that happened tonight."

His mouth quirks the smallest amount. "I've got you in my arms."

"Rule number eight." I flex my fingers against his waist. "Next time, though, let's skip the haunted house."

He nods. "That's rule number nine."

"I need to sit down for a minute." I don't trust my legs right now. We move to one of the benches in the garden space, and I blow out a breath. "You were kind of scary back there."

"Scarecrow scary?" He sounds almost sad, and I realize how that might have come across. Like maybe his behavior contributed to my fears.

I turn as much as I can to face him on the bench. "No. More like...'touch her and die' scary. It's a good thing."

Ten minutes ago, I wouldn't have listed that as one of my top-tier micro-tropes, but it's up there now.

"That's pretty close to what I was thinking." He presses a kiss to the side of my head. "I'm sorry that triggered your old fears."

"Me, too. Not how I imagined our first date going."

"How did you imagine it going?"

Whatever actual plans I might have had are hard to remember when his gaze falls to my mouth. "I mean, we would definitely be our goofy selves."

His gaze holds steady. "Check."

"And we would have fun because I always have fun with you." My answers are getting breathier by the second, but I have very limited defenses against his intense focus on my lips.

"I always have fun with you, too."

Oh, good gracious, does he have to use that deliciously low voice?

"And at the end, we'd definitely have a kiss."

His gaze snaps up to mine. "Are we at the end?"

"We can kiss in the middle, too."

He leans in just enough to graze his lips over mine in a tease that lights up all my nerve-endings.

"Rule number ten," he says before closing the distance again.

Text Thread

Georgia: Want to go to movie night with Harper's big family this weekend?

Georgia: They're projecting a movie onto the side of a barn

Miles: No horror movies, I hope?

Georgia: *The Nightmare Before Christmas.* Not scary at all

Miles: You know Jack Skellington is a scarecrow

Georgia: What? No he isn't.

Georgia: Are you serious?

Miles: He gets down off of his stake in the opening scene

Georgia: No...?

Georgia: He's the pumpkin king not the scarecrow king!

Miles: Did I just ruin the movie for you?

Georgia: A little bit

Georgia: Jack's the only good scarecrow

Miles: Am I still invited?

Georgia: I'll need you to hold my hand during the scarecrow part I've apparently missed my entire life

Miles: Done

Georgia: Just as a heads up, Eliza's husband might bring his copies of your books for you to sign

Miles: ...

Georgia: And Eden's husband might, too

Georgia: MAYBE!

Georgia: But probably yes

Georgia: Just a totally casual, impromptu book signing

Miles: I'll try to prepare myself

Georgia: Sam will not bring your books

Miles: Go, Sam

Georgia: But he will probably give us a hard time

Georgia: And Eliza definitely will

Georgia: Maybe Harper

Miles: Will anyone be there who won't ask for an autograph or comment on our relationship?

Georgia: There's a couple of babies who haven't heard of you

Miles: Can't wait to meet them

Chapter 27

Georgia

This party is the antidote to Ava's. Blankets and camp chairs are spread out across the sprawling lawn, a picnic table displays tons of treats and classic movie theater snacks, and steel ice buckets hold drinks. Not a fairy godmother or a fancy Jack Skellington piñata in sight.

Miles and I walk across the gravel drive in front of the barn where an assortment of cars and trucks are parked. I've got his hand held tight in mine, a plastic container of cookies in the other. Pretty sure both hands are sweaty.

I was thrilled when Harper invited me to this—I love her extended family, and an outdoor movie night sounded like the perfect way to wrap up October. But as we approach the six or so other couples already mingling around the food, this feels an awful lot like hard-launching a relationship.

Nerves skitter through my stomach, but I'm not quite sure what they're for. All the gazes surreptitiously dancing over us? The inevitable questions I won't know how to answer? Or the fact that I've never had any kind of relationship to share before?

I hope Miles knows what he's getting himself into. I sure don't.

Sam watches us walk over like a cat with a canary stuffed in his mouth—the canary being every single sassy thing he can think to say about Miles and me. Luckily, Harper gets to us first.

"We're so happy you two could join us. Here." She takes the cookies from me and adds them to the snack supply. "I think you know everybody."

All the women here have been to romance book club at least once, and I consider them friends. I don't know their husbands as well, but I've met them at some holiday event or another.

Like June's husband, Ty, who's holding their baby while he talks with one of her brothers. Little Lucy's wearing a hat that looks like a pumpkin top, and her face is nothing but dark eyelashes and chubby cheeks. He's got her cradled to his chest like his whole world is right there in his hands. It's too dang cute to see the big rancher so happy.

Or Eliza's husband, Dean, who's listening to some animated story she's telling. He's a little like Miles—he doesn't seek out the spotlight in groups like this. But he watches Eliza like she's got a light all her own.

And then there's Eden's husband, Booker, who's heading straight for us. Because there's plenty of cuteness to go around, he's also carrying a baby. Noah's got a tiny tuft of black curls on the top of his head and the biggest brown eyes you ever saw.

Baby fever is a myth. A myth that's got me in its grip, urging me to smell both of those babies' heads, gently press their rounded cheeks, and touch the tiny divots in their sweet little hands. *I will not.* But only because their fathers are huge, and unsolicited baby-touching feels like a quick way to get thrown out of the party.

Eden joins us with their toddler, Bee, on her hip. "Miles, you know my husband, Booker."

Miles nods, and the two men shake hands. Booker's pretty

much always got a smile on his face, but this one feels like a kid finding out he's going to Disneyland.

Or a Disney adult going to Disneyland. I don't judge.

"I have to ask—are you really the Miles Forrester who wrote the Quantum Station series? I heard it from Eliza, and it feels like the kind of thing she'd say to try to wind me up."

Miles laughs softly. "It's true."

Booker shifts Noah in his arms, and I get the full force of the baby's adorable, toothless smile.

"Does it make me too much of a fanboy if I tell you they're two of my favorite science fiction books I've ever read?"

Miles's expression flickers from high to low like a newfound thrill is duking it out with his humility. "Not too much of a fanboy at all. I appreciate hearing that."

Oh my gosh, this man doesn't know how to take praise. He struggles enough when I tell him he's a great boss or when I compliment an idea he's had for the bookshop. But it's so much worse when the praise is for his writing.

"I've been reading science fiction since I was a kid. I genuinely couldn't believe the Quantum series is your debut. Nothing against debuts," he adds quickly. "It just reads like so many of the greats. Not that you lifted anything from them. Your books are totally unique. But familiar, do you know what I mean? But fresh."

He glances to Eden, and his shoulders sag. "I'm doing the thing, aren't I?"

She runs a hand over his arm. "A little bit." She turns to Miles. "We're just really excited to know...well, that we already know you. Booker because he's a big fan, and me because I'd love to have you speak at the library sometime."

"I hadn't thought about, uh...speaking engagements." Looks like humility's winning out again.

"It'd be very casual. We have several writer and reader

groups I'm sure would love to hear from you. And we'd be happy to host a meet and greet to feature your books."

"Well..." My man is lost in a sea of uncertainty.

He's always willing to step up and help out everyone else, but he doesn't know how to handle it when someone wants to give some of that attention and support back. He deserves to be celebrated—for his creativity, for his success, for *himself*.

I slip my hand into his. He looks down at me, and I try to convey all the encouragement and affection I can into my smile. I can be his champion, too.

"No pressure," Booker adds, adjusting his wiggling baby. "We're just psyched that you're part of the family."

Eden nudges him with her elbow, eyes wide. Her correction is probably more obvious than his blunder.

"Ah, I mean the Magnolia Ridge family," Booker says.

Nice save, coach.

"I'd like that," Miles finally says. "We should talk more about it."

Eden's soft smile reappears. "That's great news. We're not staying long tonight because of these little ones, but I'll talk to my director at the library and get in touch with you soon."

Booker leans closer. "If you're up for it, we started a sci-fi enthusiasts club at the high school a couple of years ago. We mostly talk Star Trek and Star Wars, but it'd be a big thrill for them if you have a chance to join us some night."

"Really? They know my books?"

Booker's got a teacherly "duh" face on. "Everybody's looking forward to book three. We need to know what happens to Aster in the end."

"You're going to love it. Best of the trilogy." I can't resist sharing a tiny bit of book gossip, however vague. And maybe I want to brag that I've already been allowed to read it.

Perks of being Miles Forrester's...best friend. Slash girlfriend.

"Yeah? So it's a happy ending?" Booker jokingly narrows his eyes on me. "Sad? Ends on a mystery that will never be solved?"

I put on my most solemn face. "No spoilers."

"All right, keep your secrets." He turns back to Miles. "You can think about it and get in touch. We'd love to have you anytime."

"I will. Thank you." Miles looks like he's not quite sure what he's agreeing to, but he's willing to try. That's the most important part.

"Now, you'll have to excuse me. I've got to go change my little man." Booker and Eden wander away, heading for the farmhouse across from the barn.

"It's our turn now." Eliza's got her husband by the hand and leads him closer as if they've been waiting in line all day. "This is Dean. He *loves* your books."

"El," he says softly.

"You do," she counters. "You've read them both like four times."

"Three." He turns to Miles. "My wife is enthusiastic."

He gazes down at her as if her enthusiasm is his very favorite thing.

"Three reads is a lot to me," Miles says.

"I can't believe I bought them from the man who actually wrote them."

Eliza pipes up. "Miles is sneaky. Like someone else I know."

"I don't want to make this weird—"

"I'm more than willing to do it for you."

Dean smiles down at her before turning his attention back to Miles. "I don't read a lot of fiction. Booker makes recommendations now and then, and...well. I'm glad I read yours."

Eliza shakes her head. "We should have rehearsed this. He

means your books are hilarious and twisty and impossible to put down and full of super cool characters and a couple of really awful villains who we hope get theirs in the end."

Dean nods. "What she said."

"Also, is Aster ever going to get with his second in command or is that just a merciless tease at this point?"

Miles laughs.

"No spoilers," we say at the same time.

"Talking in unison already? That's fun." She bobs her eyebrows at me. "We're going to go snag the best blankets before Harper and Sam get there. We're glad you're here, Miles."

They grab some snacks and head into the yard on the shortest route to the set of blankets farthest from the screen.

"Can the babies come back and talk to me?" Miles says when they're gone.

He looks adrift at sea, like his cruise ship sailed away without him, and he's all alone on the vast ocean on an inner tube. I step closer to his side and put a hand on his chest.

"Are you okay with all this?" This man *needs* to be clapped and cheered, but I don't want to make him actively uncomfortable. I just want him to see how much he's adored.

"Yeah." His stunned expression breaks, and his sweet smile peeks out. "I'm...processing."

"Which part?" Hopefully not the "Welcome to the family" bit Booker accidentally threw in there. Premature much?

"Having readers? Writing's a lonely job sometimes. I talk to the people in my head and make them come alive on the page, but that's solo work. I have some online writer groups I've connected with and a critique partner I trust. I hear from my editor and my agent now and then, but I've mostly been removed from the reader experience. This is...new."

"Good new or bad new?"

Honestly, he still looks pretty stunned. "Awkward, but really good."

"Can we please plan a meet and greet at the store? I know you've got more local readers who would show up just to say hi and get a book signed. Put yourself out there a bit. Give people a chance to show how much they love you and your books."

"I don't know how an event like that will go. I'm used to blending into the background."

"Well, that's too bad, Miles Forrester. You are not a background guy. *You* are the main character. You're the star of the show all the way."

He goes on watching me like *I'm* the star of the show.

"Seriously. And not just because of your career or the bookshop, but because you are the kindest, most thoughtful, most generous—"

He leans down and cuts me off with a kiss. It's brief, but his huge smile when he pulls away says it all.

"You're right. We should have a meet and greet. I need to get my social media started—one platform is probably all I can handle, though. But I should to be out there *somewhere* so I can talk to readers. And more writers. Basically, I need to stop trying to do it all on my own."

Am I grinning up at him like a goofball? Yup. I do not care. "I should probably be jealous that I'll have to share you."

He dips his head closer to mine again. "You never have to share."

Because I can't have nice things, Sam walks over to interrupt our moment, disintegrating the butterflies bouncing around in my chest. He's wearing the biggest smirk ever while he loads up a plate with snacks.

"Miles, I think it's only fair to warn you." His intro hits an ominous note. "You've got a reputation in the family."

Miles looks from me to Sam. "Because of Willa's party?"

He nods. "I was at Grandpa's last week, and Dad turned up while I was there. He told us how you called him out for how he talked to Georgia."

Miles squeezes my hand tighter. "I did."

Ooh, I do love me some defiant Miles. Super rare item, but worth a small fortune.

My brother grins again. "Well done. Dad actually thought we'd take his side in it. I think it shocked him when Grandpa said you were completely in the right."

I wish I could have heard that, to be honest. Grandpa's the best.

"Hopefully he'll start to see it, too," Miles says.

I don't need Dad to see it anymore. Having Grandpa, Sam, and Miles in my corner is more than enough.

"I wouldn't hold my breath. Dad's not in the business of accepting when he's wrong." Sam finishes loading his plate. "But hey, Willa loves that stuffed axolotl you gave her, and Finn never shuts up about how great you are at board games. So you've got all of the important Donnellys covered."

He winks at me and leaves us to join Harper.

June's little nephews start running around, yelling at everyone that it's dark enough to start the movie. Miles and I grab some food and select our blankets. The camp chairs in the very back would probably be more comfortable, but they don't offer the same snuggle opportunities that being together on a blanket does.

We sit side by side, and I pull a quilt over our legs while we wait for Ty to start up the movie projector.

Miles is quiet. Not unusual for him, but it leaves my stomach unsettled anyway. I did bring him here, knowing full well he'd be accosted by a couple of fans and harassed by my well-meaning brother at a minimum. Then there's the "welcome to the family" of it all.

"Was this a lot?" I whisper. "Did my family and friends make you question the wisdom of joining me at events like this?"

My attempt at a casual laugh comes out too high-pitched. *Tell me you're not joking without telling me you're not joking.*

Miles turns to face me. This close, we're practically within kissing distance. Which I hope is still on the table.

He blinks, like he needs a second to process my question. "I was watching the little kids."

He nods toward the barn, where June's nephews are doing some coordinated move that must be the latest elementary school dance craze. Right in front of them, hogging the spotlight, their little sister shimmies her butt.

She's actually got some decent moves for a three-year-old.

"Oh. They're the opening act."

"They belong to..." he prompts.

"June's brother." I point off to the side where Wade and Annie are already cuddled up on a blanket.

"Her other brother is over there." I gesture toward Jed, who's fussing over his wife and making sure she's comfortable in her camp chair. The way he looks at her, you'd never guess the guy was once a sworn commitment-phobe. "You know Callie from romance book group."

"Right. He's the one from Evans Orchards. Best peaches in town. Mom used to buy from their family for her bakery."

"Oops—forehead kiss. Time to look away before he moves on to other kiss locations." I've been around them enough to know it's inevitable.

Miles moves his arm around my back, resting his hand on my hip. "I never had this kind of big family closeness. I've got two older cousins, but they've been in Houston since college, and don't visit a lot."

"I never had it either. I'm lucky all of these siblings and cousins adopted me into their group."

Miles kisses my temple. "They're lucky to have you be a part of it."

I think my heart does a full cartwheel.

The movie finally starts, and Miles points out the very brief moment Jack Skellington appears as a scarecrow.

"I can't believe I never realized that's what he is."

"Selective perception," he says, snuggling me closer. "You didn't want to see it because you already liked him. Knowing the truth would have ruined it for you."

"Okay, Mr. Science."

He kisses my face again. "That's Mr. Science Fiction to you."

I lose track of the movie pretty quickly. Not just because snuggling under a blanket with Miles is an absolute delight, but because that phrase he used keeps clattering around in my head. *Selective perception.*

Maybe it's true. Here I am, surrounded by a bunch of happy, committed couples. Couples who are exactly what Harper and Eliza told me a few weeks ago—each other's biggest supports, best friends, and champions. People who see past the mess and the imperfections to the best version possible of the other person.

I rest my head on Miles's shoulder and watch as Jack opens Sally's gift of an ethereal butterfly.

Maybe not all love is fictional, after all.

Miles helps me carry the leftover treats Ty sent us off with into my apartment. Somehow I brought home more goodies than I took out to the ranch.

"I'm going to throw all of this into a dish and make candy casserole," I tell Miles.

"And people say a vegetarian diet is unhealthy."

"My dentist loves it." I swallow. "Thanks for coming tonight and putting up with everything."

"I had a great time. Thanks for not getting mad I ruined one of your favorite movies."

I chuckle. "You didn't ruin anything. You make everything better."

And then we're silent. Watching each other. It's not uncomfortable, exactly, but it is...charged.

"Do you..." I start.

"Yes."

No notes. Just yes.

We snap together in a hungry kiss, his hand at the back of my head, mine clutching at his shoulders. He slips his other hand around my waist, pulling me as close as possible. I love Miles for exactly who he is, reserve and all, but I really, *really* like it when he's bold.

He takes charge in a way he doesn't often let himself do out in the real world, and I'm more than happy to follow where he leads. His heated touch consumes me like a wildfire until there's only sensation—his mouth on mine, my hands tracing down his chest, the weight of his arm around my back.

He slows the pace, relaxing his grip on me and gentling his movements. His deliberate caresses are a conversation all on their own. *I care for you. You're precious to me. This is entirely real.*

Awareness spreads through me, aching and soothing at the same time. I've had the perfect match right here and didn't even know. He's better than my imagination, or a book hero, or even an actual special ops guy. I don't want any of them—I only want my best friend.

He takes a detour along my jaw and down my neck. Curse this gloriously chunky sweater that stops him on his path before he can reach my collar bone. He traces his way back up, and when he kisses behind my ear, I think I've melted. No thoughts. Just a smooth brain, here to enjoy his caresses and nothing else.

He returns to my mouth for a tender kiss and then touches his forehead to mine. "I should probably go."

I'm tempted to tell him to stay. So tempted. But we don't need to rush. We've known each other five years, yes, but our bigger feelings only started developing a couple of weeks ago. We can spare a little more time to sort those out.

Plus, I am the novice to end all novices. So. Slow is good.

"Smart." I run my hands down his shoulders to grip his biceps. That MMA training does quality work.

One of his eyebrows darts up. "Do you need a minute alone with my biceps?"

"Yes." I squeeze them a little more. I'm brazenly feeling him up and I regret nothing.

He laughs softly. "Maybe I should return the favor."

His hands slip from my back around to my shoulders, down past my honestly not-that-impressive biceps to land on my elbows.

"You're right," he says, eyes alight. "Elbows are sexy."

I laugh and pull out of his grasp. "For that, I'm going to throw you out."

"It was genuine. I think everything about you is sexy." He narrows the distance between us to lightly kiss my mouth. "And beautiful." He kisses one cheek. "And marvelous." The other.

I cross my arms over my thumping heart. "Well. Then I suppose it's okay."

He just smiles at my pretend pout. I'm not that great of an actress.

"Goodnight, my Georgia."

But seriously, when did this man learn to be so swoony? Did he take online courses, and I never knew?

"That's not fair, though. I can't say 'Goodnight, my Miles' in return. The alliteration sounds goofy."

Even though right now, the *only* thing I want to say is "my Miles."

"How about 'Goodnight, *the* Miles?'"

I put my hands on his shoulders and steer him backwards toward the door. "Goodnight, 'skating on thin ice' Miles."

I pull open the door and he stops just inside the threshold. "Goodnight, 'one last kiss' Miles?"

I pretend to mull it over for as long as I can manage. Which is about six-point-three seconds. I lean up to press a soft, sweet kiss to his mouth.

He grins like Willa seeing her ornate piñatas.

"Goodnight, my Georgia," he whispers.

"Goodnight, my Miles."

Text Thread

Georgia: How formal is formal for the Andromeda Awards?

Georgia: I'm trying to decide what to wear

Miles: You mentioned a dress once

Miles: Slinky something

Miles: I forget exactly

Miles: But you should wear that

Georgia: Slinky dress made an impression

Miles: I have an active imagination

Georgia: How big of a scene am I allowed to make when you win?

Georgia: Can I whip out noisemakers?

Georgia: Throw confetti?

Georgia: Unfurl a banner that says *In your face, science nerds?*

Miles: They recommend sitting reverently with your hands folded in your lap

Georgia: I doubt it. I saw the pictures from last year

Georgia: Those writers know how to party

Georgia: Can I at least kiss you until it gets really uncomfortable for everyone in the audience, and they throw us out?

Miles: Go with that one

Chapter 28

Miles

I'm in a literal ballroom filled with some of my writing heroes, here to find out if I've won a prestigious award in my genre, and all I can think about is that dress Georgia's wearing. *Slinky dress.* If my eyes have left her for five full minutes tonight, they owe me an apology.

The butterscotch-colored dress hugs her upper body, with little flutter sleeves that hang off her bare shoulders. The gauzy material drapes over her legs all the way to the floor, both concealing and enticing, with a slit that...well, I'm trying not to think about the slit too much. It's got a high back, with another slit here that cuts straight down between her shoulder blades. Every glimpse of that strip of skin on her back drives me crazy.

She catches me watching her. I haven't been subtle, so it's happened a lot.

"What?"

I lean closer. "I'm just committing this moment to memory."

"It's not my usual style." She lightly pulls at the material at her hip, making the skirt sway. "I thought about throwing my chunky sweater with bats sewn all over it on top to make sure you'd recognize me."

"You'd still look fantastic in the bat sweater. It's not just the dress. It's you."

Do I know what she's done with her hair, partially braided away from her face while the rest hangs loose over her bare shoulders? No. Could I explain exactly what's different about her makeup tonight? Probably not. But she glows like a harvest goddess at my side.

I don't know how I got this lucky.

She puts her hand in mine, intertwining our fingers. "We're here to celebrate you."

"That's not what I'm celebrating tonight."

She rolls her eyes at me, but her smile says she's pleased.

It's technically cocktail hour, but since I don't drink and Georgia rarely does, we're awkwardly standing around empty-handed. I'm not good at approaching people I don't know in a crowded room, and even worse at it when those people have written some of my favorite books.

"Is there anyone you want to meet?" Georgia asks.

"Yes...but no. As a fan, absolutely. I could approach that man there, whose series got me through college. Or that woman over there with the big crowd around her? Her books have lived rent-free in my head since middle school. But to walk up to them as a peer?" I shake my head, an unfortunate lump lodged in my throat. "I don't know if I can do that."

I fully realize I'm up for an award tonight, but that doesn't help me shake the sense I don't belong here.

Georgia runs a hand along my suit sleeve, comforting my mini freak out. "But you *are* their peer. I understand that you've been a fan of their books since before you started writing, but you have fans now, too. A lot more than just Booker and Dean."

She's not wrong. I still don't want to move from this exact spot.

And apparently, I won't have to. A man walks up to us with his hand out, a big smile on his face.

"Miles Forrester," he says as we shake hands. I'm legitimately unsure who he is, but he carries himself as if I should know. He doesn't offer his name, either. "Up for the Rising Star. First awards ceremony?"

"Does it show?"

"You've got that wide-eyed look about you. You'll get used to it. We all write our books the same way—drunk and on a deadline." He laughs at his joke and then throws back the last of the liquor in his glass.

"I like your Aster books. Interested to see how you wrap things up. Good luck tonight."

He walks off, and it's like the seal has been broken. I won't say everyone approaches me after that, but I meet more authors than I can properly keep track of. Experienced authors, new writers, and people I've never heard of but likely will one day.

It's overwhelming meeting so many people. And the notion that they actually want to meet me? Bizarre.

I get asked when my next book is coming out. If I'm part of the larger Texas sci-fi writers' association. Someone suggests I should level up with a new agent who'll bring in a bigger advance on my next series. Another author tells me his key piece of advice is to take leadership courses so I can properly manage my "team."

I'm grateful for my agent and editor, but the only person I care about having on my team is Georgia. I've never been able to manage her very well, and I wouldn't change a thing. She's the one who's always at my side, ready with a fresh idea for the bookshop or eager to listen to me talk through plot holes. She's my best friend in every sense, the person I trust the most, and can be my truest self with.

I am madly, deeply in love with this woman. I just need to find the right time to tell her.

Surrounded by increasingly tipsy writers is not it.

The emcee announces it's time to find seats in the next room so the ceremony can begin. I take Georgia's hand and move with her through the crowd, wishing we were alone. Maybe dancing somewhere, since I'd like a legitimate reason to touch that flattering dress and hold her close. I really don't care, as long as we're together.

We sit down, and Georgia leans closer, a hint of pumpkin spice moving with her. "In this crowd, I feel like noisemakers would have been perfectly appropriate."

There are ten awards, and nobody's quiet when the winners are announced. We stand and applaud for everyone as the crystal prizes are handed out. Thankfully, winners aren't allowed to make a speech when they win. They walk up, receive the award, get a picture snapped, and move along.

I shift my face even closer to hers. "Thank you for being here with me tonight."

She beams at me. "I'm proud of you, no matter what happens."

"No matter what happens, being with you is the best part of the night."

Cheesy, but perfectly true. The nomination is flattering, and it's a new experience to be with so many authors like this. But the thing keeping me in my seat isn't the hope of an award.

It's her.

I want her to chase her dreams just as much as I've been able to chase mine. I want her to have these moments for herself, too. To have her talents be celebrated and fully seen. Even if that means she leaves the bookshop so she can pursue her art full time.

But again, not the right moment for that conversation.

I don't know exactly how I thought the evening would go. I don't want to say I came here expecting to lose, but I didn't drive down to Austin planning to win, either. I know my books are good, but I wouldn't have called them award-worthy.

Until suddenly, they are.

It takes my brain a few seconds to process it when the emcee calls my name. Georgia gives my shoulder a little shove, snapping me out of it. I move to the podium in a daze, my ears ringing with applause. The next thing I know, I'm walking back through the maze of tables, a surprisingly heavy crystal award in my hands signifying I'm a *Rising Star*.

That this room full of science fiction authors think *my* career is worthy of notice. It's hard to comprehend, honestly.

Georgia's standing and cheering louder than everyone else. I move without thinking. I set down the award and lift her into my arms, pressing my face against her neck until she laughs. I spin her around once, letting her skirts twirl around us, before I put her feet back on the floor.

I kiss her like it's inevitable, one hand on the back of her head and the other sliding up the soft fabric of her dress to the thin bare strip of skin on her back. For one brief moment, we're the only ones in the room. There's just Georgia and me, breathing in time, our mouths and hands moving together in celebration. And the only thing I'm celebrating is *us*.

I kiss her until we're breathless, and even then, I only stop when the wolf whistles start up. Applause rises again as we draw apart.

"I always knew it would be you," she says.

I want that sentence to be about so much more than an award.

We sit back down to cheer for the last two winners, and I don't think I've ever smiled this hard. It's for the award, sure. It's a thrill and an honor to be recognized by other writers this way, and I'm unlikely to ever forget this night.

But mostly it's that Georgia's the one here with me.

When all is said and done, it's a relief to leave the conference center. My excitement hasn't faded, but my enthusiasm for socializing has. I just want to go someplace quiet with Georgia so I can slow down and process.

Outside the venue, the cool evening air greets us. She shivers, apparently feeling the drop in temperature from when we got here this afternoon. I slip off my suit jacket and wrap it around her shoulders.

"Miles," she says softly. "Will you take me somewhere?"

Has she read my mind? I pull the coat lapels closed over where she's clutching my award to her chest like a baby. "Anywhere you want."

She gazes up at me and pulls her lower lip between her teeth. The sight urges me to take her place and be the one to nip at her soft lip. Her earlobe. The soft juncture at her neck. But then her teasing smile peeks out.

"Can we get Whataburger on our way out of Austin? The finger food they had in there was not enough. I need fries."

I laugh and kiss her forehead. "That's my girl."

I have never been so eager to go to a drive-through in my life.

Chapter 29

Georgia

If the awards ceremony was a dream come true for Miles, right now we're living out my dream. We're in his apartment, snuggling on his couch. My legs are in his lap, and one of his hands gently traces over my calves where they're exposed by the slit in my dress. The lights are low, and we've been saying goodnight for at least half an hour.

Oh, and? He's wearing his glasses.

Basically, it's everything I'd hoped. Sure, we're still in fancy clothes instead of my gray sweatpants fever dream, but the awkward way my bodice pokes me in the armpit at this angle helps remind me it's not all in my head.

"Can we change Dogeared's website to say *Owned by award-winning author Miles Forrester?*" I ask.

He grazes his fingers over one of my kneecaps. "Too showy."

"Can I get you a plaque for the front desk that says *Ask me about my major award?*"

He fights a smile. "That makes it sound like I won a leg lamp. But also, I wouldn't want anyone to ask."

"Can I get a custom bumper sticker for you that says *My award is in my other car?*"

He pulls me closer so I'm nearly on top of him. "We're going to keep the award quiet and be very subtle and casual about it."

I tap a finger to my chin. "That doesn't sound like me."

He runs the tip of his nose over my ear until I shiver. "No. It doesn't."

"I never doubted you would win it."

"I know. Thank you for always believing in me."

I rest my head against his, careful not to skew his glasses. "You don't have to thank me for that. You believe in me just as much."

"I do. And I was thinking tonight that I should prove it by finally firing you."

I let my head fall to his shoulder, collapsing against him. "I guess there's a reason your award doesn't say *World's Most Romantic Man.*"

"Georgia." He shifts me so we can see each other again. I do not appreciate looking into his eyes when he's being this sincere. "You needed the job at the bookshop when you first started out, but you don't need that safety net anymore. If illustration is your dream, you should embrace it."

I cup his face in my hands and gaze into his stupidly attractive hazel eyes. "Miles. I'm going to pretend you didn't say any of that."

"But, Georgia—"

I stop him with a kiss. "We have more fun things on the schedule for tonight."

His mouth tries to look unhappy, but his eyes are all heat. "What kind of fun things?"

"Like..." I kiss him again. "Figuring out where we should we put your award."

"That's not fun. But I like the 'we.' I want all the 'we.'"

I sit up straighter, despite his hands on my waist, holding me to him. "Should we put it in the bookshop?"

He makes a sound in the back of his throat. Indistinct but a definite no.

"It doesn't go here on your coffee table." I slip out of his grasp and stand, gesturing at the chunky award. The crystal is out of place with the video game controller and stack of library books.

He stretches one hand out to me. "Come back. We're in the middle of something."

I grab the hefty award and stalk around his living room, searching for the best spot. "Maybe on your bookshelves?"

I set it on one of the shelves, but it disappears against the colorful books and movie memorabilia. The curse of a see-through prize, I suppose, but there's got to be a good place for it.

"Georgia. Please."

Miles sounds so pained, I turn to look at him.

"I need to kiss you," he says. "Just once. Softly. Before I die saving my crew from an exploding nebula."

Cruel of him to remember what I said and quote it back to me like that. "If you had any throw pillows, I'd chuck them at you."

"Exactly why I don't own any."

"It was a really good idea though, wasn't it?"

He nods. "I considered using it, but I didn't want to have to add you in the acknowledgements."

I make a face at him and go back to my hunt. "I think some actress keeps her Oscar in her bathroom. Want to do that?"

"Not even a little."

"Yeah. Sounds kind of unsanitary. How about on your desk?"

I stand in front of it, but there's not really space for the award anywhere. It's messier than it was the last time I saw it. Like he's much too busy exploring the worlds in his creative brain when he's sitting here to ever clean off his desk.

"Why do you have so many pencils?" They're all over the desk and cubbies. One has rolled onto the floor by his chair.

"I'm in the brainstorming phase. I need to be able to write down ideas any time."

That explains the ones I saw next to a notebook on his kitchen counter.

"Well, this is a mess."

"You should see my nightstand. Sometimes I have to write a line or two in the middle of the night."

I'm not going to think about him sitting up in bed scribbling away right now, thanks. I'm trying to focus and failing pretty miserably. He keeps tossing curveballs at me.

"It should go up here on the desk shelf, so it can remind you just how awesome you are when you're writing." I gather up the loose pencils from the desk and put the crystal award in its place of honor.

Miles Forrester, Rising Star. It's even got a shooting star etched deep in the glass. I love it.

I turn to him and wave the handful of pencils.

"Just throw them in a drawer somewhere. Then please come back to the couch."

Oh boy, will I ever.

I open the drawer beneath his laptop, expecting to find a treasure trove of pencils waiting to be sharpened, but instead I find a sheaf of papers. The top one begins, "Dear Georgia." They're letters. I fan them out a little, and the others are addressed similarly, all to me.

"Miles?"

"Not...that drawer." He stands and moves nearer but doesn't quite close the distance.

"What are these?" I haven't touched the letters again. I'm just standing here with a handful of pencils, staring at them.

"They're, um..." He exhales, and I meet his gaze.

He looks...sad? Unsure? Why can't I read him right now? My heart squeezes.

"Is it something bad?" I don't even know what the "bad" could be. I just know I don't often see Miles like this. He's had so many little secrets lately. What else could he be keeping from me?

"Georgia, no. They're letters I've been writing to you. When my feelings overwhelm me, I sit down and write them out."

"Your feelings?" Why am I so lost right now? I hate this confusion clouding my thoughts.

He inhales long and deep. "I love you."

"I—" I almost give in to the urge to tell him I love him, too. It's an automatic reflex, like someone tapped my heart with a tiny mallet and the words sprang right to my tongue. I can't say them, though. It's too much, too soon. Isn't it? "You mean..."

I let that prompt hang between us. Because maybe he means it in a friendly way?

"I mean I am in love with you. Hopelessly."

My heart races so hard it hurts. "But we just started seeing each other differently a few weeks ago."

Miles shakes his head slowly. "I've seen you that way for a long time."

The squeezing in my chest grows tighter. My heart is a pencil in a merciless grip, and it's about to snap in two under the pressure. "How long?"

"Two years." He says it almost in apology. Is he sorry it's such a huge amount of time? For not telling me sooner? Or is he sorry that he finally has?

"Years." I barely breathe the word. I can't fathom it.

"I never meant to deceive you, Georgia. But I couldn't tell

you how I felt when you didn't give any indication you felt the same way."

I stare at the letters. I don't try to read the top one, but the word *love* jumps out at me anyway. There are so many pages in that drawer, the letters practically spill out of it. I can't imagine him writing these, pouring out his heart...to me? He's got that kind of love and affection for me?

"I thought we were just having fun." Even as I say it, I know it's wrong. Miles would never have that kind of fun. He'd never play with someone's emotions. This was never just about flirting or kissing...but I don't know if I'm ready for more. I've been so careful to avoid even the most superficial dating relationship for ages now, I can't just dive into *love*.

"It's not just fun for me."

His soft voice burrows into my heart. I want to turn around and comfort him, but I don't know what to say. I can't comfort myself right now. How could I comfort him? I'm not even sure what I'd be comforting either of us *from*, let alone the right way to ease it.

"I want something real and lasting with you, Georgia. If you don't want that, I won't bring this up again."

That's good. A very Darcy move. But it's also bad. Could he just...never mention his feelings for me again? Maybe he could —if he's gone this long hiding them, he could probably box them up again if I asked. The question is, do I want him to?

"I...I don't..." I can't think straight. My heart is a mess. It was wild enough realizing Miles and I could be kissing friends a couple of weeks ago—I can't sort out emotions this big on the spot.

"It's okay." He moves closer to pull the stack of letters from the drawer. "You can take them. Read them or don't, whatever you're comfortable with. Just come find me when you've had a chance to think about it."

"Miles." I don't even know what I'm asking of him, I just know I need clarity.

He gently takes my shoulders and gazes down at me. Then he presses an achingly soft kiss to my forehead. "Whatever you want, I'll understand."

I don't deserve him. Maybe I never have.

Letter

Two years ago

Dear Georgia,

I think of myself as a writer, yet when I'm with you, I lose all grasp on words. It's probably for the best. I can't tell you how I feel, so I'm going to write it. Maybe unleashing some of my feelings on this innocent piece of paper will help me manage them the next time we're together.

I'm in love with you. I don't know when it happened. I suspect it's been coming on for a long time. Your friendship has gradually become the most important relationship in my life. Your smiles the only thing I want to see. Your laughter the only thing I want to hear. The realization today was a jolt straight through my ribcage that seared your name on my heart.

I know, I know. This is already so cheesy it's clogging my arteries. You would probably laugh until you cried if you read it. I can't help it. I've had relationships before, women I cared about. What I feel for you goes so much deeper.

It's not just the difference in time and knowing myself better.

The difference is *you*—your heart, your humor, your willingness to do absolutely anything for the people you care about. The way you throw yourself wholly into the things you enjoy. The way your joy shines through your art. The way you think you don't trust anybody, but you have a circle of people you fiercely love who truly love you back.

I am one of those people. I'm not delusional enough to think that you love me the same way. But I am in the group of people who adore you. Utterly and completely.

I should probably burn this. That's the traditional thing to do with unsent love letters, isn't it? Is this one of those "felt cute, might delete later" bits you tried to explain to me the other day?

I love you, Georgia Donnelly. I wish I could tell you.

Yours always,

Miles

Letter

One year ago

Dear Georgia,

Working side by side with you is turning out to be the greatest joy and keenest torment of my life. You don't mean anything by the little touches you bestow on me each day, I'm well aware. And yet, I feel them like a flame on my skin. Your hand on mine when you take charge of my laptop. Your shoulder nudging me to drive home a joke. Your fingers ruffling through my hair.

That last one almost kills me every time.

Today, you told me about the hero in a romance book you're reading. It's messed up to be jealous of an imaginary person, but I'd like to punch him in the face all the same.

I would be that man for you if you'd let me. I would support you and protect you, encourage you and be entirely dedicated to you. I would cherish you, Georgia.

I would never be able to kill a man, no matter how villainous or deserving, so in that respect I suppose I can never match up to him. All hope is lost.

Still. I hope anyway. I hope one day you'll see how much I've cared for you all along. If you never do, I still hope for the deepest, most genuine love to find you, whoever that might be with.

This one's definitely going on the burn pile.

I love you, Georgia.

Yours always,

Miles

Letter

One month ago

Dear Georgia,

I adore your enthusiasm. You don't like holding back, and I love to see how things play out when you throw yourself into something new.

Except for your latest scheme to find me a date. A girlfriend. The love of my life.

I wish I could tell you how misguided your efforts are. All you have to do to find her is look in the mirror.

I know you're doing it because you care about me and want me to be happy. How can you not see that I am happy? Every day with you, I'm happier than I've ever been. Is it horribly cheesy to tell you that you are the glorious sunshine of my life, and I'm content just to bask in your glow?

Yes. Very. But fear of cheesiness hasn't stopped me from writing the rest of these letters.

What am I going to do with you, Georgia? Should I take you

by the arms and tell you that the only woman I ever want to date is you? Should I admit everything I've been concealing for so long?

Should I just recklessly kiss you in the bookshop and see what happens?

I can't tell you how many times I've imagined doing just that. However, it's certainly the most drastic option, with the highest likelihood for a messy outcome. So kissing you senseless is off the table.

To be very, very clear: I desperately want to kiss you senseless.

Georgia, in all your searching for my dream woman, I hope you will consider yourself. Because you are all I want.

I want a love based on true acceptance and friendship.

I want a love that's unconditional, without hidden strings or requirements.

I want a love where we can laugh together, even when days get hard.

I want a love I can rely on in good times and bad.

I want a love that's passionate, even though we know passion is a choice.

I want you.

I can't believe I'm saying this, but I hope you fail at something. I hope you fail in your quest to find me a date to the awards ceremony.

And I go on hoping you'll realize that you love me just as much as I love you.

I didn't know I was a hopeless romantic until I met you.

I didn't know I could love this hard until you.

Yours always,

Miles

Chapter 30

Georgia

I barely sleep. When I wake up—way too early, I might add—I finish painting the finally non-squeaking rotating bookcase on my balcony. Then, when it's late enough my neighbors won't get mad at me for using power tools, I finish putting the hinges and doors on the bike bookmobile. I even paint Dogeared's logo on the wooden box.

I think too much. Try not to think. Go back to agonizing over every little thing. Every word I can remember that Miles said last night. Everything I can think of that he's said to me in the last *two years*. Maybe worse, I try to remember everything I've said to him.

Two years is a lot of time to scroll through. Good days. Bad days. Embarrassing sick days. Triumphant business days. Days when I hugged him an obnoxiously long time. Days when I could have been nicer. Days I was just *me*. And apparently every single one of those days...Miles loved me.

Does not compute.

My phone rings, and my very hopeful lizard brain expects to find Miles's name on the screen. But it's my dad.

Sure. Why not? Might as well round out my morning with some criticism.

"Hey, Dad."

"Georgia." Weird pause as though I called him. "How are you?"

Not good, Dad. I am not good. But the cause is not something I want to share with him.

"I'm fine. How are you?"

"I'm...uncertain. I've been thinking about what Miles said at Willa's party."

I genuinely can't believe it. Of all the surprises I've had in the last twenty-four hours, this might be the biggest. Miles loving me almost makes sense because he's always had a capacity for love. Dad pondering whether or not he made a mistake? Unprecedented.

"And your grandfather pointed out some things."

Lord, give me strength. My father can't apologize to save his life.

"I may have been unfair to you, Georgia. I had Ava show me some of the covers you've done, and some of the comments people make about them online. Exuberant praise, to be precise. I didn't know the extent of what you do."

I'm kind of surprised Ava came out swinging in my corner, too. She's more likely to worship Dad than go up against him. It's nice of her, though.

"Your work is unusual," he goes on. "It's difficult for me to encourage that because I want you to be successful."

Once again, he's pitting success opposite my art as if they're two unrelated concepts. "I am successful, Dad. I'm making a good living on my art *and* working at a store that I love. That's success to me. And if you can't see that—"

"I will try."

I need to mark this day down on my calendar. It's the closest thing to an "I'm sorry I was wrong" I've had from him in...ever. "Are you feeling all right?"

The slightest chuckle. "I am not as wholly unfeeling as it may seem. I want what's best for all my children."

"Then try to see the same in Sam's career, too. He's good at what he does, even though he's not in an office crunching numbers."

He makes another sound, and I suspect that's enough negotiating for him today. "I will try."

Try is apparently all I'm going to get. That's a lot for him. It's not nearly enough, but for him it's significant.

"Thank you."

"Ava wants me to be sure you know you're invited for Thanksgiving."

We've almost got a month to go, but I won't forget. Holidays, at least, keep a spot on my mental calendar. "I know."

"And Miles is invited, too. If you want."

Even Dad and Ava are getting in on the Miles and Georgia train. And now I'm back to feeling sad and confused.

"Thanks, Dad. I'll let him know."

We hang up, and I kind of stare at the wall for a while. *Miles.* He's always the answer. I just can't figure out the right question.

I can't do this alone. It's time to call for backup.

Georgia: Can I come over? I'm spiraling
Sam: Get over here

When I walk through his apartment door, I head straight across the living room and fall face-first onto his couch.

"That's dramatic." He sits down on the coffee table and nudges me with his knee. "What's going on?"

I turn my face sideways so I'm not talking into the couch cushion. "Miles is in love with me."

"Everybody knows that."

I get up on my elbows. "You do not."

"Dude, I saw it the night you pretended he was sick, and Harper and I brought the littles to Dogeared. It was all over his face."

"What was?" I read over thirty of Miles's love letters to me, and I'm still fishing for confirmation of what's in them. I'm a mess.

Sam nudges me harder. "He couldn't take his eyes off you. He watched you like you were a Christmas angel fluttering around in his store. The usual lovesick stuff."

"You never told me that."

He flashes this small, sympathetic smile. "You were so oblivious. I figured knowing wouldn't help anything."

I flop back down. "I know now."

"You're dating, right? I thought that loving you would be a thing you would encourage."

"Not like this. Not where he's loved me for two years and I had no idea. Not where he thinks I'm—" All the ways he finished that sentence in his letters flood my brain.

Amazing.

Glorious.

Hilarious.

Perfect.

So many more.

"Not where he cares about me this much," I finish weakly.

"So, you just wanted a fling."

"No!" I sit up so I can glare at Sam properly. He's goading me, but I fall for it like I always do. "I don't want a fling or anything casual. But it's just..."

I don't know how to explain. Sorting out my feelings is like staring at a mountain and having to move it piece by piece. Where to start?

"A little too real right now?" he offers.

I can't seem to swallow properly. All I can do is nod and clutch at one of the throw pillows on the couch.

"Do you love him? Because a lot of what I have to say depends on your answer to that."

I flop backwards across the couch, pressing the throw pillow over my face. It hurts to breathe.

"Is that 'I don't know' or 'I don't want to say?'"

I move the pillow just enough to speak. "I don't want to say."

Saying the words will make it all too real. Can't he see I'm already freaking out just *thinking* the words?

He sighs. "Maybe I should call Harper."

"She already gave me her pep talk. I know what she'll tell me."

"Which is?"

I put the pillow back over my face. "I don't want to say."

He takes the pillow away and tosses it on the floor. "Tell me what you're afraid of."

Against my will, my gaze finds his. We're teenagers again, and Mom and Dad are telling us they're divorcing. That actually, they stopped loving each other a long time ago. That, you know what? Maybe they never *really* loved each other at all. That the last six months of our lives together were a lie. At minimum.

My heart is in my throat, and it's hard to swallow. But Sam understands.

"It's so much more to lose," I whisper. And because spiralers are gonna spiral, tears start streaming down my face and into my hair. "It's too much. That kind of love...everything he said in his letters...it will hurt so much worse when it's gone."

"Oh, George. Come here." Sam helps me up and sits down next to me. He hugs me hard, squeezing out more sobs than I thought I had in me. I rest my head on his shoulder and cry it out.

It was so long ago. I can't still be messed up over my parents splitting up. But I can, and I am.

"Georgia." His soft, tender voice just makes me cry harder. "That kind of love, the kind you don't want to lose? That's the only kind you should ever want. Because that means you'll both fight for it. Right?"

I nod, a little bit in awe that he can be so frantic sometimes, bouncing from one activity to the next, and yet be so logical and wise sometimes, too. I do not wish to tell him that at this juncture. But it's true.

"It might shock you to know that I'm not a perfect husband."

A strangled laugh bubbles out of me. I still sometimes can't believe this goofball is a husband in the first place. *Perfect* was never on the table.

"I make mistakes with Harper. Say the wrong thing or say nothing when I should open up. Do something selfish or thoughtless. But I always work on fixing it because I know she's the one I want. Today, tomorrow, forever. I'll never stop coming back and fighting for her. For us."

I haven't cried so hard since that teen romance movie where both the main characters die of cancer.

"It's scary to trust that you'll both keep fighting for each other. But you have to take that leap sometime." He shifts to look into my weepy eyes. "Would you catch him if he needed you?"

I sob even harder. "Yes."

Because the feeling filling me up and wringing me out isn't just fear. It's love. I love Miles Forrester so much the realization is barreling through me like a monster truck. And I think maybe I've loved him a lot longer than I ever suspected.

How long has Miles been the person I want to talk to every day? The one I go to with my worries? My celebrations? How long has he been the person whose opinion I seek out first? The person whose gentle affirmations and encouragement mean more than anyone else's? How long has he been the first thought in my head when I wake up and the last when I go to bed at night?

Years.

"I think I need to go talk to him," I finally say.

Even though the thought of doing that, of admitting *anything* absolutely terrifies me...the thought of not having Miles in my life anymore is worse. And I don't just want our friendship. I want it all.

"Sounds like a good idea. But first—what's this about letters?"

I shake my head. I read through them too many times to count last night, and went to sleep hugging them to my chest like they're my emotional support letters. It felt wrong to leave them when I came here, but I don't want to share them with anyone either. I left them underneath my pillow as if they needed protecting. Or just needed to stay tucked safe in my bed.

"I can't tell you. But they're...something special."

He nods. "Sounds like Miles is 'romance book hero' material to me."

I've been so ridiculous. I couldn't see what I had all along.

"He's better."

Chapter 31

Miles

Saturday morning at Dogeared is a non-stop crush of people requiring drinks, books, and pastries, all served up in record time. I don't mind the distraction today. Staying busy keeps my mind off of Georgia.

Actually, that's an absolute lie. Georgia never leaves my mind. If I were Arlo, I'd have that song play on repeat all morning just to hammer it home.

I want to know how she's feeling. If she read my letters. I laid my heart bare in those scribbled words, never thinking she would see them. Now that she has, were they too much for her? Too little? She's not on the schedule today—will she come in anyway like usual? Sit down in a cozy chair and sketch? Give me some hint of how she's doing? Or will she need more time to process everything?

I've always enjoyed Georgia's impulsivity, but I don't think she'll be impulsive about this.

I want to believe I know how she feels, but her expression when I told her I love her haunts me. She was confused, but also almost pleading for me to take my confession back. Like she didn't want it to be real. It's that look on her face that maybe she'd rather I never said anything that sticks with me the most.

"Not that cinnamon roll." The elderly woman on the other side of the counter makes a face at the roll I'm sliding out of the case for her. "The ones in the back look lumpy. I want the one in the front. On the left. *My* left."

I apologize and box up the specific cinnamon roll she wants. She pays, shooting me a last judging look as if to question my cinnamon roll making skills before she leaves.

It's true. My rolls didn't turn out as uniform as usual. Possibly due to distraction and dire lack of sleep.

Bailey, a young woman who's been attending the romance book group for several months, steps forward to peer into the case. "I'll take one of the lumpy ones."

A short laugh exhales out of me. "I appreciate it."

"Oh my gosh, they're pumpkin cinnamon rolls? I love it. I'll have to try a recipe like that. Not at work, of course. Don't worry about competition. We're not allowed to experiment."

"Not allowed?" I pass her the boxed cinnamon roll.

She opens it immediately, grabs a fork from the napkin station, and takes a bite. "That's really good. You get a hint of pumpkin, but it's not overpowering. But yeah. We have a set baking schedule at the grocery store on rotating days. Surprise, surprise, I'm always scheduled for sheet cake day."

We've never really had a conversation, but that doesn't seem to deter her.

"And you don't like sheet cake day?"

"I guess it's good experience, and my piping lettering has leveled up. It's just not what I imagined I'd be doing when I got my culinary certification, you know?" She points behind me. "I got an email the romance group's books are in for next month."

"Right." I find her copy and ring her up, wheels turning. If Georgia were here and heard even half of this conversation, I know exactly what she would do next. "Are you looking for a different job?"

Bailey hands me her card to pay. "Always. I keep checking job listings, but there's never anything posted. I'd rather not have to drive down to Georgetown for work, so...I make sheet cake."

Maybe local places want to hire someone, but they haven't gotten around to posting their listing. Maybe local places *need* to hire someone, but they've been too stubborn to do it.

Guilty.

"Would you be willing to do register work, too, or just baking?"

She pauses, fork frozen mid-air, staring at me. "Is this a hypothetical? Because working here would be a dream job."

"It's not a hypothetical. It's long overdue. We had an employee quit over two months ago and haven't replaced her. I do all the baking in-house, and I wouldn't mind sharing those duties with someone else."

She bounces on her heels. "I would be willing to work the register. Does that mean I can talk about books with random people?"

"Ideally. Would you like to come in for an official interview?"

"One hundred percent."

We decide on a date and time, and I mark it on the shop's calendar. It's a small step, but Georgia will be thrilled when she finds out.

My first impulse is to text her the good news, but I understand that she needs some space right now. A text—even a happy one telling her I've finally taken the advice she's been giving me for months—could feel like I'm trying to rush her.

"Hey, boss." Arlo walks in looking more cheerful than he has in weeks. "How was the big night?"

"You heard about that?" I hadn't spread news of the awards around much.

"Is Georgia likely to keep something like that quiet?"

I have to smile. "Not at all. I won, surprisingly."

"Congratulations! That's impressive. Does this mean we can put out a display of your books now?"

Am I going to keep fighting this? I don't love the feeling that I'm catering to my own ego...but it's smart business. And like selling coffee I don't drink—just because I don't like it doesn't mean I shouldn't do it.

"I guess we probably can."

"Cool. Are you ready to be fought over in the corn maze?"

At the top of the list of things I don't like but still should do...

I'd meant to bring up the maze with Georgia last night, but things went sideways before I got around to it. Sitting in that cornfield waiting for a strange woman to find me is the last thing I want to do today, but I can't back out on a commitment to my mom and aunt. And I want to help out the Cortez family however I can.

Still. The timing couldn't be worse. As though I need more time alone with my thoughts.

"Nobody's going to fight over anyone. Wait. Do they do that?"

"It probably depends on who's in there. Last year, I went with Remi." He winces but recovers quickly. "All the women were after that new veterinarian with the big Instagram following. They were calling him Hot Doc everywhere, so...yeah, there's probably some roughhousing going on in the maze."

I'm not sure what's worse—the idea that nobody's fighting over me or the idea that they are.

"Any chance you want to take my place?"

He laughs. And laughs. "No way. I prefer to meet women

the old-fashioned way: on an app where they have to reach out first."

"Are you looking again?"

His smile falls just a touch. "No. I don't know if I'll be ready for a while. But when I am, you can bet I won't be looking for love in a cornfield."

What are the odds the woman who finds me this afternoon will feel the same way?

Chapter 32

Georgia

Fun fact: I never actually rode the bookmobile bike before today. It's heavy, impossible to pedal, and—get this—a cruiser bike. No gears. I'm starting to understand why this dumb thing was free in the first place.

It's taking me three times as long to ride to the store as it would have if I'd walked. I'm sweating through my undershirt despite the cooler weather. And I suspect the back tire already has a flat. But at least I'll be able to pull up to Dogeared and give it to Miles months earlier than I'd originally promised.

It's pretty meh as far as grand gestures go, but it's all I had at the last minute.

When I park it in front of the store, it's an incomprehensible joy to get off that bike seat. My poor behind wasn't ready for riding miserable miles on a seat I should have replaced when I fixed it up. Maybe my new fitness goal will be to get strong enough to easily ride it to the farmers market and back every Saturday.

Ha. Good one, Georgia.

I straighten my sweater that's striped like a candy corn, and push through Dogeared's door, ready to make my love declaration to Miles. As scared as I've been to risk my heart, I wouldn't trust it with anyone else but him.

Only, he's not at the front counter. Arlo's there, talking about a book series with one of the guys from the fantasy reader group. I wave at him and head for the back room, but Miles isn't in the kitchen, either. So...where is he? He's *always* in the store.

Maybe he got another migraine?

As soon as the fantasy fan leaves with his purchase—of an entire series he hasn't even finished book one in yet, no less—I go up to Arlo. "Is Miles sick today?"

"He's doing the corn maze thing."

The Kissing Corn Maze careens around in my head.

"What?" I run over to the front window and pull the flyer off the glass. There's Miles's cute little face printed out in orange and gray, right next to today's date. I completely forgot about it. Never put it on my calendar because why would I? And I'm terrible at checking my calendars even if I had. "No, no, no."

The bachelor portion of the Kissing Corn Maze starts in just over half an hour. My stomach bottoms out. I can't let someone else win my man. I have to get over there. I head for the door but stop short.

I didn't drive here. And I definitely can't pedal the bookmobile bike out to Mackay Farm. That would take me days. Maybe if Sam can get here right away—

Ava walks through Dogeared's doors with the littles following behind her. As usual, she looks remarkably stylish for doing nothing but wandering around Magnolia Ridge.

"Georgia, I'm so glad I caught you. Do you mind if I leave Finn and Willa with you for a little while this afternoon? I need a dose of retail therapy, and you know how they get so bored with shopping."

My little siblings each hug me on their way to claim two of

the bookshop's cozy chairs. Ava's already heading out the door without even confirming with me that I can babysit. Which, to be clear, I can't.

"Ava. I'm not working today."

She barely pauses in the doorway. "Then it's that much better!"

"No, it's not." I pull her outside onto the sidewalk so Finn and Willa don't overhear. I wait for the door to shut before I go on. "You can't keep bringing them to me to babysit without warning."

She rears back, a perfect pout forming on her face. "I thought you liked spending time with them."

"I do. I love them. But I also love having my own life. I need you to give me some advance warning. Call. Text."

Amazing how her phone works whenever she's planning a party or a holiday gathering, but never does when she needs last-minute babysitting. She just appears, like a rabbit in a hat shoving her babies onto the magician.

Ava's shoulders sag beneath her fashionable wool coat. "I just want you to have a close relationship with them. The way you do with Sam."

Oh. Well...that's asking a lot, considering the age gap between us and how young they are. But I guess her springing them on me makes a little more sense in that light.

"We are close. I love them, and they love me. But sometimes I have things to do. Like right now. Except—" I look up and down the sidewalk as if a taxi might be waiting. I don't think even ride share apps get much use in this town. "I think I'm going to miss him."

She looks me over and perks up again. "Miss who?"

I sigh, but I might as well tell her. "Miles is one of the bache-lors in the Kissing Corn Maze at Mackay Farm, and I totally forgot about it. I was going to go down there, but I rode here on that."

I toss a hand at the bookmobile bike. Super cute as a book display. Super impractical as actual transportation.

"You were going to go down there, and…" she prompts.

"Tell Miles I love him, obviously. But now I don't have a way to get there."

It's fine. It's not like the Kissing Corn Maze ends with a wedding or something. I'll just tell him how I feel after his date.

With a woman who'll probably figure out how incredible Miles is a lot quicker than I did.

"Oh, yes, you do have a way to get there." Ava pushes open Dogeared's door. "Kids, come along. We're going for a drive."

Fifteen minutes later, Ava drops me off outside Mackay Farm's front entrance.

I open the door and start to get out. "I owe you one."

"I think I've owed you for a while."

I turn back to her, and she smiles softly. She's doing her best, in her own way. Mothering her kids and trying to ensure they stay close to me and Sam. That means something. And she totally came through for me today.

I scoot closer to hug her. "Thank you, Ava."

She hugs me back, but then pushes me toward the door. "You're welcome. Now go get that man."

"Go kiss Miles!" Willa screeches.

She had a *lot* of questions for me from the back seat on the drive over. Most of which I deflected, but our next family get together will put me straight in the hot seat.

"Or don't," Finn adds.

But preferably do, I say under my breath as I close the car door behind me.

I go straight to the ticket booth to pay my fee. There's no line, thankfully. Maybe there won't be as many women out there as I'd feared.

"I'd like a ticket to the corn maze bachelor thing, please."

The woman behind the corn-shaped cutout gets this knowing look on her face. "Twenty dollars."

I pass her the bill. "Is it very crowded today?"

She nods and slides me a pink wristband. "It's our most successful fundraiser yet. You've got about five minutes before they drop the rope. And a whole lot of competition."

Terrible pep talk.

Mackay Farm is massive. Thankfully, huge directional signs are everywhere, indicating where their featured areas are. Pumpkin patch. Apple launch. Bouncy houses. Petting zoo. Wagon rides.

Naturally, the corn maze is the farthest from the entrance. I jog past toddlers being pulled in wagons along with their pumpkin hauls, a live music stage, and food trucks. The smell of apple spice donuts frying gets my stomach growling, but there's no time for treats.

When I reach the corn maze entrance, my heart sinks. It's teeming with people. Maybe a hundred women wait to be let in, and at least twice that many people crowd around watching. Even if I were to join them, the odds are extremely low that I would be able to find Miles before anyone else does.

Worse, the reality of the situation finally hits me—he's *inside a corn maze*. And it's not small and contained like the fake one at the Abandoned Manor. It's so gigantic, I can't see where it ends on either side. I actually thought I could run around in there instead of curling up in the fetal position and hyperventilating?

"Georgia!"

I turn to find Miles's mom and aunt waving me down.

"We were just checking out the potentials," Cece says with a wink.

"What are you doing here?" Lydia asks.

I gesture vaguely at the corn. "Well, I..."

I can't tell his mom I love him before I tell him. Can I? Then again, my stepmom and the littles already know, and none of them are likely to keep it quiet for long. And I don't want them to. I don't want to hide it.

"I wanted to win Miles. I'm in love with your son."

They both light up and come in for hugs at the same time, each exclaiming about what great news this is.

"But I don't think I can do this." I look past them at the towering stalks of corn. "I have very specific fears about cornfields. Running through that is literally my worst nightmare."

I'm already getting a little sweaty just looking at it. Two "friendly" scarecrows guard the entrance. There could be more inside. Just the thought of them waiting around blind corners makes my stomach cramp.

Lydia squeezes me gently on the arm. "I'm sure he'll understand."

"I'll just call him and tell him before it starts." I move to get my phone, but Cece stops me.

"They took the men's phones away to ensure nobody can cheat. Each man has a map to get out once he's been claimed, but that's it."

"Ladies, are you ready to pick your bachelor?" the announcer asks over the loudspeakers.

The waiting women crush even closer to the entrance. A lot

of them are dressed like they're prepared for a marathon—athletic leggings and sneakers everywhere. Most are roughly my age, but some are considerably older. As they crowd around, it starts to look more like they're ready for a rugby match than a love match.

I'm wearing a candy corn sweater, jeans, and Converse and haven't shoved someone out of my way in my life. I am zero percent prepared for the Kissing Corn Maze.

"Begin!" The rope falls away, and women stream into the field, laughing and jostling at each other.

Well, that's it. It's too late. I'll just stay with Lydia and Cece and be here waiting when Miles comes out.

With some other woman on his arm.

Not really an ideal moment for a love declaration, but maybe it will be one of the older women and she'll be understanding? But what if it's one of the younger women, and she's not?

Even if it's all for charity, I don't want him going on a date with anyone else but me.

The last of the contestants disappears into the field. My heart rate amps up higher and higher. I know the stupid, scary, stupid-scary thing I'm about to do roughly three seconds before I do it.

"I'm going for it anyway," I yell, and dart forward through the crowd.

Lydia and Cece cheer me on, but their hurrahs are quickly lost in the noise of all the people I have to push past.

"Coming through!" I shout, my eyes on that small break in the corn. I do *not* look at the scarecrow guards.

A man who works at the farm tries to step in front of me, but I dodge him, raising my arm to reveal my pink wristband.

"I'm a contestant!"

"You're a little late," he yells back.

Yeah, about two years late. I'm not wasting any more time.

I dash through the corn, and I'm immediately back in the fake maze with the haunted scarecrow. Sweat beads down my back and the nape of my neck, and my hands are balled into tight fists. The faster I move my feet, the faster I can get to Miles. And then the faster we can get out of this demented version of fall fun.

It doesn't take long to catch up to the very back of the crowd of contestants. They clog the narrow maze aisles, and I slow to a walk. I'm never going to find Miles first if I wait around at the back.

"The man I love is in there!" I shout.

"Join the club," one of the older women shouts back.

It was worth a shot. Fine. It's time to get pushy.

I slip past everyone I can, ignoring the tiny ball of shame in my gut that normally stops me from even considering cutting in line. But this isn't a line. It's a weird free-for-all, and *my Miles* is up for grabs. You bet I'm cutting.

Some of the gals push back a little bit, but most just laugh as I barrel past. Someone says, "Way to be desperate," but I don't care. Watch me be desperate for Miles.

After a while, we've hit enough forks in the path that it's less crowded but considerably more confusing. No surprise, I've never been in a corn maze before. I don't know if there's a strategy to it, or if you just take your chances and hope for the best.

I hit dead-ends and have to turn around. I find more toy scarecrows than I care to acknowledge, each one sending a jolt of panic up my spine. I stumble on one set of turns that, after three times through it, I realize is running me and everyone else in it in circles. They're not exactly making it easy to find the guys.

That's the point. Still.

But ladies are having success. I come across one dead-end

and see a man who's already chatting up his winner. It's not Miles, thank goodness, but it just proves how unlikely it is I'm going to come out of here with him.

Someone could already be with him now. Ignoring the stitch in my side, I run faster.

I stumble around another corner and find a man who hasn't been won yet. He smiles wide, but I turn around and retrace my steps.

"I'm sorry," I shout behind me. "It's not you. It's me!"

The fewer women I see around me, the quieter the cornfield gets, and the quicker I run. It's too spooky to be alone like this. Do the farm owners do a sweep of the maze every night to make sure nobody's lost in the cornfields? It's broad daylight, but I have a very clear picture of what it would be like in here, lost in the dark.

Nope. Not going *there*.

I keep running, but I have no concept of where I am in the maze. With zero sense of direction, I could be circling back toward the entrance. All I know for sure is that I haven't reached Miles yet, and I can't stop until I do.

I turn a corner, and finally, *finally* I've found him. I might cry.

After this morning, tears are a very real possibility.

Miles looks at me for a second like he can't believe it's me, and then his face lights up with the biggest, brightest smile.

"Georgia," he breathes as I jog the last few feet to him.

I stop in front of him, breathing too hard to speak, the pain in my side reminding me I am not and have never been a runner. But I can grin back at him.

"What took you so long?" he says.

I launch myself at him, laughing as he scoops me up. I'm sweaty and covered in corn silks and still majorly freaked out to be in a cornfield in the first place, but I found him.

I pull back so I can see him clearly. "I didn't want anyone else to find you. You're mine."

This delicious look of triumph crosses his face before he leans down and kisses me. He lifts me up, encouraging me to wrap my legs around him. Oh, yes, let's do. We're frantic and happy, and for a few glorious minutes, I don't even care that I'm in a cornfield.

I'm with Miles, and that's all that matters.

"Tone it down, girl. You got him," a woman's voice behind us says.

We break apart, and he guides my feet back to the ground, but I don't let him go. I cup his face in my hands.

"I love you, Miles."

The sheer happiness on this man's face makes my heart sing. *Mine, mine, mine.*

"I should have realized it a long time ago. Yes, I love you as my best friend, but I love you as so much more than that, too. I love you in all possible ways. On your good days and bad days and everything in between. You're the best person I know, and the sexiest bookstore owner on the planet, and I am in love with you. Desperately."

"Did you read my letters?"

"All of them." Several times over, but we can get to my sleepless night later.

"Then you know already that I want you. And only you."

I kiss him again softly.

"You have me. Now, can we please get out of here? This corn maze is really freaking me out."

Chapter 33

Miles

When I gave Georgia the green light to throw a signing party for me at Dogeared, I did not expect her to print out so many pictures of my face. Posters featuring my author photo stare down at me from the walls. She plastered it on flyers she spread through town and on the bookshop's website. She even printed out bookmarks with my face on them.

She's extra. But it only makes me love her that much more.

I've been signing books for a while now, chatting briefly with everyone who comes by to meet me. It's still disorienting, to be honest. I kind of like being the anonymous guy nobody notices. But Georgia won't stand for that where my writing career is concerned.

I mentioned I love her, right?

I recognize a lot of the people filing through the bookshop, like the bulk of Georgia's adoptive extended family. Sam and Harper already congratulated me, both on the books and on winning over Georgia. Dean and Booker got their copies signed, and Eden finalized the plans for the meet and greet I'll do at the library in a few weeks right before Christmas. Even members of the family who admitted to me they don't read much came out to support me.

Mom and Cece are here, along with my cousins. I hadn't expected them to drive in from Houston just for this, but it's a nice surprise.

Plenty of people I don't know wander through, too. Georgia posted about the signing on Dogeared's website and several other book group pages across Texas. We even posted it on my Instagram, which has slowly gained traction over the last month.

I can't pretend to enjoy having this much attention fixed on me, but I evened it out by pledging a percentage of tonight's sales to go toward the Cortez girl's recovery fund. As busy as Arlo and Bailey are up front, it looks like that should be a pretty good amount.

Owen and Josie walk up hand in hand, and they each put a set of my books in front of me.

"I figured I should have my own copies," he says with a shrug.

"And mine are for my dad," Josie says. "He's a big fan of this kind of space cowboy stuff."

"Space cowboys. I like that." Owen's devious smile tells me I'll be hearing that term during sparring for the foreseeable future.

Georgia's grandfather, Glen, is a few customers behind them in line. He slides my books across the table to me. "Make them out to 'Grandpa, who knew all along.'"

He winks and hands me a pen.

I guess my secret pining wasn't quite the secret I thought it was.

"It's a good turnout tonight, son."

I suspect he talks that way to everyone, but I like having him call me "son."

"It's all thanks to Georgia."

He nods and takes the books. "Most things are."

I watch her talking animatedly with someone across the room. Naturally, she's wearing a sweater embroidered with books. She catches my gaze, and the heated look she sends my way is enough to make me want to flip the table and declare an end to book signing for the night.

I don't, only because that would ruin all her hard work.

One person I don't expect to see in line is Georgia's dad. He and Ava have my books with them, but he's also got a few rom-coms Georgia illustrated tucked under one arm. He catches my curious look.

"They're for Ava," he says quickly. But he holds one out to admire. "Nice cover though, isn't it?"

He sounds like he's not quite sure, but he's made up his mind because Georgia had a hand in it. I like the progress.

"Beautiful cover," I confirm.

Willa splays a hand on the table in front of me. "We get to pick out books for us. Mama said we can't read your books yet because they're boring."

Ava puts a gentle hand on Willa's shoulder, laughing as though she'd rather put that hand over her mouth. "I didn't say they're boring, darling. I said they're not for children."

Willa nods. "Because they're boring."

Probably not the phrase you want repeating through the room at your book signing, but I adore her too much to ask her to stop.

"Which book are you getting instead?" I ask.

She slams down a brightly colored book with a delicate fairy on the cover. "Her name is Sparkle Gardenhome."

"Sounds about right."

"I'm getting this one." Finn shows me a middle grade sci-fi about a field trip to Mars gone wrong.

"Good choice."

"But Dad says maybe I can read yours after he does and sees what it's all about."

"You'll have to let me know what you think."

After the line dwindles away and guests have all checked out, Georgia and I linger in the bookshop. We often spend a little extra time in the store after closing, when the lights are low and we can just enjoy being surrounded by books.

Also, one of the cozy chairs is positioned exactly right among the shelves to be hidden from any windows. Georgia calls it the Make-out Chair. It's my favorite place in the store. We wander through the stacks, and I sit in the secret chair, pulling her down to sit in my lap.

"Can we burn those posters of my face now?"

She giggles, getting comfortable against me. "Absolutely not. They're going in my bedroom."

"I'll never be able to set foot in there again."

She side-eyes me. "Seems doubtful."

We both know not even the prospect of seeing my own giant face would keep me out now that I've been invited in.

"Thank you for tonight," I tell her. "It went better than I'd dreamed."

"You need to dream bigger. This was just the beginning."

I press a kiss to her neck. "I have some big dreams."

"Oh, really?" She burrows closer, tilting her head away so I have more access to her soft skin. "Like what?"

"Like...you and me..." I kiss up her neck and nibble on the shell of her ear.

"I love it so far," she breathes.

"All alone..." I taste along her jawline.

"Please go on."

"A weekend away."

That makes her stop and turn. "Really? A weekend away?"

"I've got a place in mind. A cabin in the middle of nowhere.

Perfect for stargazing. And...other things." Sam told me about the remote lodge, and I've been eager to take Georgia there ever since.

I won't mention the outhouse and outdoor shower until it's absolutely necessary.

Probably also shouldn't mention her brother goes there with his wife.

Maybe I should find a new place.

"But you don't take time off." She's not reprimanding me, just stating fact.

"I know. But it's time to change things." With Bailey taking on most of the morning baking, I'm freed up to focus more time on my writing. She and Arlo work so well together, I don't need to be in the bookshop at all hours anymore. "Someone told me once I need to be careful not to burn out."

"You should definitely do everything that wise woman says." Georgia grins, and her gaze drops to my mouth. "And, you know. You could burn just a little bit. For her."

"Believe me, I do."

I kiss her, slow and perfect, tasting a hint of spice on her mouth. This woman is everything I want, everything I could have hoped for. Everything I need.

"I have other dreams," I say softly.

"Tell me."

"You, working full time at illustrating. Pursuing *your* dreams."

She draws back and spins so she's straddling me. But she doesn't have a come hither look on her face. It's more...come at me, bro.

"You know what? I think I need a more secure position at Dogeared. Something where I can't possibly be fired by you."

I love the spark of flame in her, even when it's directed at me.

Or maybe I especially love when it's directed at me.

"I didn't mention firing." I figured she would put in notice on her own one day. With a very politely worded letter I would keep in a drawer forever.

"It's implied."

"What kind of secure position do you have in mind?"

"A partnership. On a more official basis."

"I'm willing to make anything official that you want." And I mean that literally, but it's probably too early to say it straight out.

A smile touches her mouth, and she starts to lean closer, but stops herself. "I'm serious. I want to be partners with you in Dogeared. I want to keep making plans for the bookshop and finding fun ways to make it better and help it grow."

I slide my hands over her waist. "What about your art?"

"I like doing both. I'll keep making covers for as long as that lasts. One day, maybe I'll branch out into other things. But I don't want to make art one hundred percent of the time." She runs her hands under the inside edges of my sport coat, sliding them along my chest. One hand pauses over my pounding heart. "I don't want to turn my art into my job and wind up resenting it. I want to do enough to keep it new and interesting and keep on loving it, but not so much *I* burn out."

"That's smart. I accept your offer. We should be partners."

"You can't just accept my offer. I have to buy you out or something."

"Well." I drop my voice low. "I'm sure we can come to an arrangement."

"That's naughty. You're naughty." Her grin somewhat dampens her scolding.

"I didn't specify anything. We'll sort it all out. I just want to be sure that this is what *you* want."

"It is. As long as you need me, I'm staying."

I tug her closer. "Then you're going to be here for a very long time."

She melts against me, kissing me with every ounce of her bright enthusiasm. Then she jolts back. "We need to shake on it and be professional for a change."

I shake her offered hand. Very professional.

And then we stay in the bookshop for a long time, being very unprofessional.

Epilogue

GEORGIA

It's not us. It's not. They're fictional characters, and their names are Ryder and Lily. He's trying to save his family's struggling Christmas tree farm, and she's the attorney trying to foreclose before Christmas Day.

Yes, Ryder wears glasses and has messy hair like Miles. And yes, Lily's wavy blond hair is somewhat familiar, but her fun sweater does not make her *me.*

I stare at the illustration on my tablet, searching for some way to make it clear I wasn't inspired by me and Miles. I am not going to be so love drunk that I put us on every cover where it even remotely makes sense. I sketch out work boots on him and put spike heels on her.

There. Very unlike us.

"Hey." Miles stops right beside my chair and leans in close to inspect my work. He kisses the top of my head. "We look great."

We're hanging out in Dogeared after closing like we sometimes do. He's deep in drafting his next book and likes to work in the quiet of the bookshop. The only distraction in here is me.

And honestly, I can be pretty distracting. But I try to let him work. Most of the time.

I save the file and close the app. "It's not us."

"I know." He holds out a hand to me. "The spring samples Bailey left are cool now. Do you want to try them?"

"Um, try delicious treats? Don't mind if I do."

In the back, Bailey's left us mini versions of six desserts to try. We always carry a few staples in the café, like Miles's mom's cinnamon rolls and vanilla scones, but they've been changing up the menu every few months, too. Give the treats case a little razzle-dazzle every now and then.

It looks like she's switching from the dark chocolate muffins and warm, spicy loaf cakes we had all winter to bright, light lemon bars and strawberry turnovers. I try each one, hoping they don't expect me to rule any of them out. They're all delicious.

It's only after I've taste-tested every one—and then some— that I realize Miles isn't taste-testing with me. I rinse my hands in the sink and head to the front.

"What are you—" I stop on the other side of the curtain.

The lights are out, but candles glow throughout the bookshop. I have the ridiculous thought that candles aren't safe next to this many books, right before realization stops my breath in my lungs.

Miles stands in the middle of the bookshop. "I've thought of a bonus epilogue for Captain Aster."

I take a few steps closer. He knows the right lures to use. "Can I read it?"

His smile peeks out. "I haven't written it yet. But I think it will show that he's going to get that happily ever after you've always wanted."

"With his second in command?"

We're not talking about Captain Aster and his second any more than my latest book cover isn't Miles and me.

"It will show that he finally gets the woman he's been in love with for so long."

"How will he do that?" It's hard to sound bold when you're on the verge of jumping up and down.

"It'd probably go a little something like this." He reaches into his sport coat, pulls out a small box, and lowers himself to one knee.

I ignore the fireworks going off in my chest and try to memorize this moment. He hasn't even said anything, and it's all I can do not to tackle him already. And sob. A crybaby tackle is in order.

"Georgia, I've loved you for a long time now. And I promise you, I'm never going to give up on you. I'm going to go on loving you, and supporting you, and laughing with you for as long as I live. And I'd like to do that as your husband, if you'll let me. Will you marry me?"

I join him on the floor, my tears making him blurry. "I love you so much. I would love to marry you."

He kisses me, and we get just a tiny bit sidetracked from the proposal. When we finally break apart, he slips the pale purple gem on my finger.

"It's a vintage amethyst," he tells me. "Seemed a good fit for my thrifting-loving girlfriend."

"It's beautiful." And exactly the thing I would have chosen. He knows me too well.

Or precicely well enough.

"And I'm your fiancée now," I add. Crazy. But the best thing ever.

He grins and moves us over to Make-Out Chair to settle me

on his lap. "I didn't ask your father's permission. I didn't think you'd like it very much if I consulted him first."

Dad tries a bit more than he used to, but Miles is right. I wouldn't have wanted him to feel like he could pass judgment on this decision before I could.

"But Sam and your grandpa knew what I was planning. And they gave their blessing, which felt just right to me."

"You're going to make me cry even more. Did Sam give you a hard time?"

"A little bit. Wanted me to ask you if he should throw away Maverick's number."

I laugh, burrowing my face in his neck. "He's the worst."

"I told him he can throw every guy's number away. You're mine."

Yeah. That's the good stuff. "Say it again."

He gets this delightfully intense look on his face. "*You're mine.*"

Then he kisses my cheek and wraps me even closer in his arms. This is everywhere I want to be.

"I can't wait to live my whole life with you," I tell him. "I want it all—love and laughter, joy and babies—"

He stops my list with a kiss. "No spoilers."

Get a short novella of Owen and Josie's love story when you sign up for my newsletter. Keep scrolling for more!

Coffee Break with the Billionaire

Read the next book in the series, Coffee Break with the Billionaire by Holly Kerr!

When a billionaire meets a small-town barista, the treats will be sweet and there will be lots of swoony star gazing as their worlds collide in this closed-door, slow-burn, friends-to-lovers romance.

Cinnamon Rolls and Pumpkin Spice series

Read the rest of the Cinnamon Rolls and Pumpkin Spice Series! Each book is a standalone, full-length, closed-door romance that can be read in any order.

Hating the Cinnamon Roll CEO by Camilla Evergreen
Falling for Autumn (Again) by Jen Atkinson
Paris, Pumpkins & Puns by Marion De Ré
Fall With Me by Amanda P Jones
Cinnamon & Spice Conundrum by Leah Busboom
Cinnamon Roll Set Up by Genny Carrick
Coffee Break with the Billionaire by Holly Kerr
The Friendly Fall by Kristine W Joy

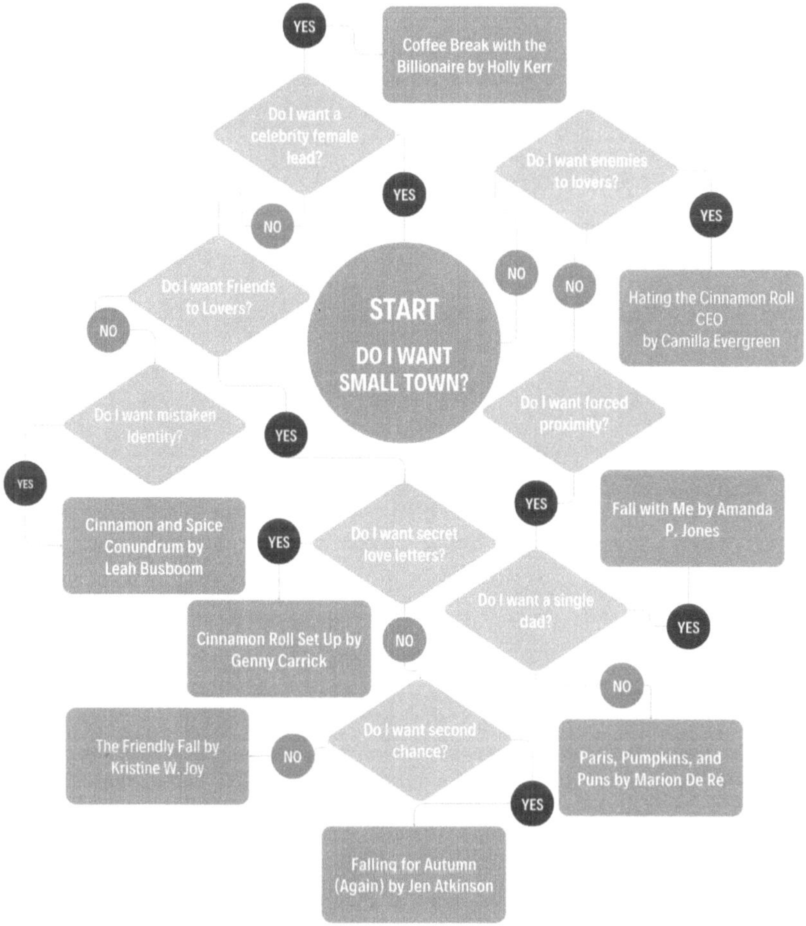

START
DO I WANT SMALL TOWN?

Do I want a celebrity female lead?
YES — Coffee Break with the Billionaire by Holly Kerr
NO — Do I want Friends to Lovers?

Do I want enemies to lovers?
YES — Hating the Cinnamon Roll CEO by Camilla Evergreen
NO

Do I want Friends to Lovers?
NO — Do I want mistaken Identity?

Do I want mistaken Identity?
YES — Cinnamon and Spice Conundrum by Leah Busboom

Do I want forced proximity?
YES — Fall with Me by Amanda P. Jones

Do I want secret love letters?
YES — Cinnamon Roll Set Up by Genny Carrick
NO — Do I want second chance?

Do I want a single dad?
YES — Fall with Me by Amanda P. Jones
NO — Paris, Pumpkins, and Puns by Marion De Ré

Do I want second chance?
NO — The Friendly Fall by Kristine W. Joy
YES — Falling for Autumn (Again) by Jen Atkinson

Also by Genny Carrick

Acknowledgments

Thank you for reading Miles and Georgia's story! It was so much fun to visit Magnolia Ridge again. I dropped a hint about these two way back in Stay this Christmas, and I'm thrilled to finally give them their HEA! I hope you enjoyed this shy, pining hero and his sweet but slightly oblivious best friend.

To Claire, Amanda, & Sam, thank you for your feedback! It's so much easier to release a book knowing you already love it!

To my editor Cindy, thank you for helping me get this ready for publication and pointing out all the pesky places I needed (or didn't need) commas!

To ND Grant, thank you for this super cute cover! I love how you brought Miles & Georgia to life!

To Camilla Evergreen, Jen Atkinson, Marion De Ré, Amanda P. Jones, Leah Busboom, Holly Kerr, and Kristine W. Joy—thank you for inviting me into the fall fun! It's been a pleasure joining forces with you!

To my husband, the original shy hero—I adore you & your genius brain. None of my fictional heroes are you, but all of them exist because of you.

And to my children, I can only hope to be as funny as you two are!

About the Author

Genny Carrick is a fool for happily ever afters, especially if there's a whole lot of laughter along the way. She writes rom-coms about sassy women, the cinnamon roll men who fall for them, and swoony moments outdoors whenever she possibly can.

When she's not lost in romantic reads, she's probably up to something crafty or trying to get her dog and two cats to love her.

After a quick detour in Texas, Genny recently returned to her true love, the Pacific Northwest, and lives with her brilliant husband and two hilarious kids.

Stay up to date with book news at gennycarrick.com

9 781957 745176